The COWBOY'S Last Song

Wild Texas Hearts

Book 2

Deborah Garland

Edits by:

Julie K. Cohen
Samantha Soccorso

Cover Designed by Kudi Design

Published by Deborah A. Garland

MORE BOOKS BY DEBORAH GARLAND

The Lords of Gotham Billionaire Series

*Reluctant Billionaire *includes bonus novella The Good Billionaire*

Daring the Billionaire

Bossy Billionaire

Rebel Billionaire

Fiery Billionaire

Tori Chase Reverse Harem Romances

Wild For You

In Too Deep

The Princeton Allegiant Vampire Series

Drawing Bloodlines

Guarding Bloodlines

Matching Bloodlines

ACKNOWLEDGMENTS

I wrote the original version of this book eleven years ago. It was my first completed novel and the book that made me think, I could be a published author. Eleven years and hundreds of edits later, including three massive story shifts, here is the couple I refused to give up on. I was determined to tell Jamie and Harper's story. Again, so much thanks to my writing partner Julie K. Cohen for her comments. My beta reader extraordinaire Kia B gave me valuable comments too. I have so much more to say about this book and its journey. Check my website for a heartfelt post about how an idea one August night in 2010 turned into this novel.

As always, thanks to my husband for letting me live my dream of being a full-time author.

Chapter One

Jamie

"Anytime you're ready, Chloe." I tapped my dress shoes patiently, leaning against my bedroom dresser.

"Chill out, Daddy. You don't have many tie options." The little muffled voice drifted out of my walk-in closet.

"Maybe I don't need a tie." I fingered my favorite charcoal Stetson off the peg and placed it smoothly on my head.

Being a clothes horse with expensive suits and ties had taken a backseat to nannies, a 529 college plan, and lawyers. I'd spent almost every penny I had to get custody of my daughter after Chloe's mother died in a horse-riding accident five years ago, turning both our lives upside down.

"You're signing a new recording contract today. You need a tie." All four-foot-nine inches and the utter love of my life marched out of the closet with a blue and gray striped tie. "Here."

"Nice." I took it from her and tugged her long braid, glossy and dark like my hair. "Thank you. What would I do without you?"

"Not wear a tie, obviously." She shrugged her shoulders and dove onto my bed. "Can I check your emails?"

"Sure."

"Uncle Cam sent you a text." She made a good assistant for an eleven-year-old. "He's picking us up in ten minutes."

I knotted my tie and tucked the silk dress shirt into my slacks, catching a glimpse of my hip tattoo. *Layla.* It hit me. Chloe was a little lady. Growing up. And soon she'd be asking tough questions. Starting with: why hadn't I married her mother?

Your mother didn't want to marry a broke musician working on a drinking problem probably wasn't the right answer.

When Layla died, I went from being a long distance, FaceTime, see your kid occasionally father to a full-time single dad who had to buck up and fly right for once. Before getting custody, I'd lost my first two recording contracts for just plain ole stupid behavior. My journey from Nashville rising star to damaged goods in seven years had been brutal.

"Are you looking forward to this summer, Clo?" When my daughter didn't answer, a stab of worry sliced through me.

She'd been spending July and August each year with Layla's parents back home in Wild Heart, Texas. That concession was key to me getting custody. Cord Renner, rich for those parts with money to burn on lawyers had always hated me and fought like a sumbitch to keep Chloe from me.

"Chloe? I asked you a question.*"*

"Yeah. I miss Sweet Bell." Her mentioning one of Layla's horses always made my stomach cramp.

Layla's parents adored their granddaughter and she was well cared for with them. So far, everyone on Renner Ranch respected my *no horse-riding* rule. It tore me up every summer to leave her there, but I needed those months to tour and promote my albums to maintain some visibility with my fans. The ache still crippled me, though.

After being dropped from a third label for the dreaded 'poor album sales,' my confidence was running on tractor fumes. Leaving me to wonder if my bad boy persona sold more albums than my music.

When Cam, my best friend and manager, worked magic to secure me a recording deal with Blue Rock Records, I knew it was my last chance here in Music City. An independent music label didn't scare me as much as facing Harper Montgomery, Blue Rock's Talent Relations VP.

"Is your school bag packed up?" I studied my daughter through the mirror, her legs scissoring against the unmade covers on my bed. "I told them I'd bring you in after lunch."

"Yeah." She kept her eyes on my phone, swiping at my pictures, even rolling over to take those selfies I loved.

Since getting custody, I'd been pushing and punishing myself, zigzagging across the country to hit every possible arena during the summer months. Going into my phone and seeing Chloe's smiles when she wasn't around made those two grueling months on the road bearable.

On the road, far away from my daughter, I lived in the shadow of the bad boy I once was: the country music god who only cared about singing on stage, boozing it up after a show, and enjoying an occasional, discreet, *consenting* woman.

When the doorbell rang in several twangy chimes, Chloe twisted around and flew off the bed. "I'll get it!"

"Let Marta answer it." I tried to snag Chloe's arm to kiss her forehead, but she slipped away.

She grew distant this time of year. Probably a defense mechanism to cope with being away from me for a couple of months. Not seeing her everyday destroyed me, too, but she did a better job of hiding it.

After one last look in the mirror, pinching and tugging on the silk suit to survive the early June Nashville heat, I secured the Stetson more firmly on my head and left the bedroom.

Watching Chloe twirl for her uncle Cam showing off her new pale blue dress, squeezed my heart. Thank God for that man. Layla's big brother had stayed solidly in my corner during the brutal custody battle. Cam was the bridge between me and the rich Renner clan who took possession of Chloe every summer.

"Ready, J?" Cam was not only my manager, but my best friend. "Nice suit."

"I picked out the tie." Chloe put her hands on her little hips.

"I was just going to say that was the best part." Cam took out his keys and handed them to Chloe. "Clo-Clo, can you wait in the car?"

"Not *in* the car, it's ninety degrees," Marta, my current nanny, objected loudly from the kitchen.

"Do you need to talk to Daddy alone?" Chloe rolled her eyes at Cam.

"Yes," Cam answered, pursing his lips.

"I'll be outside." Chloe opened the front door, gave me a smirk, and disappeared with Marta, who carried her school bag.

"You okay, J?"

"No." I laid flat palms on the console next to the front door. "She hates me."

"Chloe doesn't hate you."

"Not her."

"You can't be talking about Marta, that woman has the sweetest gig ever. You're usually around all day, you barely go out at night, and Chloe goes back to Texas every summer."

I glared at Cam. "I'm talking about Harper Montgomery."

"Oh, *that* her." Cam's eyebrows arched and he said, "Harper," with a little more apprehensive care this time.

Harper. The woman who wrote my first big hit, the song that launched my career and propelled me to instant stardom.

The woman who asked for one night in my bed seven years ago.

The woman I turned down.

I needed that very woman to write me another hit song and save my career.

"You had an awkward moment with Harper seven years ago. Has she reached out to you at all since?"

Awkward moment all right. I refused to sleep with one of the most beautiful women I'd ever laid eyes on. "If she did reach out to me, I never got the message."

"All messages go through me. Do you think I'd hold back a call from the *Nashville Hitmaker*?"

"No." I blew out a breath and snuck one more look in the mirror.

"This is a good day, Jamie. I think you're gonna be very happy with Blue Rock. Niche labels have been very successful in recent years."

I rubbed my chin. Damn, I forgot to shave!

Losing three contracts in seven years because of stupid choices I made on the road already made me a tragedy, and now I looked strung out as well.

I'd come full circle or was it a vicious circle?

"Okay, let's do this." I prayed Harper had forgotten all about that night.

Harper

How could this be happening? Over my objections, no less. But alas, Jamie Miller was signing a recording contract with Blue Rock Records. I wondered if he even knew I was the VP of Talent Relations.

With the stroke of a pen later that afternoon, Jamie would be the *talent* and I'd have a *relationship* with him. The singer I'd worked all summer with seven years ago and kept it mighty professional which wasn't easy given his off-the-charts talent, the face of a god, and a smile that lit up a honkytonk more than any neon sign. And that wicked sense of humor of his had left me giggling like a school girl.

In an emergency VP meeting, Gregory Blue, my CEO, asked the marketing team to pass out Jamie Miller's press package including photos. I glanced up to see if anyone was watching me melt down as I slid the media kit open.

I'd ruined everything with Jamie. The night before he left to sign his first record deal, I had a few shots of whiskey in me and put myself out there, I propositioned him for sex. One night. Something I'd never done with a man before. And in an instant, I'd made myself look like all the groupies he encountered on the road. Losing all my credibility with the man.

When Jamie Miller turned me down, I'd never been so embarrassed in my life. It'd been a hard climb back all these years, getting over that one stupid move.

Staring at his press package, I ordered the butterflies

in my stomach to calm the heck down. I stuffed away the hypnotic headshots in a folder as if they meant nothing—as if those remarkable green eyes didn't jump off the glossy prints to greet me.

As a songwriter and a producer for country music's biggest stars now, my daily routine included a steady parade of beautiful men.

Jamie Miller was a ten-car pile-up on the highway. He possessed that lethal combination of killer good looks and an amazing voice.

After the rest of the meeting passed in a blur, I slipped out the conference room's rear door, avoiding the stampede of Blue Rockers who wanted a glimpse of country music's gorgeous bad boy waiting in the lobby. Dazed, I dug my high heels into the carpet to bolt to my office with my assistant Maisy in tow. I had to collect my senses in private.

"Harper, wait!" Michael Bradley called out, following me out of the conference room.

I ignored him and kept walking, afraid the emotions storming through me would show all over my face.

"Your mother called again, Harper," my assistant said, glancing behind us.

I sighed. "Did she leave a message?"

"Yep. *Poppy, this is your mother calling again. Just because you're a big shot label executive, you can still call your Grammy-award-winning mother.*"

"You're starting to sound like her." I gave a small smirk, but the repeated messages meant there were probably issues at Gigi's rehab facility. Again. Something else to deal with.

"Harper Montgomery, I know you can hear me!" Michael's voice boomed down the hall, stopping everyone from moving.

"Wha-at?" I turned sharply in his direction, a tendril of my long dark hair nearly hitting him in the face.

As if the smell of my hair aroused him, he took a moment before saying, "You're being unreasonable about this whole Jamie thing."

"You signed someone over my repeated objections." I shot Michael a burning stare.

"You were overruled on this one. By a landslide, I'm afraid." Michael crossed his arms against his broad chest. "And last I checked, I run Blue Rock's A&R department. *Artists and Repertoire.* I sign the artists."

"And I have to keep their butts in line," I snapped back, even though Talent Relations was in the rearview for me. I had my eye on the CEO throne. Gregory Blue had announced his retirement a few months back. But ignoring my opinions on signing Jamie shook my confidence to the core making me wonder if Gregory thought I didn't have what it took to run his record company.

"I don't get what you have against me signing the man," Michael argued. "You wrote his first big hit."

"And since then, he's managed to lose *three* recording contracts. Excuse me if I don't want Blue Rock to be his sloppy seconds."

"Fourths," Maisy mumbled.

"Right, *the fourth* in line to pick up the pieces. We're better than that, Michael."

"Jamie knows he has a lot of ground to make up." Michael stood firm. "I was given assurances all that nonsense on the road is far behind him."

I expected Jamie to show up at Blue Rock's doorstep either with guns blazing to repair his damaged reputation or just blazing mad for being held back. Did Gregory Blue have a soft spot for hard luck cases, or did he believe a Jamie Miller hit under the Blue Rock label would put our little music company on the map before he retired?

"He's not signed yet, so that means he's still all yours. *Your* prospect." I dug my heels back in to attempt another escape.

Michael scooped away everything in my arms, clumsily brushing against my breasts. After a strange look passed between us, he said, "Jamie's being brought to my office right now. I'm gonna sign the contract in a few minutes. He brought his manager. Come with me. We'll welcome him together."

"You want me there?" My eyes wildly looked for any reflective surface to catch a harried glimpse of myself. "You never asked me to a signing before."

"We don't sign someone like Jamie Miller every day."

No kidding.

"Sounds like you have everything under control." I clawed at Michael's muscular chest to pry my stuff free.

"Some CEO you'd make if you don't even want to welcome an artist who will hopefully make us all a lot of money."

I dropped my hands at my side, shock and awe rolling through me. Did Michael actually go there? *Was I being unreasonable?* Was I letting my personal humiliation get in the way? I had been laser-focused on bringing out the best in my artists. Let the Blue Rock stars shine while I stayed in the background.

Under no circumstances did I ever have the mind to get involved with one of them. Before Jamie Miller reentered the picture, that had been as easy as catching mosquitos with a glass of warm lemonade next to a swamp.

"Let's just level set our understanding with him right away. Set the tone of what we expect. Together." Michael drew up close to me, leaving no space for Maisy to hear what was sensitive label business between two VPs. "You know how important this contract is. We need this for our survival."

"I know that." I folded my arms, my throat tight with heat at just the *thought* of making eye contact with Jamie.

Much of the wow factor he projected had melted away as we built what I thought was a solid friendship. Then I went and messed things up by suggesting we sleep together.

"Maisy?" Michael dumped my phone, iPad, and folders in my assistant's free hands. "Do *not* give Harper any of this back until she meets with Jamie."

When Michael spun and trekked away, his backside shifted exquisitely in his tight dress trousers.

Michael had been a godsend of a friend from the day I arrived in Nashville and stayed in that friend zone. As the years wore on, an emptiness I couldn't vanquish had hollowed me out. I didn't want to believe only Jamie Miller could complete me. When I couldn't find those same prickles of excitement anywhere or with anyone else, I'd focused on my career. Driven to be one of the very few female CEOs for a music label. It *was* a goal. Now at thirty-three, it was a blessed life raft because I had nothing else in my life.

Except for a troubled mother, a string of hits with my name on them, and royalty checks hitting my bank account every month. From a distance, I had it all. Up close, anyone would see how lonely I was. Which was why I never let anyone get too close.

Sighing, I turned back to Maisy and frowned. "You're not going to give me back my stuff, are you?"

My assistant shook her head. "You might as well go say hello to Jamie."

Annoyed, I trudged to Michael's office, hoping with all my might Jamie had forgotten all about our little misunderstanding in Austin seven years ago.

Chapter Two

Harper

The glass sidelight to Michael's office gave me a quick lay of the playing field. With his wide shoulders pitched confidently back at his dark cherry desk, Michael looked very much like the strong and powerful A&R VP every artist would sell their soul to get five minutes with. Peeking out of the wing chairs across from him were two pairs of very manly legs, one stretched out farther than the other. Jamie Miller. The man was so tall he could block out the sun.

I'd not been pining for him all these years, but the unique magic Jamie made with his music had gotten into my soul and I never shook him off.

Summoning all my strength, I tightened my hand around the satin nickel door lever. Jamie couldn't look as heavenly in person after all these years. The music business wore people down. Like it wore my mother down.

As soon as the door opened, a towering god in an exquisite suit shot out of the chair. My breath caught as my gaze wandered up Jamie Miller's six-foot-four frame and his hypnotic green eyes made my stomach do somersaults.

Hell's bells, Jamie Miller was *more* gorgeous than I remembered.

"Harper Montgomery?" A young girl sitting on the sofa under Michael's window spun me around.

"Yes?"

Sweet round cheeks flushed and eyes went wide. "I can't believe it's really you!"

Everything else in the room suddenly blurred out

when the little lady slid off the sofa and rushed toward me. The same jet-black hair and Jamie's vale green eyes shined from the little face.

Name, name, what was his daughter's name?

"Hello, honey. And you are?" I decided to play dumb.

Finding out Jamie had a daughter only deepened my hurt that despite the friendship I thought we'd had, he hadn't trusted me enough to open up about his child. Did he think I'd be turned off?

"I'm Chloe. Jamie Miller's daughter."

My head fuzzed out hearing those words said out loud. "It's wonderful to meet you, Chloe."

"I *love* the song you wrote for Daddy."

Ah ha! That was how Chloe knew who I was. "That was a long time ago."

"It went to number one. It was Daddy's first big hit." She pushed her hands in the air. "He plays it for me all the time. He sometimes sings it to me when I'm not feeling well."

My throat grew tight. What could *that* possibly mean? He sang *my song* to the daughter he never told me about.

"Hello, Harper." The deep baritone voice made my body spark with heat.

I pivoted and soaked in the well-defined jawline and devilish almond-shaped eyes under thick, dark eyebrows. My shameful request for sex from him roared loudly like a dog whistle. But only he and I could hear it. And the way he stared at me, I knew instantly, he'd not forgotten.

When Jamie had swaggered into Remy's honkytonk that summer in Austin, the world stopped spinning. *I hear you write songs,* he'd said to me. I was lucky I could write because my voice had disappeared.

Seven years later, time stood still again as I struggled to speak. "Hello, Mr. Miller."

With confident footfalls, he crossed the room. A picture of power approached me and I had to steady myself. That amazing suit was quite different from his stage gear, perfectly fitted jeans and long sleeve shirts, most with his signature laced-up neckline. Or bell-bottom chinos laced up the side and iridescent skin-tight mesh tops with the fabric stretching to accommodate his biceps flexing while he played his guitar.

The grip of Jamie's fist as he claimed my hand dangling helplessly at my side was tight and warm. "It's so good to see you again." His familiar Texas drawl felt like velvet rubbed across my skin.

He sang even better.

Slipping my hand free, I said, softly, "So, this is Chloe." My heart squeezed, saying the name.

His green eyes beamed with pride. "Sure is."

"How old are you, sweetheart?" I crushed the moment, though.

Jamie's head dipped and he muttered, "She's eleven."

I reached out and smoothed my fingers down the long braid draped so sweetly on Chloe's narrow shoulder. "I'm sure everyone tells you this, but you look exactly like your father."

"I know." She adorably rolled her eyes.

"Harper Montgomery, it's good to finally meet the king and queen's daughter," Cam Renner gushed with a firm handshake.

My crown always peeked through eventually and

wedged itself into every introduction. I was country music royalty, Gigi Montgomery and Billy Cross's princess. Having those two as parents had set vicious expectations from everyone in this damn business. Labels wanted me to record. Artists wanted songs. Producers wanted my magic touch on the mixing board. All I had wanted was to make Nashville stars shine. Jamie would be a challenge given the layer of tarnish he had all over him.

"Mr. Renner." I smiled and shook his hand.

Cam nodded and stuffed his hands in his trouser pockets. "We're very happy to be at Blue Rock."

"Same here," I answered with a veiled attempt at sincerity.

A quiet fell over the room as nervous glances bounced around like a beach ball at an outdoor summer concert. Cam's shifty eyes to Jamie and quirky smile suggested the manager knew about our brush with awkwardness. A good manager should know all potential pitfalls an artist can tumble into.

Talent and crushing good looks aside, Jamie needed to work his tight ass off to earn points with me. Just like *all* my artists. No one got a free pass.

"Contract all signed?" I asked with a breath of an impatient exec. *I have a mother to not call back.*

"We were waiting for you, darlin'." Jamie took the pen and bent over Michael's desk.

The view of his ass made me lose my balance and I had to grip onto the back of a chair.

After Michael countersigned and sent handshakes all around, I locked my hands behind my back, signaling I had no intention of touching Jamie ever again.

Nodding, I said, "You don't appear to need me

anymore. Carry on." As I spun to get the hell out of there, I caught Chloe's gleaming smile once more. "Nice to meet you, Chloe."

"Harper, wait." Michael's voice stopped my escape. "We have something to discuss with you." He waved me toward one of the guest chairs.

So close.

"I'll wait outside with Chloe." Cam snagged the little girl's hand.

A shiver ran down my spine as Jamie's daughter's eyes stayed on me as she left the office. My focus was only broken when Gregory Blue appeared in the doorway.

"What can I do for you, Gregory?" I asked.

After seven years, I still worshipped the man and would do anything for him. He'd given me a home, an escape from all the record companies throwing contracts at me. Only because I was Gigi's daughter. Gregory hired me for me, not my pedigree.

"I'm here to talk to you and Jamie," my CEO responded and took off his classic white cowboy hat.

Me and Jamie? I glared at Michael. "What's going on?"

Michael snagged me by the waist. "Will you just have a seat already?"

I sighed, complying. Michael and I worked well together, ignoring the frequent sexual tension that sometimes reared its head. We were better as Blue Rock's dynamic duo.

Any other man who tried to crack my walls had slogged away defeated. "Okay, okay. Talk to me."

"You didn't tell her?" Gregory asked Michael.

"I didn't want to steal your thunder," Michael

answered his boss. Our boss.

My wild eyes shot from man to man. "Tell. Me. What?"

"We need you to write a song for Jamie," Gregory said with a smile that usually got the man whatever he wanted from me.

Usually. "No." I unfolded myself from the wing chair and prepared one heck of a storm-off, but Chloe's glossy black braid caught my eyes through the sidelight to Michael's reception area. Damn it. Looking back at Jamie, I said with a tight chest, "I saw the song list from your demo. You have plenty of material. You don't need a song from me."

Jamie's pleading grin penetrated me. Damn, that man. That song I wrote for him seven years ago had put me on the map, labeling me the *Nashville Hitmaker.* Plenty of my other songs dominated the charts, but the song with Jamie always had something different. Something more. Something…personal.

Maybe only I could tell the difference.

I sighed, my brain running the usual interference with my heart. If having one of my songs on Jamie's record made his sales go through the roof, it would give me a leg up in my fight to be CEO when Gregory retired. I was the favorite, but nothing was a foregone conclusion. The board had to approve any decision Gregory made.

"I have to think about it," I gave in. "Let me check my schedule and I'll get back to the executive producer."

Michael and Gregory exchanged tense glances.

The CEO nodded and said, "If you could decide by the gala tomorrow night, marketing would like me to make an announcement as soon as possible." Gregory's elite foundation raised money for music programs in the Nashville area and the annual charity ball was where he liked to show off Blue Rock's new artists.

"I really want to work with you again, Harper." Jamie flicked his gray Stetson with his finger, the motion slamming me back to his last night in Austin. *That* night.

After I'd handed over the demo CD I'd made for Jamie, I offered him a drink. Even opened a buck-thirty bottle of *Elijah Craig* for him, for Pete's sake. He'd worn that same sexy charcoal Stetson, his green eyes hooded under the front dip. I couldn't help myself. He was leaving the next day for Nashville. As politely as any good southern girl could manage, I laid my hot little hand on his groin, but he jumped back, finished his whiskey, apologized, and bolted out of my river-front apartment.

Nodding tightly, I opened Michael's office door counting the steps to get away.

"Will I get to see you again?" Chloe broke away from Cam.

For a moment it got so quiet that all I could hear was the sound of my heart pounding. I glanced over my shoulder. Jamie watched us with a confused look on his face. "Clo, Harper is very busy and—"

"I, uh…You'll probably see me again, Chloe. Daddy's launch, for sure."

"Chloe doesn't go to my launches." Jamie's firm jawline tightened. "School night and all."

Yeah, I hadn't gone to any of my parents' record launches either. I certainly never got invited to watch them sign contracts. Jamie wanted to share today with his daughter. My breath stuck in my lungs. I'd read this little girl's mother had died, poor thing. At least Gigi was still alive. I had a chance to repair that relationship. A returned phone call would be a good start.

I shook those thoughts out of my head. "Then some other time, for sure." Something about that sweet face got to me and I wouldn't disappoint her.

"I want to learn to play the guitar. Maybe you can teach me?"

"Clo," Jamie scoffed and quickly, but tenderly, took Chloe by the shoulders. The way she sank so softly against him, just a small movement, spoke volumes to their close, loving relationship. "Harper Montgomery doesn't—"

"You know your father plays guitar, too." I couldn't help but feel ice on my shoulders, sure that my father never held me so sweetly.

"I know." Chloe shrugged.

This little girl made me melt. With her dark hair, she could have been me at that age. Except she was clearly better nurtured. Gigi and Billy had lived on the road while I bounced from relative to relative all over Texas.

"Well, Chloe, I'll be writing a song for your father. When it's done, I'll be happy to teach you how to play it."

Jamie's breath hitched and he mouthed, *thank you*.

"Welcome to Blue Rock Records, Jamie Miller." I turned on shaky legs and with a fuzzy head wandered away trying to remember where my office was.

Chapter Three

Jamie

The last place I wanted to be was a *gala*. On a school night. Thankfully, Marta had agreed to stay with Chloe for a few extra hours.

When the first sip of whiskey passed my lips, my shoulders relaxed. I had two free passes to have a drink: Chloe would be fast asleep by the time I got home and Cam had picked me up in a limo.

The tension kicked back up when I spotted Harper gliding through the 1920's industrial warehouse turned upscale venue. All male eyes in that damn room were on her, too, dressed in a red satin mini dress that hugged her curvy figure a little too nicely. She looked downright spicy, like the bourbon hitting my tongue.

Mmmm. An ancient growl echoed deep in my chest. Harper's shimmering dark hair and cerulean blue eyes threatened to bewitch me again. The more I watched her, a spark that I'd hoped would be long doused grew with dangerous intensity. I'd had an opportunity to find out what was underneath her clothes seven years ago and I blew it.

Harper Montgomery wasn't a woman who handed out second chances. Or was she?

I moved in her direction, but a man's voice and face came out of nowhere.

"Jamie Miller?"

"That's me." I assessed the gentleman, older, suit, slightly wrinkled to go with his face and chalky white hair.

"Ronny Kravet." He moved a drink to one hand and

held the other out to shake. "Blue Rock, CFO and Marketing."

Ah, one of the *money men* at Blue Rock. As much as Michael touted how they were different from the giant labels, the *money men* still held considerable weight in business decisions.

"Pleased to meet you." I felt the need to snap into apology mode for my last album's pitiful sales.

I was high-risk. The fact that no other Blue Rock artist in that room even talked to me, meant either they thought partying and enjoying life a little too much was contagious or they despised me.

"I appreciate the chance Blue Rock is taking on me, sir." I shook the man's hand firmly which may have intimidated the little jerk since I stood almost a foot taller.

Even Harper was taller than this guy.

"You'll have an opportunity to properly thank me." He winked.

"Excuse me?"

He cast a sidelong glance around the venue. "You'll see." Ronny Kravet slithered out a door that looked like it led to a back-of-house corridor.

That's what I got for hiding in the corner.

Gregory Blue's voice stopped me from chasing the guy down the hall to ask him what he'd been getting at. "I want to thank everyone for coming. I especially want to give a huge shout out to The Rivermen and their producers for the unbelievable success of their album *Shine On*. Morgan, now that was a producing victory, right there." Gregory raised his glass of whiskey to a group of men standing in the corner. The Rivermen were a trip. They dressed like hippies and twanged every word. I didn't know if it was an act or if those guys were for real. Gregory continued after the applause. "And Harper, man-oh-man, girl, another multi-platinum song, dominating the airwaves."

But it was easy to get whiplash watching people come and go in this business. One wrong move, I could be next.

"I also invited a new artist, specifically to remind him that this is his goal," Gregory continued. "To have an album sell so well you can live beyond your wildest dreams."

I sure as heck didn't hope multi-platinum was now the goal for every record.

Thanks, Harper.

"Jamie, Jamie Miller, where did you disappear to, son?"

I gave a small wave at everyone who turned around and looked at me.

"Oh, he's being modest," Gregory said with a comical wave of his hand. "If you've seen him on stage, you know what I'm talking about. We've got plans for that album of yours. And in a few weeks when it's released, I know you won't let us down." Gregory raised his glass in my direction.

I returned the gesture and let the rest of Gregory's speech fade away until Cam's voice found my ear.

"What's got you all bent, J?" Cam swirled his Jim Beam in a crystal tumbler.

"Nothing," I responded, not looking at my manager.

Cam had come a long way from the scrawny rancher's teenage son who followed me around from gig to gig after I'd given him some music lessons. The poor guy was tone deaf, though, and hopeless in the music department. It was the business part he locked into and wowed me every time with one fantastic deal after the other.

Don't feel too sorry for Cam's ruined career. Life rewarded him with a big dick he liked to brag about. "For someone who just signed a multi-million-dollar contract, you should be happy."

"I'm happy. And I made sure to smile earlier while shaking Gregory Blue's hand in front of all his foundation donors. Can we leave now?"

"No. The more I can show you off not acting like a jerk, the better for me. My job is hard enough." Cam nudged me on the shoulder. "Harper is looking at you." His stupid sing-song voice taunted me. He usually only used it when a warning followed.

"I didn't notice Harper was watching me," I lied and glanced down at my glass remembering she had been the only woman who compared the flecks of gold in my green eyes to the drink I liked to knock back after a show.

"I can't place her expression." Cam put his drink down on a high-top table behind us.

I can. The fire in Harper's eyes rang loud and clear, except it was confusing as all get out. I'd committed the *never turn down a beautiful woman* sin.

"There's a sea of beautiful women here." I pointed in the opposite direction to change Cam's focus. Harper's hypnotic stare was knocking me off balance. "Don't worry about Harper."

"I worry when any woman looks at you." Cam squinted, then took out a pair of glasses. "It usually means work for me. I've been your friend long enough to know what's behind a woman glaring at you. I saw it on my sister enough times."

"Low blow, man," I shot back with a harsh scowl, surprised because we hardly ever discussed my botched relationship with Layla. "Who cares if Harper's looking at me?"

"She's your label executive. Call me crazy if I don't want her *or* Michael ticked off at you."

"You don't need to remind me." My musical connection with Harper had been powerful that to this day, I still heard her voice singing beside mine every time I sang our song to Chloe.

Ah, fuck, something about that woman scrambled my head. We were cut from the same cloth, both of us growing up in Texas was the least of it. We'd been so in sync that summer and she'd felt like my missing half.

I'd loved Layla, but she grew up on a horse ranch, and riding was her life. She would have considered living my dream on the road, in a bus, bouncing between low-grade motels night after night an utter nightmare. Chloe hadn't been part of the plan. My daughter was a surprise.

"Don't worry about Harper," I repeated and took a controlled sip of my drink. I'd reached the drinking-in-public limit Cam had set for me.

My manager cleared his throat. "Maybe *I* have a shot with her."

I grabbed my friend's suit jacket in a burst of jealous rage that spread through me so fast it frightened me. "You do *not* go near her."

"Sheesh." Cam straightened his jacket and reclaimed his glass. "I was kidding."

"Two *Elijah Craig* shots, please. Neat."

I turned my head to see who ordered the whiskey that always gave me goosebumps.

Michael Bradley glanced my way and took out a

twenty from his wallet for the tip jar. "Staying out of trouble?"

"For now," I answered and strode up to him. He gave me a full once-over and for the first time I wondered with shock why Michael never made a play for Harper. They worked together for years. Or…had he? Had she turned him down? Was the man pining for her? All these years? Wow. Then again…so was I. Was I? Pining for Harper? "Good drink."

"It's Harper's favorite."

I know that. I may have known that before you. Except, Michael didn't know she preferred it over ice. At least she had seven years ago.

I looked her way again noting how ram-rod stiff she stood talking with that Blue Rock money man.

The bartender poured the expensive bourbon into two crystal tumblers that sparkled under the sconces shooting reds and yellows across the bar. The amber goodness looked like liquid gold in a glass. My throat itched, needing one more soothing burn down my throat.

"I'll take a shot of that whiskey too," I said to the bartender. "Neat."

Michael masterfully balanced the two glasses in the palm of one hand and offered me a grin. Speaking low, he said, "Harper and Ronny Kravet don't get along. I have to get over there before she rips his head off."

"What are they disagreeing about?"

Michael tossed me a once-over.

"Great." I choked on my warm sip then sighed bitterly.

"Don't worry, Harper fights like a warrior for her artists. You're in good hands with her." Michael winked.

My fist tightened around my glass and when Michael

disappeared, I barked at the bartender. "Yo! One more of these shots. Rocks."

Sweet Harper could shoot whiskey like a six-foot cowboy and I geared up to rescue her with the kind of buy-back she actually liked.

Harper

I bit my lip, holding back some choice expletives for Kravet, a weasel who was suggesting we make Jamie a shirtless pin-up boy.

That Kravet runt wanted every singer's album cover to look like an erotic novel's book jacket.

Jamie had a daughter. One old enough to know how to Google.

"Sex sells, Harper," Ronny Kravet droned on.

"So do amazing songs." Where on heaven's plains was my drink?

I'd have fetched it myself, except Jamie was hovering at the bar. Every time I looked over there, he'd gotten more and more comfortable and even started staring back at me.

"Gregory gave me license to direct marketing dollars to Jamie however I want. That means I have a say. I'm telling you my angle as a courtesy—"

"*Courtesy*?" I wrenched forward, sending him back since I was taller than him. "I'm a VP, too."

"So, *act* like it, Harper," Kravet snapped. "This company is drowning. Why else would we sign that train wreck?"

My stomach heaved listening to someone call Jamie with his platinum talent a train wreck. Bad boy, yes. And everyone has off-albums. Yesterday, Jamie seemed like the same decent man I'd met years ago and he was wonderful with his daughter.

"Jamie Miller is no green debut artist," I argued. "He's seasoned. He's had to wrangle the big boys. Sony. Warner. EMI. I assume his manager learned a few tricks, too, and will push back against anything not in Jamie's best interest. You're the CFO, but you still report to Gregory. I'd move forward cautiously with these heinous ideas."

"Listen, you little—"

"Whoa!" Michael's voice boomed, shaking me up.

Kravet cleared his throat. "Excuse me." He drained his beer glass and slinked away.

"Do you want me to go punch him in the head?" Michael handed me my drink.

"It's not worth doing something stupid." I couldn't get that tangy whiskey to my lips fast enough. Warm, though. Yuck.

"Can *we* talk about Jamie's album?" Michael asked cautiously.

"Sure," I murmured into my glass, resolved not to make any kind of mistake with Jamie again.

"Gregory wants it fast-tracked. He was in the middle of recording when EMI dumped him. So, we need that song."

"I don't feel this one, Michael," I confessed with a sigh.

"What's up? We both know writing a song is second nature to you. You can bang one out in a day if you had to."

"If I had a weekend, it could be a masterpiece." Or a summer.

I cleared my throat, wondering if I should just admit what happened: *I asked Jamie to lay me down and he said no.* Except Michael might think he'd offered a multi-album contract to a complete moron.

I let my cheek rest on the side of the glass. "How did the rest of the meeting with Jamie go?"

"After you stormed off?"

"Sorry."

"I made an excuse for you." Michael would always have my back. "We good?" He clinked my glass.

"Yes." My drink was empty and there were more messages on my phone from Gigi. "I need one more of these."

Michael glanced over my shoulder, and whispered, "Be careful what you ask for, Harper."

I gave a peek and my body turned hot and hard. Jamie sauntered up to me, holding a sparkling glass of fresh *chilled* whiskey looking like a cat who'd eaten an entire pet store of canaries.

Jamie

I watched the muscles in Harper's throat tighten when Michael walked away, his eyes narrowed suspiciously at us. The stare Harper laid on me, however, touched a nerve. It felt new as if she almost didn't recognize me. Yeah, I changed in the last seven years.

Once upon a time, I was a singer nobody heard of and she was a local songwriter hiding under the Austin stars. I'd proved I had what it took to be a star. Anyone doubting my talent ate crow ten times over. But while I'd slowly slid down the favor pole like a squirrel violating a bird feeder, Harper's star had risen up, up, and away. She was the *Nashville Hitmaker* with a mile-long platinum-artist waiting list for her songs while I held on for dear life.

"Hello, Mr. Miller," she said in a seductive drawl, different from the stiff VP greeting, I'd gotten yesterday.

"You know you can call me Jamie." My right eyebrow dipped at her.

The bluest eyes I'd ever seen peered over the rim of her glass as she sipped the whiskey she never thanked me for. "Your daughter is cute as a button, *Jamie*." Those eyes pierced me with the question I suspected she'd been dying to ask: Why hadn't I mentioned Chloe at all that summer? The answer at the time had been messy.

"She knows it, too." Chloe was the best thing to happen to me and now all I wanted to do was gush about her.

Being a full-time single father had scared the heck out of me at first, but it made me a better man. My daughter only saw the good in me. Because during those ten months out of the year, I *was* a good guy. Boring, spending my days in a writing cave, pushing out music for the next album. Making my pathetic dinners for us, helping her with homework, and taking her for ice cream on the weekends.

That train of thought managed to calm me down.

"You don't need me to prattle on about your success. Your parents must be very proud," Harper said, sounding upbeat.

"They are, according to their holiday newsletter," I responded with a slight head shake.

"Do they still live in California?"

"They do. *According* to their holiday newsletter." I hadn't opened up to many people about not seeing or speaking to my parents too much. Harper had been one of those few people.

"Well…you've changed since that summer." The

sound of her voice stroked something I'd not felt in years. Seven, to be exact.

"That's one way to put it." I had a nice house, a few expensive suits, and one killer watch. Everything else was representative of an artist living royalty check to royalty check. "So, this is awkward, huh?" I lowered my mouth close to hers, the tart smell of expensive whiskey on her lips tickled my nose.

"You have no idea," she muttered and swigged her drink.

The room's tall acoustic ceiling had the cooling system working overtime and failing. The day's heat lingered into the evening and kept the party room balmy, sending trickles of sweat down my back.

I'd known it would be difficult to face Harper again. I hadn't expected it to tie me up in knots. How had I forgotten how nice she smelled? The pleasant blend of expensive perfume and her shampoo must have imprinted on my brain because images of Harper laying her hand on my package with lust in her eyes came screaming back at me.

Damn it, falling for Harper Montgomery was not on the flippin' to-do list.

"So, I need to get this song written." I shifted my weight to relieve the tension in my pants. "All my other tracks are mixed. I want to send everything out to be mastered together."

"I can't promise this one will be a hit."

"I have every confidence it will be. You're the most incredible songwriter. Those Grammys and CMAs for songwriting I watched you accept weren't participation trophies."

Harper looked up from her glass, her narrowed eyes

settling on me. "Do you want to work on the song with me?"

My body stilled and my extremities numbed so quickly I almost dropped my drink. I drew the glass to my mouth and spoke with my lips pressed against the rim. "You actually want to be alone with me again?"

Harper's otherwise glowing skin turned pale. "Mr. Miller, I can assure you, I will not be asking you—"

In a heartbeat, my control snapped. I leaned in close enough to touch my lips against hers. "I wanted you that night, Harper. But if I'd gotten into your bed, I'm pretty sure I wouldn't have been able to leave Austin to go sign my contract. I could have gotten so completely lost in you. You have no idea what price I paid to get where I was at that moment. Being with you would have eaten up any luck I had left."

Harper held her throat. Her eyes went all glassy and her cheeks looked like they were on fire. Breathing heavily, she gasped, "I need some air."

I put our glasses on a nearby table and with my hand on her back, I steered her past the open doors to a secluded corner by the outdoor bar.

A blue shine from the moon lit up her intensely black hair. It was almost as dark as mine. I usually went for blondes like Layla, but something about Harper had captivated me seven years ago. And now. "Better?"

She tilted her head back. "Yeah. Thanks."

It was best if I kept my eyes anywhere but on her face. Because, goddamnit it, I wanted to kiss her so bad. Those lips, full and shiny with lip gloss, were driving me crazy.

Shoot. I coughed and shifted again, cursing my choice to wear dress slacks and not tight jeans that would have kept what she did to me a secret.

Finally, I pushed out, "And, yes. I would like to work on the song with you. Very much."

She looked shaken by my intense stare. "I'll have the producer build more time into the recording schedule so we can write it. Together." The word *together* fell clumsily from her lips. "Next week, maybe."

Her blue eyes studied me, questions blinking out of her eyelashes like a frantic Morse code, SOS call.

"I look forward to hearing from you." I gripped her hand, my thumb pressing into her palm, making her lose her breath.

The flash of light in the sky registered as my heart sparked to life. I'd felt more alive at that moment, than in such a long time. My body craved to feel something, anything, again. Without thinking, I killed the space between me and Harper and put my lips on her mouth.

More shocking, she didn't push me away. Her hands held me at the waist and gripped me tighter while I deepened the kiss. Her silky-sweet tongue tasted like the whiskey and tingled me the same way.

I held the back of her head, the soft compliancy made my heart pound. After all this time. The flame I'd doused for her roared back to life.

Side to side, I moved my jaw, sipping at her lips, sucking on her tongue, tasting the inside of her mouth. With every beat, she held me tighter, whimpered louder, but still whisper-quiet, only for my ears. Her voice sang in my head while I lost myself in the kiss, just as I suspected I would.

Damn, I didn't want it to be *this* good.

Crying. I was crying. No, Harper was. No. No one was crying. It had started to rain. In sheets. A quick summer storm of fat drops drenched my skin and yet, Harper hadn't stopped kissing me. So, what the heck, neither did I.

"Jamie?"

I flicked my eyes open to see who called my name. Wiping the warm beads of heavy rain from my eyes until they focused, I saw Cam standing in the downpour watching me kiss my new label executive.

"Oh no," I mumbled, my lips still touching Harper's.

"Harper!"

Her eyes now flashed open. "Oh shoot. Is that...?"

"Oh shoot, is right, darlin'."

Michael and Cam stared at me holding the VP of my record label tight in my arms. The two men stood there getting soaked, seeming just as unphased by the pouring rain as Harper and I were.

Michael moved first, striding up to me with bewilderment in his eyes. Cam wiped his mouth and kept in step with Blue Rock's A&R VP.

Harper backed away, acknowledging how drenched she was. Michael gently put his hands on her shoulders. "You're getting soaked out here."

She nodded and let Michael lead her away, but her blue eyes stayed on me as she gazed over her shoulder. Looking...sad.

Michael removed his suit jacket and firmly laid it across Harper's shoulders as he hustled her out of the pouring rain.

Shaking, I drifted my gaze to Cam, who after a moment, smirked. "You just couldn't help yourself, killer, could you?"

"No." I got out of the deluge, but now a different type of storm headed my way.

Chapter Four

Harper

"Are you really not going to say anything?" Michael asked from the driver's seat of his convertible Corvette with leather seats he and I were ruining because we were both still soaking wet.

And I was rode-hard tired from my guts being ripped out from me.

I smoothed my hair, pushing more water down my back. At least I was no longer burning up. "That was…" Hell's bells, the best dang kiss I ever had. "That's not going to happen again."

"No kidding." Michael downshifted at the off ramp from 440 to Oak Hill.

With my nerves shredded, I counted the minutes until I could get behind my gate and into my house where I could fall apart alone. But I suspected Michael had no intention of doing a curb-side drop off. Even being under a deluge of water, Jamie's cologne lingered on my skin. I smelled it every time I moved.

Bad. Bad. Bad.

"Please don't make a big deal about this." I leaned my head against the heel of my hand. "It was just an impulse."

"After all the women he's seduced, I didn't think you'd fall for that."

"That?"

"Whatever sweet talk he laid on you."

"We were talking about his daughter. And the song."

"He's even more devious than I thought." Michael checked his mirror and changed lanes. "Using his kid and music to get to you."

"He wasn't trying to *get* to me." I knew Jamie didn't have to try very hard, that's what scared the daylights out of me. "We got caught in a moment. He knows there could be nothing between us."

Michael glared at me briefly and then turned on my block. "Okay."

I let go of my breath, swallowed, then said, "You're not coming at this from another angle, are you?"

"Other angle?"

"Are you the A&R guy looking out for his artist or my over-protective best friend?"

Michael stopped short, just missing my gate. "Do you need protecting?"

I thought about that.

"No," I finally answered. My internalizing how I felt about Jamie rang like a dull hum off my skin.

Michael stared out his windshield. "And can you still write that song?"

That kiss in the rain had left me shaken and unsure of myself. I was terrified anything I wrote now would reek of innuendos masked as my feelings. But with that kiss in the spotlight, I had to prove more than ever what a professional I was. How I could string lyrics together that didn't touch my heart. "Of course. Piece of cake."

Only being alone with Jamie again, and *not* falling for him again and *not* losing my heart felt like a Herculean effort at the moment with the feel of those damn lips lingering on my mouth.

"Go inside and dry off, Harper." Michael pulled into the paver-stone apron in front of my gate.

"Why don't you come in and dry off, too?" I slapped his wet shirt.

He shot me a smile. "I can use a towel and one more

shot of whiskey."

"Deal." I clicked the security app on my phone to open the gate.

I bought the southern colonial with a center hallway and grand staircase after songwriting royalty checks rolled in regularly.

Past the arched walnut door, a line of windows let in the moonlight and I followed the drops of light to the kitchen while Michael lingered quietly behind. Until he grabbed my arm and pulled me against his body.

"What are you—" My breath caught noticing movement inside my kitchen.

The petite frame of a woman sat at the lighted quartz island.

"What in God's name?" I cried out.

My mother turned her stool around and eyed me up and down. "He won't answer my calls. That's why I've been praying to the altar of bourbon all these years."

"What…what are you *doing* here?" Only then did I notice several Louis Vuitton cases strewn about in the corner.

"Isn't it obvious?"

"Let me guess." I set down my sparkly evening bag on the kitchen island, shaking off the heart attack. "They wouldn't let you do shots in rehab."

"Yeah, they kind of frown on that thing. Oh, hello, Michael." My mother's smile widened noticing him finally. "Am I interrupting something?"

"No," Michael answered quickly, drawing a glare from me. "In fact, it's late and I need to get going. Gigi, good to see you."

My mother shook a head of her signature blonde ringlet curls, only they looked somewhat dried out and saggy. "I guess you two idiots haven't gotten out of your way, yet."

"I'll see you tomorrow, Harper." Michael squared his shoulders and high-tailed it out the front door.

Take me with you!

"Did I really not interrupt something?" Gigi's genuine befuddlement made me wonder if I'd been terribly naïve about me and Michael.

We worked well together, but I felt strangled with worry that perhaps I'd been leading Michael on.

Musicians were known for pulling themselves up by the bootstraps, turning scaring heartache into gut-wrenching songs. I'd worked with one artist who sang a song so suffocated with emotion that when I'd met the woman who broke the singer's heart, I wanted to punch her in the face.

Perhaps Michael's Luccheses didn't have straps.

I thought about next week's music auction where I planned to donate one of my father's guitars. Now I worried asking Michael to go with me sent him mixed messages.

"Poppy!"My mother's prodding kicked me out of my thoughts. "What is going on with you and Michael?"

I spit out a *zzzt-zzzt-zzzt* ending *that* conversation. "Are you seriously not going to address why you're here and not in that expensive California facility I'm paying for?"

"Come on, Poppy." Gigi rifled through the credenza next to my dining room table. "I can think of better ways for you to spend *your* money." She emphasized it was on my dime because I had Gigi's money locked up in a trust.

"I doubt they'll give me a refund. It's not a hotel you can just check out of."

Gigi opened and closed my kitchen cabinets. "If I raised you right, you have your mama's favorite hooch tucked away. Eighty proof is for amateurs." Shamelessly prying open a wrapped bottle of 1792, and pouring a healthy shot into a crystal tumbler, Gigi announced, "I'm through trying to be clean." She swigged it down, her long curly blonde hair slipping back.

I felt a wisp of sympathy. My mother had been battling demons of alcoholism for decades. I had refused to *ever* record music. Gigi had been dragged away from her career kicking and screaming.

When Gigi and Billy's band fell apart because of her substance abuse, the relationship with my daddy turned sketchy at best. Not that it was ever great. After the poop hit the fan, Billy turned his back on *both* of us. The man had divorced his wife while she was in rehab. Talk about kicking someone when they were down.

I'd been left with a mess to clean up.

While my mother had been in and out of rehab, my father went to Houston to be a DJ. I'd heard whispers he was spinning records for one of the radio stations there under an alias. I didn't have the energy to pick at that thread.

So yeah, Billy and I didn't talk.

My mother leaned in and took a delicate whiff. "Whose cologne is that? Not Michael," she asked, sipping from her glass. "His fresh aquatic cologne is nothing compared to this woodsy, spicy scent."

How she could still smell was beyond me. "No, it's not Michael. It was…Jamie Miller."

My mother lowered her glass. Yeah, word of Jamie Miller, with his looks and talent had made its way to California and Gigi's rehab centers. "And have you turned into a groupie while I was away? It's widely known he *loves* those."

"Michael signed him to our label." I chose not to dignify the groupie comment.

"And just how do you celebrate with newly signed artists these days?"

"Mama!"

Music was everything to my mother at one time. Maybe if she stopped thinking about *not* drinking and focused on something else.

I put down my glass and pried the matching tumbler away from my mother, who frowned. "Come have a listen to his demo. Even you with all your awards will agree it's the best darn thing you've ever heard."

I steered her into my music room, brought up the demo on my computer, and after a few guitar licks, Gigi stumbled into a seat.

Her eyes strayed to me as I gyrated to the rhythm. "How long did it take for this good ole boy to get you into bed?" my mother asked.

I gasped. "If you can believe it, he just kissed me."

"You're all caddywonked over a kiss?"

I slumped into the seat next to her. "Looks that way, doesn't it?"

"We are gonna need more alcohol if this is a long story." Gigi shook her empty glass.

"We should probably eat something. There's lots to tell." I pulled myself up.

Despite the whiskey Gigi had knocked back, she managed to assemble random ingredients from my kitchen into an interesting midnight snack. I never had a normal childhood and it startled me to realize her concoction may have been the first home cooked meal

Gigi ever served. Mac and cheese from a box didn't count.

After Gigi also did the dishes, I knew I had myself a house guest and was too exhausted to drag my mother to the airport.

The evening had been…nice.

Gigi offered to stay in the pool house. It was the best thing for our fragile relationship. Once I realized she wasn't spiraling out of control, I tiptoed back into my music room.

I in no way had enough of Jamie Miller. The musician, no. The man? Yeah, I was done with the man.

Reclaiming my glass, I finished the one-hundred-proof of velvet gold. The smooth drink mixed deliciously with the smoky taste in the air from a nearby wood firepit that crept into the house. My tongue moved across my lower lip, remembering how Jamie kissed me. I tipped back my glass and sighed as the last of the tangy heaven splashed against my tongue.

Jamie was my artist. Talent Relations had a unique role at my label. The gentle ear when no one else would listen. A glorified life-coach. Musicians were known to have…issues. I knew. I grew up with a couple of doozies.

I trudged off to bed, firm in my goal to just give Jamie Miller a rebirth. He could significantly boost Blue Rock's revenues and appeal to other artists like him who wanted small label love and not big business chill.

I *could* resist him, couldn't I? There was only one way to find out.

Jamie

After leaving the gala, I felt Cam's stare burn a hole

through my skin. I evaded his questions the whole ride and shoved a wall between us. For the entire ride home, he looked like he was dying for details of how Harper's lips ended up on mine.

I pretended to read emails all the while hoping to see a text from Harper. Some kind of message that would tell me Michael wasn't furious and fixing to tear up my contract.

"Have a good night," I said when we arrived at my house.

"That's it?"

"Yep." I slapped my best friend on the back, getting out. "I'll talk to you tomorrow."

"Sure," Cam said, sighing.

A life without Cam was unfathomable. We'd spoken every day since we were teenagers. I never would have gotten through these past eleven years without him. It still amazed me how he stayed out of my on-again/off-again romance with his sister, trusted me not to hurt her.

At one time, I didn't think I could live without Layla. That had been a sad slow erosion, though. Starting with her breaking up with me for what had been the final time. Right before I had my very first show booked in a Nashville honkytonk.

She'd then called me to tell me she was pregnant and then didn't pick up her phone again for weeks. When I'd gotten home to Wild Heart, she told me she was keeping the baby, but didn't want or need anything from me. She was a rich rancher's daughter and I had two nickels to my name. No shit she didn't need me. But Chloe needed a father.

I tiptoed softly through the front hallway of my house. It was dark and quiet at that hour. The deep shadow on the wall reminded me of those few steps I took before a stage light shined down on me and the thunderous cheers from thousands of screaming fans deafened me.

A light from a lamp in the corner of my living room pulled me out of my reverie and found me along with Marta's concerned glance. My clothes hadn't dried much.

"I was going to ask if it was still raining, but I have my answer," Marta said, putting down the book she was reading and rising from a rocking chair.

"There was a roof deck at the gala. I got caught." Kissing Harper Montgomery. Literally and figuratively. "Chloe get to sleep okay?"

When Marta didn't answer right away, the hair on the back of my neck stood up. After a stare lingered between us, she said, "She gets restless this time of year. It's hard for a child to change their routine. I checked on her after an hour or so. She's sleeping soundly, now."

I nodded, relieved. For a whole host of stuff.

The stout, fifty-something nanny had been a godsend when I hired her three years ago. Other nannies had been a nightmare. Singers who wanted a break in the music business or minxes trying to seduce me as if I'd cross that line. My judgment hadn't always operated on all cylinders, but I wasn't *that* big of an idiot to sleep with my kid's nanny.

"Thank you again for staying." I toed off my wet shoes.

Marta was Chloe's nanny, not my housekeeper, and made no attempt to wipe up the water I dripped all over the hardwood floors.

"Good night, Jamie. See you tomorrow." Marta

settled her purse under her arm and strolled out into the warm night that turned foggy after the rain.

Once the front door closed, I removed my clothes in the living room and tossed them down the stairs to the basement where the washer and dryer were. I kept my wet briefs on in the unlikely event Chloe woke up. When I reached my bedroom, I changed out of those and slipped on a pair of sweats and my favorite merch tee-shirt.

No one understood that I was restless, too. Counting down the days until my life was going to do a one-eighty. A boring single dad from a small Texas town one day, to a Nashville music god with lights in my eyes and people screaming my name. Performing was what I'd wanted my entire life. My one and only goal. It was a good thing I achieved it because I didn't have a backup plan. That may have been what pushed Layla away.

The odds of being a success were so far against me, despite my talent, despite my looks, despite my dedication. No one ever thought I'd make it.

It took one song: Harper's.

I wandered to the other wing of the second floor. My heart eased seeing Chloe sleeping peacefully, even twisted up like a pretzel. I fixed her skewed blankets and kissed her forehead. Always shocked that in those quiet moments how she smelled like Layla.

I shuffled back to my bedroom and lost the urge to keep the past buried. I pushed aside my first Stetson, revealing several shoeboxes stacked in the back of my closet. All that was left of my life with Layla. Pictures. Letters. Postcards. Chloe would want to see those pictures one day. I told myself I kept them for her, but I was quite good at lying to myself.

Then there was the other box, the red shoebox on the opposite wall. Inside, I took out a phone. I plugged the charger in and fired it up. My phone from seven years ago. Right before I signed my contract. I'd had money for a much fancier phone after that and didn't need that bottom-of-the-line piece of junk.

But I never got rid of it. Inside were pictures. I'd downloaded all the pictures of Chloe years back. Those sat on a laptop somewhere. No, I had pictures of the other woman in my life. Harper. We became great friends that summer. All the time spent working on my song bonded us in a way I didn't think would ever break. Except when she asked for one night in bed with me, our bond cracked like it'd been shot with liquid nitrogen. I'd told Harper the truth earlier, I wouldn't have been able to leave her behind to go to Nashville. Sure, she would have pushed me, no one wrote a song that spectacular to just go unsung. It'd already been torture living my music dream without my daughter, without Layla. How many other women was I supposed to leave behind?

On a scale of one to ten, Harper hadn't physically changed much in seven years. It startled me how the face smiling at me was so recognizable and familiar. The woman I wouldn't kiss.

How could I have been *that* stupid?

A beep to my working phone caught my attention.

Cam: *Harper is still writing the song for you …*

I slept with a smile on my face. It was just a kiss, one that neither of us expected. But it felt like the beginning of something I wouldn't be able to walk away from…not again.

Chapter Five

Jamie

"Her *house*?" I broke a guitar string when Cam told me I'd be writing with Harper at her house. "What…how…why?" Yeah, *that's* what I wanted to know the most. *Why*?"

Being shuffled around and kept in the dark about important details had been the part of my career I found most unnerving.

"Logistics," Cam answered. "The two studios Blue Rock usually rents out are closed for renovations. The others are booked solid. Plus, it's just to write a song, no need to pull rank and pay a premium to get some studio time."

All expenses to make the album were on my dime. My financial statements showed I was flush with enough cash to splurge here and there, but if I wanted to keep Chloe in her private school, pay Marta the salary she deserved for everything she did for us, and then get my daughter into a good college, I best save my pennies where I could.

"When?" My daddy brain kicked into gear, as I replaced the guitar string in my basement studio.

"Hang on." Cam opened his iPad and began swiping which meant he was moving stuff around. When I wasn't touring, Cam doubled as a personal assistant.

I cursed when Cam told me the writing session with Harper would be in the evening. Unlike seven years ago in Austin when she was freelancing her skills, Harper Montgomery was a nine-to-five girl now. The night she'd offered conflicted with Marta's schedule and Cam had dinners with promoters for my upcoming summer tour. The limited events most of the year didn't call for me to set up a string of sitter backups.

That meant one thing…

*

"How much longer, Daddy?" Chloe asked from the backseat a few evenings later.

Most of the week she'd been moody. Quiet, but punchy when I'd tried to talk to her. With a month or so to go before leaving for Texas to stay with her grandparents, her demeanor slowly shifted like she was mentally preparing for the time away from me. Sure, some kids went away to camp for an entire summer. Two months, limited supervision, and nothing but playtime wasn't the same as living with her grandparents who watched her like a hawk, didn't let her ride her horse, and playdates weren't Faye Renner's concern. Making sure Chloe grew up to be a proper southern lady was more important to Layla's mother.

A different kid sat in the backseat of my car, right now, though. A smile had not left her little face.

"Soon." I gripped the steering wheel following my phone's GPS directions to Harper's house.

Yeah, I was bringing my daughter to a writing session with Harper Montgomery.

When I gave Harper a heads-up about the schedule conflict for Chloe, she'd immediately said, "Oh, bring her along. Does she swim? I have a pool."

Chloe had tagged along to writing sessions before which were as common in Nashville as sipping sweet tea on a back porch. Many of my writing partners had kids and Chloe played well with others. Those writers meant nothing to Chloe. She'd been hung up on Harper because she'd written my first number one hit. Chloe's favorite song.

My nerves were shredded seeing Harper again. Unsure of myself. About what I was feeling and what the right move was. Working alone, without the prying eyes of a producer or engineer would allow me to finally confront all those unknowns. After what happened at the gala, I wasn't sure what type of executive she was going to be with me.

How would the kiss affect our working relationship?

This was different now. I was in a sense…her employee. Contracted by her, as an exec with the label. And *my* career and ass were on the line.

The view along the road after I got off West End Avenue before it turned to 70 South graduated from small brick Victorians, stacked side by side, to southern colonials with cement fences and lots and lots of trees.

"Very *nice*, Harper." I nodded in approval, talking to myself.

Seven years ago, I was living in an Austin fleabag motel and she had a one-bedroom apartment overlooking the Colorado River.

I'd received a text warning me not to turn into her driveway too quickly. When my Range Rover came within inches of a large wooden gate I understood why. It opened while I caught my breath. I pulled into the mouth of a wide circular driveway and parked next to a concrete tiered fountain gushing with water.

Growing up in Wild Heart Texas, I'd been accustomed to large, frosty, palatial estates with acres and acres of farm or cattle ranches. Like Renner Ranch, the home Chloe lived on every summer. The same home where Layla grew up.

Harper's house had a warm quality lingering over it.

The smell of butterscotch and vanilla from nearby ponderosa pine trees was about to overtake my senses, but Harper appeared on the top step of blue shale floating stairs twisting down to her driveway. Her flared skirt, loose embroidered top that hung off one shoulder, and sandals were a sharp, but exciting departure from the sleek business suit she'd worn last week. Given a choice, I preferred her in tight jeans and a tank top. That's what I'd remembered her wearing our summer in Austin.

Chloe snapped out of her seatbelt, opened the door, and rushed to hug the woman I couldn't.

Jeez, my daughter had met many leading ladies of country music, a few actresses, even a royal who'd attended the same charity event I'd gone to one afternoon. Meeting those women, Chloe reacted with a yawn and a question about where to get more ice cream. The electricity buzzing through my daughter over Harper Montgomery was baffling. Smoothly stepping out of my SUV, I kept my cool, even though I felt just as giddy over seeing Harper.

After getting my guitar out of the back, I noticed Chloe had gone stock still except for her jaw hitting the gravel below our feet. I followed the stunned gaze and had to hold on to something, too. Just not Chloe or we both would have fallen over.

I blinked in surprise. Unsure if I was seeing correctly. Gah! I wanted to smack myself. How could I have forgotten Harper Montgomery was the daughter of the legendary singer, Gigi?

The woman was enough of a star that she only needed one name. Harper's *father*, I swallowed hard as the name rumbled in my throat, Billy Cross, was my very first guitar hero. Among the many things Harper did correctly was to make a name for herself without riding the coattails of her insanely famous parents.

The resemblance between Harper and her mother was more evident when we were only a few feet apart and it allowed my fear to ebb slightly. Harper's long dark hair framed her face compared to the crystal blonde signature ringlet curls Gigi kept since the early nineties.

"Is that?" Chloe finally grumbled.

"Sure is, honey," I mumbled back.

Harper

I had grown used to being noticed. I even appreciated the acknowledgement from artists I was working with for my songwriting talent and achievements. The complete and utter stupefaction around my mother still set me back. I'd spent my entire life in the shadow of country music's blonde bombshell who sang with the voice of an angel.

Jamie and Chloe looking like they'd been zapped shouldn't have bothered me. But it did. They were *mine*, not Gigi's.

Whoa.

"Is that really her? Are you really, you?" Chloe said, turning red.

"It's me, sugar." Gigi opened her arms for Chloe. "And what's your name, cutie pie?"

When Jamie nudged her forward, Chloe sprang away from him, climbed the shale steps, and flew into Gigi's arms. "Chloe. Chloe Miller."

"That's some powerful hug you have there, sugar," Gigi said. "I'm Georgia Montgomery. Holy sands of time, this baby girl looks just like you," she said to Jamie, holding Chloe's chin softly.

"That's my dad." She pointed behind her, but kept her eyes on Gigi. "Can I call you…Gigi?"

"Of course, you can, sweetie," I answered, fearing my mother didn't know how to edit sassy jokes down to a child's level and worried an f-bomb would fly from her mouth. It'd taken a miracle to keep a drink out of her hands all day, telling her Jamie's young daughter would be in the house.

I felt a world of gratitude for Gigi's compliance and pushed back the resentment of how Chloe got a courtesy Gigi had often failed to show me, her own daughter.

"Mr. Jamie Miller," Gigi said with her hands on Chloe's shoulders. "I've been tucked away in those…resorts your label exec here sends me to so I've not had a chance to meet the man who nearly single-handedly transformed our music world."

It was true, many of Jamie's songs had significant crossover appeal, seducing pop music lovers into the world of country.

"Pouring it on a little thick, huh?" I murmured, but stepped aside to let country music's former first lady swallow him up. The queen deserved to take in her subjects. Gigi certainly had those two under some kind of spell.

It was hard to remember how people only saw the glory in Gigi. Not the devastation when the stage lights went down.

"It *is* a pleasure." Gigi went on. "As far as talent goes, you've given the big boys a run for their money."

Jamie climbed the steps, one powerful confident step after the other until we were all on the landing outside my door. "I hope it sure looks that way." He smiled at my mother, but the corners of his mouth turned down facing me. "It doesn't always feel like it, though."

Right there, I felt that connection I made with my artists. The ear no one else would have.

"That's quite normal," Gigi dished out her music wisdom. "And eventually you'll learn to live with both sides of what this business does to you." Words of advice from the woman who taught me how to count with an ice cube tray. "Poppy wrote a song on your debut album, right?" Gigi asked, glowing.

"*Poppy* sure did." Jamie laid an evil grin on me. I was gonna regret him knowing my nickname. "*Poppy* and I have written together before. This is a beautiful home, *Poppy*." He smirked at my frown.

I pushed my front door open, and Gigi and Chloe glided in.

"My mama had golden hair like you, Gigi." Chloe played with her braid.

I froze, realizing I hadn't told Gigi Chloe's mother had passed away. "Hey, Chloe," I said and smiled when she whipped around and gave me the same adoring smile. "Did you bring your bathing suit?"

"I got her bag right here." Jamie lifted a pale pink knapsack with the initials CM in gold glitter.

As he stepped into my foyer, he took my breath away. Beat up vinyl guitar case in one hand, his little girl's backpack in the other.

"Are you two joining us?" Gigi asked.

"Probably not. We have work to do."

"If you want my opinion on that or any other song, Jamie, when you're done with my little chickee, just come out to the pool house and let me have a listen."

"You have a pool house?" Jamie scoffed at me.

"It's just a glorified cabana with a galley kitchen, a

stand-up shower, and a small alcove bedroom. It's no big thing."

If that was supposed to make me look less spoiled, he didn't let it register on his face. He looked at me like I was bat-crap crazy. "I can't wait for the day when I have a pool house I think ain't no big *thang*," he said, shaking his head.

"And yet she put her mother there." Gigi crossed her arms.

"Bad, Poppy," Jamie snickered.

Chloe gave a soft giggle and Gigi turned her attention back to the little girl. "I want to see you swim. And show me some tricks." Gigi took the bag from Jamie.

I thought I'd have to handhold everyone through this meet and greet, jiggle the marionette strings to get everyone to do what we needed to do.

Nope.

Chloe took Gigi's hand who clutched on with the natural grace of a seasoned… Good lord, did Gigi want a grandchild? Just like that, off they went into the house, Gigi's long skirt billowing behind her.

I smiled hearing Chloe's oh's and ah's over my house. Surely, Jamie's mansion was spectacular, too.

Keeping my eyes on them, I slinked backward sailing into a hard chest of muscle pressed against my back. I froze, feeling Jamie's breath on my neck. Somewhere in the frenzy kiss last week, I'd touched him. Just the feeling of his broad chest against my back knocked me off balance.

Jamie's breathing stopped. Neither of us moved. His massive body should have frightened me. No, I liked it, liked how he engulfed me. Warm fingers pressed into my neck, and the weight of my hair gave way to a whisk of air conditioning blowing from a nearby vent.

Then wet lips, full and sensuous, glided up and down the side of my neck.

Man, it felt so good. *Too* good.

The foyer had grown darker from a passing cloud blocking the setting sun. The sconces on the opposite wall cast a warm ambient glow in its place, but made the space seem smaller, more intimate. *Too* intimate.

No. No. No. After an agonizing sigh, I turned around and gently nudged him away.

"Seriously. Whatever happened the other night can't happen again."

Jamie backed off, his face flushed. Staring straight ahead, he said, "I'm sorry." He pressed his eyes closed and seemed annoyed with himself. "I can't help it. I feel like an utter moron for not letting us cross that line seven years ago. And now…"

"Now?"

"Let's just say I won't forget that kiss," he groaned, his seductive eyes boring into me. Despite his relaxed posture, I picked up the tightly coiled strain in his voice. "But I guess I don't deserve another chance."

"It's not about another chance. I'm your label executive. That creates a working relationship between us and technically I can be charged with sexual harassment. Or worse, if your manager all of a sudden isn't happy with how the label is supporting you, and they find out we're sleeping together, you can sue the label and me personally for malpractice."

"Here I was waiting for some kind of character assassination and you're worried about workplace drama?" He shifted his guitar case to his other hand. "I think you're being a little dramatic, Harper."

"I wish I was being dramatic, Jamie, but I'm not. Have you been paying attention to the news at all? We're in a new era. The media would have a field day taking down a woman executive. They'd make a meal of me to get their point that harassment suits aren't witch hunts. Or wizard hunts."

"I try not to watch the news. Fearing I'll be on it. And not in a good way."

I nodded, we understood each other better than I could have imagined. Watching my parents deal with fame certainly gave me the tough skin to deal with loving a man like Jamie and seeing everything he needed to go through.

It was the touring and being apart, though, that I would never do to myself.

Ever.

Chapter Six

Jamie

Hugging Gigi had only reminded me my own mother hadn't hugged me in a really long time. After their move to Northern California several years back, my parents had grown apart from their superstar son, and oddly, when I got custody of Chloe, they just had no interest in either of us.

I'd been living a life of bizarre paradoxes. Layla's family fought tooth and nail to be with Chloe, and my parents didn't even return phone calls.

So, I picked up on the clear tension between Harper and Gigi. I wasn't oblivious to the complications of mother/daughter relationships.

I stopped and got choked up, realizing it was *another* thing Chloe would miss out on. Having a mother when she turned that corner and needed serious female advice.

As I passed through Harper's foyer of floor-to-ceiling windows with raw silk drapery panels the color of oyster shells, the setting sun glowed through, warming my body. Another ray of light shined down from a skylight above. Its bright cast tilted my head toward a curved staircase. The second floor was shockingly visible, open, and exposed. The feel of Harper's eyes watching me drew my attention back to the main floor.

"Sorry if my mother was a little over the top." Harper strolled into her kitchen.

"No problem, Poppy." I shoved one hand in my jean's front pocket. "I'd love to get to know her better."

She glared at me, and as we passed her state-of-the-art media room, she said, "Perhaps after we're done, you guys can play Xbox." The snarky comment was either an

59

attempt at flirting or Harper was still annoyed.

"I'd give my left…" I cleared my throat, censoring myself. "To see you and Gigi do battle on *Guitar Hero*."

Harper bit her lip and moved in closer. The blast of her floral perfume hit me square in the chest. "She can't play anymore," she whispered.

Before I hung myself with another stupid response, I asked, "What happened?"

"The drugs basically, and the booze. Her hands shake."

I tried to process how awful it would feel to have my gifts ripped away from me. I squeezed the handle of my case tighter. My lifeblood.

"Before you go boo-hooing for her, she still has her voice and I suspect she can still write songs that will do fly-by's past anything you and I could do."

Anything we *could do* echoed in my brain. I'd had a chance to get more songs from her, but I screwed up by laying the biggest insult a single man can on a single woman. Turning down sex. *And* never telling her about Chloe. I was already one step in the wrong direction by trying to feel those lips again. Even though she kissed me, willingly, desperately the other night, I was there that night in her house to reach her on another level.

"Do you want some water?" Harper asked at an open refrigerator.

"Sure," I answered, dragging my gaze away from her.

Everything about that place, the stunning and elegant house, the property in back, the pool, all reminded me someone could have money, be kind and generous, and not be a jerk like Cord Renner. I blew out a breath to get out of my head.

"My music room is this way," Harper said, holding two bottles of water.

I looked up to catch the blue sky reflected in her eyes from the row of windows over the stretch of counters overlooking the yard. But Harper quickly turned and I caught her back instead. The line of her body was almost as good a view. I crossed a small hallway and passed under a bright white arch with decorative molding.

Inside a room filled with trophies, platinum albums, signed celeb photos, and honorary diplomas, Harper leaned casually against a glossy black baby grand piano. With musical sensations for parents, it was no surprise she was equally proficient on both the guitar and piano. Shuffling papers around, she appeared unaware of the massive accomplishments around her.

I'd been so damn cocky seven years ago, not realizing who I'd been dealing with. I had no frame of reference. Now after sinking deep into the business, I knew what it meant to not only make it to the top, but stay there.

In the mix of priceless instruments, recording equipment, sparkling awards, and photographs of Harper being hugged by artists I'd kill *just* to be in the same room with, a simple, yet beat-up wicker basket drew my only verbal comment.

"What's in that?" I pointed, putting down my guitar case.

Harper looked up. "Oh, songs."

Inside the basket were reams of sheet music, blank staff paper, pages from yellow legal pads, as well as sheets torn out of notebooks. Without thinking, I reached in and took several in my hand. I loved the idea of seeing one of my favorite Harper Montgomery hits as a rough concept.

The titles and lyrics on all these pages, however, were unrecognizable. "Who recorded these?" I asked.

"No one." The uneasiness in Harper's eyes made me feel as if I'd been caught looking in her underwear drawer.

"Harper, are you going to record an album of your own?"

"No." She pried the pile from my fingers.

A nearby wall where all the platinum records she'd written stacked like honor guards on both sides of the display case drew my attention. I expected more pride in the way she viewed her achievements. Instead, I sensed nothing but emptiness.

A moment of silence passed before she added, "What you sent to us for your album, Jamie, was…" Harper's breath caught.

"Yeah?"

"It may be your apex because I can't imagine songs being any better."

"Do you really think so?"

"Some people get better and better. Just fly over the wreckage and debris of other people's crashed careers. That'll be you. I feel it."

Our eyes locked and I licked my lips.

"So…this song, do you have something particular in mind?" I asked, feeling the gravity of where I was.

"You write some killer power ballads." Harper smiled, like somehow, she knew that's what I would ask for. "I like a power ballad that opens with a piano. But we can do something different. Perhaps open with a piano and then fade into an acoustic guitar?"

"I've been playing around with a melody." I

skimmed my hand on the glossy surface of her piano.

"Show me." She nodded, scooping up a notebook. "If we're doing this together, I want to hear what you have."

What I had was a daughter who was crazy about her and my heart wasn't far behind...

Harper

Jamie and his sexy tight black tee-shirt tucked into those jeans fitted in all the right places made me unsteady on my feet. He sat down at my piano. A haunting order of piano chords drifted from my *Precious.* Jamie manipulated my baby. Took sounds from it *I* never got the darn thing to make.

A sizzle of fire shot through me. Musicians were so profoundly seductive; they tunneled deep into my soul. Songwriters needed a muse. Could it be as simple as that? *Keep it simple, stupid.* KISS.

A voice said, *Give the man whatever he wants to make him strong and sure of himself.* Jamie carried a heated burden on his wide shoulders. The world didn't deserve him beaten and broken, not when he had such talent to lift people up.

Jamie didn't glance up at me, but he knew I was watching him, the way his gorgeous mouth curled into a wicked smile. The chords vibrated through the steel strings beneath the piano's wooden lid and then filled the room. The vision of Jamie playing my piano dissolved into a watery image of him playing for me that summer. I stopped myself *then* from jumping across the piano because people were watching. This time may be more difficult.

"That's incredible, Jamie. How long have you been working on that?" I asked after he finished the vamp.

"A few days." He raised dark hooded eyes toward me. "After you left me standing in the rain, wanting more than a kiss." His smile made the ground feel unsteady beneath my feet.

My body heated up. "I'm serious."

"So am I." He cleared his throat. "I have a lot to make up for, Harper. I've made some pretty big mistakes." But then the look he laid on me, stopped my breath.

He had enough star power clout with Michael and Gregory to say he didn't want anything to do with me if my proposition had offended him.

"Your talent earned you our contract." I needed to be Jamie's mentor, not a scorned woman. "Fair and square."

"I'm sorry they signed me against your wishes."

I hated that he knew I objected to offering him a contract. It didn't make for a very good working relationship. "Are there words that go with this gorgeous thing I'm listening to?" I leaned against the piano. "Or are you just gonna torture me?"

His jaw twitched "No," he answered and let me figure out which of the two questions it applied to. "That's why I'm here. This is what I need you for."

"You *are* like me. Exactly. More than you know. You knew how this would kill me." As the words tumbled out, I wasn't sure if I was burning from the song or the fact that his music seduced me. "Do you want to stick with this melody for the song?" I pressed one of the water bottles against my burning cheek to keep cool.

He answered, "You tell me," and took the second water from me. "Is it good enough?"

"Everything I've heard from you is…good enough." I inched closer, but maintained a safe distance.

Jamie cocked his head to the side and rested his forearms on top of the fall board, above the keyboard. "Don't blow smoke in my eyes. Nothing is perfect. No one is perfect. Tell me something that's useful."

"Play that last measure again." I snapped on my producer setting.

He was right, it could use some tweaks. The opening was beautiful, but so perfect without any punch, people might tune it out.

"Again," I demanded and my cheek ticked up when he drove the notes louder using the foot pedals.

I scribbled a few verses in my notebook, letting a darker side of my writing nature come out. A haunting tale of love gone wrong in the form of lyrics that would slide effortlessly into the notes Jamie played.

"Here. Sing this." I rested a page of lyrics on the music rack.

He glanced at the paper, dropped his jaw, and stopped playing.

With the paper in his hand, he stood, his height suddenly jarring in the small space. He counted on his hands, moving his long talented fingers.

After pacing back and forth, I realized why my heart was racing. Our previous writing experience had been buried away with everything else that led up to me asking for one night with him.

The shape his face took as the ideas came to him. He kept a shocking amount of information in his head and wrote very little down. Which meant it all played out on his face, every word, every note.

Like me. It was a rare gift to be able to remember every little up and down the notes took especially when playing to find the right combo.

He sat back down, closed his eyes, and sang. His voice made words on a piece of paper gut my soul and twist me up. I remembered coming up with that idea for a song. Could my subconscious have driven it out of me knowing I'd reunite with Jamie to get this…this adrenaline rush from being with him?

He stopped singing, his lips parted as he took slow breaths. His eyes opened and found me, and I prayed I wasn't drooling. "Like that?" he asked.

I guffawed a laugh at the double entendre. Yes, I liked that and yes, I meant that. He'd taken a string of verses and mixed them all up. Like he tore up the paper and then taped it back together randomly. Only, now the song was…perfect.

Almost.

"We're close." I signaled to take over at the piano and he scrambled off the bench. The temperature under my skin rose a few degrees, brushing past him. "Why don't we shift the song after the first verse, like this." The cool, smooth keys I touched earlier that day now tingled with Jamie's warmth.

"Hmmm." He held his chin.

"This is what you have in the first verse." I softly dipped my chin into successive nods as I ran my eyes up and down the keys. "Then transition to this for the bridge," I said, continuing the fluid movement. "Keep this one off-balance. Symmetry is for amateurs and you want something that sounds different, not predictable."

"I agree." Jamie looked around and sharply crossed the room.

I gasped when he picked up *my* acoustic Gibson, and not his own. My guitars were on the short list of things in the house I'd save in the event of a fire.

It sat just as comfortably in his grasp as it did mine. After giving the tuning pegs a few turns to adjust to his dramatically low octave, his fingers smoothly ran up and down the mother-of-pearl inlaid fingerboard.

"Ah, perfect," Jamie purred.

I couldn't stand being left out, my fingers itched so bad they almost burned. From a closed guitar case tucked in the corner, I took out the axe no one had seen in years.

My father's. If my Gibson hadn't been held by the strap, it might have crashed to the ground, Jamie looked so shaken. God love him, he played it so cool, but I knew he recognized it.

Fingering my Gibson, he strode up to me and let me see the notes, so I could repeat. Within a minute, I strummed through the song's second verse of chords, but stopped when I realized I was the only one making music.

"Let's switch." He pulled the Gibson off his shoulder and reached for the axe.

I released Billy's Strat gently into his chest and snatched my Gibson. Needing a moment to take the look of want from my face, I turned around and let the feel of the guitar guide how it wanted to be held.

Remembering Jamie's notes, I strummed with my right wrist, circling in successive flicks, gliding past the custom pickguard. After getting the feel for the notes in the different keys, I turned back around.

My fingers danced across the strings, fluffing up the basic chords, adding texture and depth.

"Do that again," Jamie said, adjusting Billy's guitar, his biceps stretching the fabric of his tee-shirt as he moved.

I repeated and gasped when he played back in the

exact same order what my brain randomly commanded me. Except it was better. *He* was better.

My chest tightened watching Jamie play my father's famous guitar. He'd disappeared into his own little world. I strummed along patiently, letting my music be the white noise he needed to figure out whatever chord wars were going on in his head. When my own cadence ended and I geared up to repeat, I looked up and expected Jamie to be busy with the guitar. No, he was watching me.

"I think I got it." Jamie's head bobbed, flicking a few more strings and when he looked up, his face paled.

My cheeks flared hot. God, what that man could do to me. I'd been around musicians my whole life, sure they were my comfort zone, but no one revved up my body and eased it at the same time.

That man was dangerous. When the next seven years clocked in, would I look back on that night and kick myself for not grabbing that man and holding him down until he screamed?

I fisted the black tee-shirt, ready to lay a kiss on him that would set the room on fire. He was already holding my guitar and...

"Daddy?"

Chapter Seven

Jamie

This had to happen eventually… Chloe *seeing* me with a woman. I'd kept my summer flings off the radar, and my daughter had always been too young to really understand relationships.

An age of awakening this past school year had hit Chloe and I could feel my daughter's eyes on me all the time. Wondering about me. Wondering if I had a woman in my life. Which I didn't. Except for that colossal mistake I'd made a couple of months ago.

Chloe adored Harper. The idea of Harper, anyway. Making her part of our world, the world where some nights we ate takeout pizza or blue box mac and cheese could ruin the magic for Chloe.

One thing was certain, she was old enough to understand what it meant if Daddy had a girlfriend. Yet, if Chloe watched me kiss Harper Montgomery, a woman I suspected I could have real feelings for, that could set off a bomb that would blow too many people apart if I messed it up.

No one went running into a minefield. This was gonna take some time and some finesse.

"Yeah, Clo," I finally answered and swaggered up to her. First and foremost, she was the love of my life.

"I can't get the hairband out. It's all tangled." She stood there, wet, wrapped in a towel, her braid caught up in a secondary knot she sometimes made when she was…stressed. It'd taken hours to get the last set of tangles out. And apparently cutting the braid off wasn't an option as evidenced by Chloe's blood curling screams when I'd suggested it.

"I'm sorry, kids," Gigi said, striding behind Chloe, looking worried. "I tried. I don't want to hurt the poor thing."

Her hands shake…

"Okay, let's take a look."

That memory of me with the scissors chasing her around the dining room table must have given the poor kid PTSD. She backed up and shot her eyes to Harper. "Can Harper help me?"

Harper changed physically being called up to the plate by Chloe. Nodding, she bounded to my daughter. "Of course, sweetie. Let's go into my bathroom upstairs where the light's better."

She glanced over her shoulder and gave me a sly smile. My heart pounded watching them walk off together.

That left me in the music room with…Gigi.

Separating the famous singer from the mother of the woman I was pretty sure I at least wanted to kiss again, delayed my immediate reaction. Individually, I could handle either. Rolled into one woman, however, made my stomach flip flop.

I knew enough about Georgia Montgomery that she would appreciate my wild side, could saddle up next to me, and try to drink me under the table. Under any other circumstance, it would be the thrill of a lifetime.

"Is that?" Gigi asked, pushing me out of my thoughts.

Just then I realized what was in my hands. I froze and lifted Billy's axe away from my body.

"No. Don't." Gigi sucked in short, but steady breaths. "It's a beautiful instrument and made so many happy memories. It doesn't deserve to be in a case," she yelled, like she wanted Harper to hear her.

"Your daughter is incredible, Gigi. Every facet of her. I was so darn star struck when I met her that summer in Austin, I thought I'd made an ass of myself."

"You've gotten over that, I see."

"Maybe." I still couldn't believe who the heck I was having that conversation with.

"It's amazing isn't it?" Gigi strode through the room and sat at the piano. "Being on stage singing your own songs. Watching the audience's expressions. Letting them into our private world."

God, I'd fit in so perfectly here. Chloe, too. These were my people. I'd planned to move to Nashville after college, but Layla became pregnant. I'd quit school and stayed in Texas, but traveled around to make a living. Not that it mattered, she wouldn't take a dime from me. I got my contract, and still nothing. Then that damn horse threw Layla to the ground like a rag doll. After I'd won custody of Chloe, I bought my house here in Nashville for us.

"I know what you mean," I answered Gigi. "Touring is...the best part of this gig, right?"

"Best and worst." Her fingers slipped across the keys, only feathering them.

She can't play anymore.

Harper's words kept slamming into me, I felt them touching me.

I looked down at my own hands. "I never wanted to sit at home and collect royalty checks. I wanted to be on stage, *all* the time."

Gigi batted her golden lashes when I made eye contact again.

"You must be so proud of what Harper's

accomplished." I glanced at her awards.

Gigi pointed her finger. "I had *one* match in the box with that girl and I used it to get her a record deal. But she wouldn't sign it."

This was earth-shattering news to me. How did I not know this? I never saw Harper in that role because the woman was perfectly suited behind the scenes. Writing songs. Producing. Mentoring.

"I wouldn't wish the kind of pressure that can eat away your sanity on anyone." I let my shoulders slump. "Especially someone who doesn't want that life."

"I had such mixed feelings when she decided to work for Gregory Blue." Gigi stood and wandered slowly around Harper's music room, her long dress swaying against her ankles. "For years, I lived by the principle that record labels weren't in the business to help artists grow and develop." Her movements suggested she had been in that room before, but ill-timed bouts of hesitation suggested she didn't know her way around very well. "I've been *so* proud to see Poppy providing the support that I never got." Gigi turned in my direction and smiled.

"How long are you staying here, Gigi?"

"As long as she lets me. She tied up my money in a trust I can't touch. I need to prove myself. This home is lovely, but I need my own space."

I didn't hate the idea of Gigi hanging around with me, Chloe, and Harper. I coughed through an awkward laugh. Was I really thinking of taking things that far with her?

Once I went on the road, any foundation we would build in the next month would crumble for sure. I wasn't sure I knew how not to be a jerk on the road. Could Harper be the one to change me? Did I even want to change? Weren't Chloe and I doing just fine? Seeing how she lit up around Harper and Gigi...

Well, crap.

Harper was adamant, though, that nothing could happen between us since she was my exec.

She peeked in for an update. "We got the band out, but she wants me to do a French braid. Are you two...good in here?"

"Oh, we're doing just fine," Gigi replied. "Go make that little girl pretty. Shoo! Shoo!"

"Five minutes and I'm taking him away from you." Before Harper closed the door, she glanced my way.

Her delayed stare, filled with longing, spoke volumes.

The words were simple enough, but the possessiveness in her voice made my mouth water for her. Even if it only had to do with music, I somehow became hers.

Damn, I liked that.

Gigi let me just sit and play random measures on the piano, her eyes closed, soft hums purring from deep in her throat, her fingers tapping on the glossy surface. Those fingers held my attention. *Booze ruined her career.*

Harper returned with Chloe, her hair all twisted up in a new braid. I checked my watch. That was fast. Before I could address the medal-worthy achievement, I noticed my daughter's eyes were half closed. Then the time on my watch registered.

Time to be a dad and not a musician. Time to be a dad and not a man trying to...

To what? What could I possibly have with Harper?

When Chloe practically tumbled over, Dad-mode

cranked to full blast.

"I think it's time for us to go." I scooped my daughter up in my arms and her hands wrapped around my neck. "Say goodnight and thank you to Harper and Gigi, Clo."

"Good night. Thank you." Her breath fanned against my neck, saying goodbye in between successive yawns.

"Good night, cutie pie," Gigi said, saddling up next to us and pinching her arm. "You're such a good swimmer. Gosh, I tuckered her out for you." She winked and sashayed out of the room.

Leaving me with Harper while I held my sleepy daughter.

She stood there, staring at me. A flash behind my eyes, I saw the songwriter I met in Austin. Like a jolt back in time, showing me what Harper would have said had I told her I'd had a daughter. When I'd gone back to Wild Heart to see Chloe that summer, disappearing from the Austin music scene for a few days, I'd just said I had to go home and left it at that.

Harper would have understood. But would she have accepted *why* I wasn't raising Chloe with her mama? How Layla had shut me down for being a loser. It left me feeling I wasn't worth anyone's love.

"Thank you for this, Harper," I said.

She approached me slowly, her eyes on Chloe. I couldn't make out what she was thinking, though. I'd donate my next few royalty checks to find out.

"I think we have something," she said, her voice filling the silence, the music room now feeling alive again.

I arched an eyebrow at her.

"The song," she whispered, but smoothed her fingers along Chloe's hair. "She's lovely and sweet, Jamie."

"Thank you, I… I don't know how much of that is my doing." I clutched her tighter, I didn't want Layla to completely disappear. I didn't want Chloe to forget her mother.

"It's more than you think." Harper stepped away, her face flushed.

"I need to go, Harper." The words weighed on me, as I imagined saying that to her with a summer's worth of touring waiting for me.

Holding my guitar, Harper nodded and led me out of the music room. We ambled back through the house in silence. After opening the front door, I expected to tip my hat with my one free hand and leave.

Harper leaned in and hugged me. Me *and* Chloe. "Goodnight," she whispered in my ear. "See you…soon."

The inflection in her voice on the *soon* part filled me with hope that maybe, just maybe I'd get a chance to find out if Harper and I were as compatible without a couple of guitars and a kid between us.

Chapter Eight

Jamie

"Are you kidding me?" Michael grumbled looking at his phone

"Problem?" I asked and bit hungrily into a bacon cheeseburger.

"You can say that." Michael put the phone down on the table and went back to his blackened-salmon Caesar salad.

The downtown restaurant was choked with customers and surprisingly busy for a Tuesday afternoon. Every table had one suit and one pair of jeans—the artist business meeting giveaway. Michael Bradley's dress slacks and a solid-colored button-down shirt distinguished him from the agent sharks sizing up prey in that place.

I ate comfortably in my jeans and one of my nicer tee-shirts. It was nearly one hundred degrees.

After Michael's phone blared with three successive texts, he picked it up and answered my next question before it was asked. "I'm supposed to go to an auction tonight, but an artist I've been trying to see just announced a surprise show tonight on Insta."

"Auction for what?" I asked, ignoring the horror that there might be another artist Michael wanted to see so bad, he'd cancel black-tie plans and sit in a dingy bar at midnight instead.

"Music memorabilia." Michael squeezed the bridge of his nose. "It's something Harper and I go to every year." He narrowed his eyes at me looking for a reaction.

Like I'd fall for that. I'd done everything I could to keep the conversation flowing away from anything to do with him catching me kissing Harper.

Except the Harper topic ran over me when I wasn't looking. "Oh, you're going with Pop— Harper? Is it for the label?"

Michael looked up. "Sort of. One of our artists usually donates something every year."

"What are you donating this time?"

"Harper usually takes care of that." Michael shrugged. "I don't like her going to these things alone. But I don't want her to back out. We represent the label. Appearances are everything. It's a charity, no less. Damn it."

My feet tapped to a beat in my head as I waited for Michael to look back at me. I fiddled with my napkin to dry up my sweaty palm or I'd drop my fork. "Um, I can go." I'd threaten to fire Cam if he couldn't stay with Chloe.

Michael shot me a glare. When he opened his mouth, the shape meant something unpleasant was about to fallout.

I held up my hand. "I'll keep it professional." *Maybe.*

I'd been waiting for Michael to ream me out for that kiss. Lip locking with my label exec. The fact that Michael hadn't even addressed it, suggested Harper must have really convinced him nothing would ever happen. Which was why perhaps Michael didn't go all alpha on me, and tell me to stay the hell away from her.

Like *I* did to Cam. *Sheesh.*

Michael kept his jaw tight, until he nodded and put his phone in his pocket. "At least with *you* on her arm, no man would dare go near her," he added dryly.

My discreet flings on the road all had one thing in common: instant gratification. Harper was long term. A forever girl.

The fact that she hadn't called me in the seven days since we worked on the song made me uneasy how to approach her. At least with Michael thrusting us together, I could use it as a neutral opportunity to explain what I was feeling.

And how I was terrified because now it wasn't just my career on the line, it was Chloe's heart. My heart often felt like it got run over by a truck and I operated on emotional fumes from being dragged through the mud with Layla.

"Do you have a tux?" Michael looked down at my torn jeans.

"Suits, yeah. Tux, no," I answered touching the dark stubble on my jaw. "But I'm sure I could get one."

"Nah, a nice suit will work." After Michael paid the waitress who didn't take her eyes off *me*, he stood from the table. "I'll email you all the details. And I'll let Harper know you're coming so she doesn't freak out when she sees you." Michael took his phone out of his shirt's front pocket. "I finally got her to play nice with you."

Trying to kiss me is playing nice? Sure, let's call it that. "Okay."

"Jamie, remember, this isn't one of your shows. You're representing the label. No antics."

"I know how to behave," I grunted.

"Don't tell me. *Show* me." Michael signed the bill with a swish of his pen that fell off the table, suggesting the man was scared silly about me being alone with Harper.

*

Later that night, as the auction got well underway, I

sat glued to an upholstered bench in the vestibule. It'd been seven days since Harper and I worked on the song and I was nervous as all get out to see her.

I'd avoided all that Nashville hoopla for years. Stayed home with Chloe at night, helping with homework while the music elites whispered whatever stupid ass thing I'd done on the road over the summer. Now I had to face the nay-sayers who'd assassinated my character over the years.

A text from Michael made my heart pound. Ugh. He'd been getting Harper's voicemail and hadn't told her about the switcheroo.

Oh, great.

Now I had to ambush Harper in front of Nashville's stuffy elite. I hated not knowing how she'd react. Would she throw a shot of whiskey in my face, thinking I was stalking her, or would she try to finish that kiss?

I need a drink…

After getting a bidding paddle, I strolled up to the bar. One shot of bourbon quickly turned into two. I'd taken a car service, so I just needed to stay vertical and not slur my words. From the mirror behind the stocked lobby bar, I caught my reflection. My hair, slicked back on the sides, but soft and loose around my eyes, reminded people I was still a bad boy. Even in Prada.

I pulled the suit jacket in place and followed the flow of tuxedos and evening gowns, none of which gave me more than a curious once-over. *I'm back to square one, aren't I?*

I stepped aside from the rush of guests just beyond the entry doors to get my bearings. There were at least ten rows of chairs in front of a stage and a podium.

My eyes moved over every inch of the room to find

Harper. To anyone else, she may have melted into the sea of beautiful women. My radar was fine tuned for that woman. My body tensed up when I spotted her, standing alone in the corner holding a glass of champagne. I was oddly thankful since the whiskey had emboldened her at the gala, enough to let me kiss her.

Yet, a bottle of water and Chloe made *Harper* try to kiss *me*.

Like the sparkling disco ball on the ceiling, Harper's body-clinging halter gown glittered like it'd been dipped in liquid silver. The dramatically low-cut neckline made my chest tight. Even though she had an amazing body, I didn't care for her showing it off to other guys. When she turned around and I saw the dip it made to her ass, I nearly dropped my drink. I blew out a breath of frustration, hoping no one noticed me having a fit. Control. Slipping.

The idea of resting a warm palm along Harper's spine to get her attention electrified me more than I wanted it to. My steps across the room came to a halt when another man approached her and whispered something in her ear. I drew a ragged breath watching her walk off with the guy.

Oh, hell no!

The swell of jealous rage pumped hot sparks through me. I knew that feeling. That's when I acted stupid.

After a long hard bite on my lower lip, I continued forward to follow her, but a male voice coming out of the speakers near the stage drew my attention. "Ladies and Gentlemen, our next item up for bid is a real treat."

I reluctantly stomped to an aisle seat in the second row.

"Tonight, Blue Rock Records executive, Harper

Montgomery will be relinquishing a special instrument from her daddy's guitar collection."

What the heck? Michael failed to mention *Billy Cross* was the artist!

The room exploded into applause. Harper stepped onto the stage with a wide smile. My jaw dropped seeing Billy's axe in her hands. She was *not* giving that away to some stranger.

It shouldn't be in a case, Gigi had protested. How would she feel about it going to some rich dude adding to his collection of musical toys used as bragging rights?

I remembered how that guitar felt in *my* hands. *I don't think so…*

Harper gave several people a few quick waves and seemed overwhelmed when everyone got to their feet.

"Thank you," she began. She acknowledged the auction coordinators then segued into a speech about her involvement with the foundation and praised them for reaching their goals that year. "But wait! There's more." She took the microphone in her hand and I gripped my seat, thinking she just might sing something. "Whoever wins the guitar, also gets a personal lesson from me."

I froze. A personal lesson? All the lascivious smiles from men in expensive tuxes, licking their lips made my blood boil in rage. Good God, no.

"Okay, Harper," the MC announced. "We'll get the bidding started."

Harper took the mic in her hand and strolled back and forth on stage seducing the crowd with a story about where Billy bought the guitar, what songs he wrote on it, and other small anecdotes. My eyes followed her watching the muscles in her back jump and flex as she walked.

The bids flooded in. I didn't understand why she'd give that guitar up. I'd never met Billy Cross and didn't think I ever would. But something told me, the legend wouldn't want Harper giving it away. When the bid climbed to an amount I could live with, I held my paddle up.

My heart hammered against my chest at the impending spectacular confrontation. "Can I ask you something, Harper?" I said in my booming baritone voice that could shake the walls of a football stadium.

No one in that room may have recognized my voice, but one person sure did.

She stopped dead in her tracks. "Look who we have here," Harper said into the microphone as she took me in. "This man needs no introduction. I'm sure y'all know the delectably talented Jamie Miller."

I had heard my name introduced hundreds of times. Hearing Harper say it with pride, mixed with a hint of sexual frustration, was intoxicating. I dutifully waved to a group of people who looked like they wanted to throw rocks at me.

"What y'all may not know is that we just signed him to our Blue Rock label." She looked around and frowned seeing the negative reaction, too.

"After playing that gee-tar the other night with you during our writing session, darlin'…" *That's right jerks, she's writing a song for me again.* "I'm thinking I might want it for myself."

The surprised wide eyes were delicious and I loved how her jaw twitched.

"You can certainly bid, sir," the announcer jumped in, robbing me of the feisty response I knew Harper had for me, given the fire in her eyes. Mostly from the shock of seeing *me* with the paddle and not Michael.

"And there's a lesson that comes with it?" I added to pry a reaction from her.

"You heard the man," Harper breathed into her mic. "But clearly *you* don't need a lesson. In anything."

The room giggled, watching her sass off to me.

"The lesson isn't for me. It's for my little girl, Chloe." The faces in the crowd softened, and women clutched their hearts.

"How good of him to take some of that money we're paying him to buy this amazing guitar and a lesson for his daughter." God love her, she was trying to persuade the crowd not to hate me.

So of course, I had to fuck that up. "What was the last bid?"

"Nine thousand dollars, sir. Ten thousand and I think we can say it's yours."

My body shook at the amount, but it was for charity. "Done."

I strolled to the stage, my head held high. With heavy, confident steps, I strutted up to her and pulled her in by the waist. I laid a heart attack of a kiss on her. Gasps filled the room, but her stiff stunned lips complied as she kissed me back, her breath shaky when I stopped.

Her body burned hot under the thin fabric of the dress. Once she was in my grip, I whispered in her ear, my lips brushing her skin, "Michael couldn't make it. Something about a singer he needed to go see. He sent me."

I swallowed, taking in the stares from the crowd. They looked shocked and...disgusted. Like, how dare a bad boy like me, woo Gigi and Billy's princess.

There were murmurs all around me and finally the

auctioneer took control of the room again. I expected Harper to run off the stage, but she just…stared. Her eyes, pleading for some kind of explanation of what the heck I was doing.

I took the guitar and just like the night she let me touch it for the first time, I slung it across my shoulders, noticing she at least changed out the strap. There was a part of her that didn't want to let that axe go.

Or could it be the other strap smelled like me?

I didn't need a guitar. And she already agreed to give Chloe a lesson.

When the stage lights left Harper's eyes, we were plunged into a soft shadow. I took her hand and brought her down the steps away from the crowd.

"I'm sorry," I said gruffly.

"For what?"

"Michael said he'd tell you I was coming instead of me."

"My phone was ringing off the hook, I shut it off."

"Sir?"

I dragged my gaze from her blue eyes. *Go away!* "Yes?"

When the attendant asked for my payment, I flinched. "Um. I don't have a checkbook with me."

"I'll send you a check tomorrow," Harper blurted to save me.

"No, darlin'." I smirked and looked back at the attendant. "Do you take American Express?"

My accountant would have a heart attack when the bill came in, but as Harper had said, it was for a good cause.

I set my shoulders back and followed the man with Harper's hand in mine.

"Will you let me give you half?" she whispered in my ear when we reached the payment table.

"Nope." I took my receipt, folded it, and put it in the inner pocket of my suit jacket. "I don't go Dutch on my dates, darlin'."

Harper

Being kissed by Jamie in front of all those people had made me unsteady on my feet. His height cast such a dense shadow that the temperature dropped around me. Even though I could still sense the furnace cranked up under that suit. Just when I thought he couldn't come wrapped in a nicer package.

After we moved into the hallway, Jamie stayed quiet. His smooth, predatory gait knocked me senseless with want and need. I waited for him to pounce, but he lingered about a foot away.

I pushed through clenched lips, "I don't understand what's going on with us."

"Me, neither."

"Okay, then." I gripped my sparkly purse. "You let me know when Chloe wants—"

"Harper, I'm an idiot and I don't always know *what* to do." His voice drifted off to that dangerous octave that made me lose my mind. "Help me figure it out?"

Jamie's dazzling green eyes pierced me There was something behind them. Windows to his damaged soul smoldered with a spark of desire.

"Is it me? Am I making this difficult?" I couldn't breathe. Where was the air?

"No. It's *so* not you."

"Oh, okay." I looked down, still confused. "How did you get here?"

"I took a car service here because I knew I'd be tied up in knots and need a lot of whiskey." His powerful presence was drawing me into his web again. I felt like a butterfly tangled up.

"Wanna get out of here?" I heard myself say.

He dipped a seductive brow. "With you?"

I nodded and licked my lips.

"Lead the way, darlin'." One of Jamie's hands rested on the small of my back, while the other held my daddy's guitar. We walked down the busy VIP corridor, and I felt the thick tweed carpet under my shoes and every wisp of air from the vents made my senses come alive. With every elegant sconce and piece of trendy artwork we passed, the exit got closer and closer.

I was leaving the auction...with Jamie.

Outside, I fished a valet ticket out of my purse and relaxed as a wave of people surrounded us, deflecting Jamie from saying anything that would make me come undone. The idea of being alone in a car with him, however, had my heart thundering loudly in my ears.

My cherry-red Cadillac SUV rolled up. Jamie confidently handed the valet a crisp C-note and held the driver's door open for me.

I moved at a slow and measured pace. I should have been reserved, tucking my breasts behind crossed arms, fearing my body would give me away. Moving in his direction absorbed by his wicked gaze, I put my exhilaration for the man on display.

Jamie tugged my waist. "Is the guitar really mine, too?"

"Uh, huh." My eyes slipped closed, loving how his hands felt.

"Good. But something tells me you didn't really

want to part with it."

My throat tightened. "I didn't. But it was time…"

How had Jamie known that when I'd put on the new strap earlier, a rush of bittersweet memories of my dad playing it had flooded me with regret for choosing to give it up?

I was trying to let go of one man in my life, but with the swipe of a credit card, my daddy and Jamie Miller were staying in the picture a little while longer.

Chapter Nine

Harper

Jamie punched his address in my nav screen, instead of dictating the directions. The tension inside the car was thick and heavy. He had a child to get home to. I didn't. A child. Good grief, Chloe was in the house. Surely, he wouldn't suggest anything happen tonight. I relaxed a bit and turned on the radio.

When the slow scratchy drawl of Chris Stapleton filled the interior, Jamie slapped the knob, deadening the music.

"Jealous?" I smirked his way.

"No. I can't deal if a song of mine comes on."

"Why?" I shook my head. "That's the best part of all this madness. Hearing your voice come through the radio."

"It's not that." He held his chin and looked out the window.

"What then?"

"I couldn't bear to see you react negatively to any of my other songs."

That shocked me. "Jamie, you've achieved a great level of success. Your songs have all made the charts."

"Nothing's gone to number one since…" He glared at me.

My shoulders slumped. I took a minute to process the turn I needed to make. "That doesn't mean they weren't incredible songs. I got chills listening to every single one."

Jamie burst out into hysterics. "Darlin', seriously? You can't lie better than that?"

"Maybe I'm biased."

"Why?"

"Because I always knew you were special. So, anything you recorded, I…" I looked at him. "I loved."

"Wow. Okay. I'll let that sink in." He pointed. "Right here."

"This is beautiful, Jamie." I turned down a residential street, high-end, but not ostentatious in any way. "So homey and warm. Does Chloe like it here?"

"In this house or Nashville?"

"Both, I guess." I parked in his driveway behind his Range Rover.

"I think so. She seems happy, right?" The panic in his voice bothered me.

"She does. But more important than that, she seems well cared for. And adored." I pinched his chin and I gasped when he caught my hand.

A blast of heat crawled across the back of my neck, though, and my body stiffened. He made no attempt to keep a safe distance. Not that there was any.

Jamie plowed a hand into his neatly combed hair, causing a few glossy strands to flop onto his forehead like when he was on stage and it hung softly around green eyes. Eyes that could make me do anything. Unable to stop myself, my fingers smoothed the loose waves back.

I gazed at one of the most beautiful male faces I'd ever seen. His jet-black hair always made me curious about his ethnicity; possibly a hint of Cherokee had snuck into the family genes a couple of hundred years back.

"That's an intense stare you just laid on me, darlin'." He leaned into my lips. "But you look positively terrified. When was the last time a man looked at you like this?" He smoothed away a few hairs from my face.

Tit for tat…

I shrugged, realizing no man had *ever* looked at me like that.

"Well, *I'm* looking at you." He leaned in. "And you're not looking away." The way his full pink lips puckered tortured me.

"Because I like how you look at me," I confessed and glanced away, ashamed. Ashamed to be craving a man so much.

"I can do more than look," he whispered.

"I've heard you like variety. On the road."

"I'm thinking I may be done with all that nonsense. I won't lie about what's happened in my past. You know what happens on tour. But sitting here with you, I have zero interest in taking what I need from some willing woman I might meet on the road. Those empty encounters compared to the way my heart is pounding right now… Touching you…" He boldly tugged the gold hairpin keeping half of my hair up.

I whimpered from the magical feeling of freedom as my hair cascaded down in soft waves on my shoulders.

His large hand closed around mine. "Let's stop dancing around the reason I'm in your car right now. I know what we both want. Neither of us are those people from seven years ago. Let's stop acting like we are." He put my hand on his groin. "That's because of you, Harper Montgomery." His use of my full name chipped away at my ability to deny him. "I've been this way since I kissed you earlier."

"That's…um," I whispered, and moved my hand away.

A stare stretched out between us in the dark. Jamie's

devilish grin vanished along with my memory of the raucous twenty-something man I'd met in Austin.

"Kiss me, Harper." The man gazing at me looked…sincere. And, if possible…sorry?

Just his touch challenged my equilibrium. Did I have the same effect on him? One of the fundamental responsibilities of my position at Blue Rock was to protect my artists and sometimes save them from themselves. Musicians with top-selling albums and tons of fans were spoiled brats and we gave them what they wanted to keep them happy. Those hotel rooms didn't wreck themselves when artists didn't get what they wanted. I had to decide in that moment if I should risk Jamie's sanity during these crucial weeks of finishing his record by refusing him or give in to what we both wanted, knowing *my* sanity would be destroyed when he left to go on tour.

Could I go another seven years feeling empty? Taking the risk, I leaned into Jamie's mouth, soft at first, but a fever spread through me. Hot and fast. He reciprocated with punishing, frantic kisses.

He reached under my dress and my breath hitched when he fingered the rim of my lace panties. "That's gonna be trouble." Jamie's hypnotic kisses made me crave his taste, I couldn't get enough.

As if I were a rag doll, Jamie lifted me out of my seat and rested me on his lap.

My core rubbed against the bulge that startled me earlier and now it felt harder and bigger.

Heated and quivering, I took what I needed in that car, holding him tighter and tighter. I was so focused on his mouth that I lost track of roaming hands. He slipped his fingers into my panty and tapped against my heat.

"Wait," I whined.

"Tell me to stop," he said, rubbing my nub, making small circles that nearly sent me over the edge.

"S…"

"What's that?" he asked, moving a finger inside me.

With just a stroke, my defenses obliterated, along with all rational thought.

"Let it go," Jamie whispered. "You're close. I can feel it. It's okay, Harper."

My eyes pressed together so tight that tears tracked down my burning cheeks. After a much needed gulp of air, I opened my eyes and refocused. Through salty tears, the fogged-up glass over Jamie's shoulder revealed my startling reflection.

The woman staring back at me, the woman whose disheveled, contorted body had flushed red and hot. That was not only the real me, it was also who I really *wanted* to be.

That realization ignited one hell of a rocketing wave of pleasure. I bit down on my lower lip, muffling the scream deep in my chest. It was as if every cell in my rushing blood bubbled and exploded at the same time. My satisfaction was welcomed by Jamie's mouth roughly on mine, kissing me through the bliss. Only when I stopped shivering and slumped against his chest did he stop.

"My turn," Jamie said, shifting my weight to his right hip. "In the house. Don't go home, Harper."

I licked my lips. I was drained, but awake and on fire. "What…what do you mean?"

He leaned in. "Stay here with me tonight."

"I can't, I shouldn't. We shouldn't. Plus, your daughter is home."

"She's fast asleep."

"She doesn't wake up when you bring women home to—"

"Stop." He dragged me in by the nape of the neck. "No woman has been in my house, my bed. I... I want *you* there."

So much for subtlety.

A knock on the window, startled us. I was on his lap in the passenger seat as my car idled in his driveway behind the Range Rover.

"Everything all right?" Cam asked, his fingers tucked in the waistband of his jeans, and just then I caught the look of a misplaced cowboy from Texas.

After I crawled back to the driver's seat hoping Cam didn't get a view of my ass, Jamie got out of the car.

"Yeah," he said, composed as all get out. Sure, he didn't just have an earthquake of an orgasm. "Harper's coming in for a little while."

Slowly I got out of the car and fixed the hem of my dress, praying it wasn't wadded up in my thong. "I just need to use the um… The um…bathroom."

Cam rolled his eyes and looked at Jamie. "For songwriters, you two are terrible liars. Use protection, please." Cam swaggered down the driveway to a shiny red Ford F-350 monster truck parked at the curb.

"And you thought he'd be unhappy with how you're handling me," Jamie clipped a joke, putting an arm around me. "Now that my babysitter just left—"

"You make your manager babysit for you?"

"Cam is Chloe's uncle. Her mom's brother." Jamie stepped back and leaned against my car. "He's been my best friend since we were teenagers."

"That must be terribly hard on him to stake his

allegiance."

"I've been very clear with him about this. If he ever needed to stand with his family, I'd respect that. His father, Cord Renner, is crazy rich. I never expected Layla to give up her birthright, and I would never ask Cam to do that."

"I see."

"What do you say, Harper? You wanted one night with me seven years ago, and I was the moron who walked away. I'm not making that mistake again."

I leaned against the car conflicted as hell. I didn't trust my judgement if I got behind closed doors with Jamie. There was too much on the line. I could taste that CEO promotion. Sleeping with an artist all but ensured I'd destroy that opportunity. In today's climate, a corporate executive wouldn't be rewarded for something like that.

And I'd never bring that disgrace on Gregory.

"No one can know about this," I said quietly.

"I'm definitely on the same page about that. But only because I don't want to damage your professional reputation."

"There's something else. Jamie, I'm in line to be the next CEO of Blue Rock."

His eyes flickered in surprise, then a wide warm smile curled the edges of his beautiful mouth. "That's incredible, darlin'. I can't say I'm surprised. I felt the power you had in that place. The way everyone's breath stood still when you came into Michael's office."

I'd worried people were just terrified of me. "Thank you."

"When?"

"When what?"

"When will you know?" He crept up closer to me.

"Soon. But…" I stopped, knowing I was getting ahead of myself and that would be jumping off a cliff. Jamie was leaving for the road, where he admitted he lets loose.

What harm would it do if we just enjoyed each other? Quietly, of course. He had a little girl to protect. Not everything had to be long term. My body was so coiled up and he could unravel me so nicely. I just wished he didn't have a sleeping angel under the same roof.

My breath hitched. "Chloe? I don't want her to have the wrong idea about me. About us."

Jamie nodded and scrubbed a hand down the back of his neck. "Right. I almost didn't think of that."

"And you've really not had a girlfriend all this time?"

Jamie swallowed and moved his suit jacket. Gripping the waistband of his trousers, he gave a hard shove, exposing his hip. I stared, and the light from over his garage shined down on old English letters that spelled out, *Layla*. Jamie took my hand and smoothed my fingers against his skin, tight and warm. "Not since her."

"Chloe's mom?"

"She was the only woman I ever loved and I couldn't give her the life she wanted."

"You were young, though." I gaped, catching the first full glimpse of his body. His stomach so taut, the skin so smooth, planes of tight abs. "We're not those young twenty-somethings anymore either. We have to account for our actions."

"Keep stroking me like that, and I'm going to take the choice away from you, darlin'." He leaned into the curtain of my hair. "I want you so much, Harper."

His mouth felt so warm against my ear. Firm and

needy. I turned to catch his lips. He sipped from me like he was in a desert and I was the saving oasis. He held me so tight, and strong. His body against mine made me feel safe and protected. I slid my hands around his neck and pushed my hips against what had become an intense erection under his still unbuttoned pants.

"Got any whiskey in there?" I pointed to the house.

"Yes, but I'm not having any more to drink, until after."

"After what?"

"After I've made you lose your mind."

Chapter Ten

Jamie

I wedged open my front door since Cam had left it unlocked. Despite Chloe's ability to sleep through thunderstorms, midnight guitar wailings, and even a few of my meltdowns, I didn't want to chance that the sound of a woman's voice would be *the* trigger that woke her up.

Bringing a woman home was new territory. I'd mastered the lonely single dad life. In all the years I'd had Chloe with me full time, I'd not imagined dating anyone. My brain had stayed focused on caring for my daughter. And when the summer came, I'd drowned myself in music, liquor, and women until I couldn't think straight.

Each September that rolled around, I schlepped back to Nashville and transformed back into a lonely single father again.

Regret.

Rinse.

Repeat.

Harper had the ability to turn all of that upside down. Chloe was smitten with the woman. Talked about her nonstop since I signed my contract, choking me up. It ate at me because I knew once I went back on the road, the madness would kick up and I'd lose Harper. Chloe already lost her mother and survived. Would I dare to test my daughter's ability to love another woman and lose her, too? I didn't think *I* could survive, never mind an eleven-year-old.

Harper and I had great chemistry seven years ago when she wrote my one and only number one song.

Adding sex to that? I whistled.

"Yes?" Harper whispered, following me inside.

"Nothing. Just a little lost in thought."

"No kidding." Harper held her arms, my cranked-up A/C sent pebbles of gooseflesh across her skin. Skin she'd hidden under that dress. "This is really nice, Jamie."

"Thanks. I'd rather not clunk around and make noise right now showing you the place." I gently placed my keys in the bowl next to the door. "Are you sure you want to be here, Harper?"

She ran a hand through her hair and looked around until her eyes found the staircase. Creeping up on me slowly, she said, "Take me to your bedroom and I'll show you how much I want to be here."

A blaring siren went off in my head. I wanted to throw her over my shoulder and fly up the stairs. Even though they were carpeted, I took her hand and brought her softly up the steps.

"Chloe's room is down that hall." I pointed to the foyer that split the house into two wings on the second floor.

Past Chloe's was a guest room when she had sleep overs, and next, a room for Marta when she stayed over which wasn't often.

In my wing, my bedroom sat at the end of the hall. Before that, I had a media room and an office, separated by a rustic barn door that slid back and forth on a metal track above the frame. A touch I added that reminded me of home in Texas. My music room was in the basement where I often fed my creative needs in the middle of the night when the music monster roared to life.

As much as I wanted Harper in my bed, I wanted to

take her down there, too. Put us in our element. Surrounded by instruments and recording equipment and a sofa that I'd love to make her scream on.

Some other time.

In the anteroom right outside my bedroom, I pressed my lips against hers. The soft kiss turned urgent when Harper took me in. With every swirl of my tongue, her kissing grew deeper, more intense.

My lips swept across Harper's eyes.

"That's so sweet," she said. When she opened her eyes, feathery lashes brushed my lips. "And intimate."

"Not intimate enough," I whispered in between breaths and kisses.

I slid a strong hand up and down her spine, signaling I wanted to take control. She purred and twisted her wrists around my neck. Once again, my lips soaked hers with passionate kisses while my hands explored her body.

Harper unexpectedly broke away from the embrace. She clutched the small console table, swaying the glass container of violet Sweet Peas.

"Harper, what's wrong?"

She turned back in my direction with one hand pressed against her throat. "You are such a good kisser. That only means… You're good at other stuff, too, aren't you?"

I strode toward her and confidently took her head between my palms. I kissed her again. Every touch of my lips was followed by a brief stare that settled my eyes on hers.

Inch by inch, her heated skin revealed just how much she wanted me.

I brought Harper into my bedroom and shut the door.

Locked her in.

She stared at my bed, the horizontal runway I crashed landed on nightly without any thought of sex.

"Let me show you everything I'm good at."

Harper

I laid on the bed and Jamie blanketed me with his body. So massive. So strong. So warm against my skin.

"I love how you looked in this dress, but I want it off you," Jamie rasped in my ear.

"You first." I pressed my fingers against his chest until he sat up. "Strip."

His cheek ticked up. "You want to do dirty?"

"So dirty."

Jamie slid the suit jacket off his wide shoulders and sent it flying across the room, not caring where it landed. His strong hands yanked the dress shirt out of the trousers and slowly undid the buttons.

Damn, he wore an undershirt. Another layer.

With the shirt unbuttoned, he leaned down to kiss me. Moving his clothes all around, his cologne kicked up, the tangy musky smell making me feel warm. Sexy. "Keep going."

Jamie smirked and lifted the undershirt over his head.

Hell's. Bells.

"How…"

"Yeah, Harper?"

"How many hours do you spend in the gym to look like this?" I ran my fingers across his torso, planes of abs making him look taller.

He glanced down at himself and cinched his eyebrows together like he hadn't a clue what a god he was. "A few times a week."

This was why it sucked to be a woman. Men do a few crunches, drink a few protein shakes, and they looked like a Greek sculpture. But I was glad I wouldn't have to compete with hours spent in the gym.

Shirtless, he kissed me again. His shoulders rounded to perfect circles and then curved in to meet his deltoids. Frickin' perfect. "Keep going?" he asked.

"Yes, please."

"Now, I'm starting to feel a little dirty. Got any one-dollar bills to wave at me?"

"I'd wave twenties at you to touch this." I splayed my hands across his body again, not avoiding the Layla tattoo. It was a shrine as far as I was concerned. Without Layla, there'd be no Chloe.

"I'm yours." Jamie toed off his shoes and undid his belt at the same time. "You can touch me for free."

My heart rate ticked up. Jamie had been wild in his early days, years before he got custody of Chloe. When we worked on his song, I'd only seen him in tight jeans and plaid shirts, which he'd traded in for those V-Neck tee-shirts with the sexy laced-up fronts he wore on stage. No pictures had captured the texture and curves of his body. Or how he'd matured into a fine piece of art.

"Wanna finish undressing me?"

"Hell's bells, yes." I licked my lips and fingered the waistband of his trousers until I reached the zipper.

The bulge tucked underneath made my heart pound, and when I brushed my hand against it, Jamie hissed at the contact. "Please hurry," he whispered.

I lowered the zipper and nudged the trousers down until they puddled at his feet. Jamie wore charcoal gray briefs with a red waistband. The long length of him so evident underneath.

"I… I'm not sure I can handle you, Jamie."

"You can handle me, Harper. I promise you."

With me sitting on the edge of the bed and Jamie standing over me, ready to remove his briefs, I wasn't sure what to do next. It'd been so long since I'd gone on any kind of date. Did two people who've wanted each other for seven years go at it and double back to foreplay later?

Figuring Jamie would let me know what he wanted sent a thrilling rush through me. What would he do? How dominant would he be with me?

He stepped back and slid his hands in his briefs, but I stopped him. "No. I want to take them off."

"I'm mighty big and hard right now, darlin'. Unless…" His body visibly trembled. "Will you take me in your mouth?"

"Do you want that?"

"Every man wants that." He breathed and lowered his head to kiss me again. "I'm not sure I'll survive sinking my cock into this warm mouth."

Licking my lips, I eyed the bulge again. I gripped the sides of his briefs, never wanting to see a penis so much in my life. As the briefs slid past his hips, Jamie's hands stood at the ready to grip himself.

He caught himself before his erection hit me in the face.

Good flippin' lordy bee. He had to be so big because of his height. As he gripped the base of his shaft, standing there naked, Jamie was as beautiful as I'd imagined. And all the nights I brought myself to that place wishing it was him in my fantasies didn't do him justice in the flesh.

"You like?" he asked, all gravel and lust.

"So much." I parted my lips. "Let me taste you."

Still gripping himself, he leaned his hips in. The smell of him, soap and powder and musk filled me up. The scent of a man. The tip brushed against my lips, so soft with a dab of wetness I immediately licked.

"Fucking-A," he groaned.

I went breathless from the reaction after just one lick of my tongue against his skin. "No, fucking me. You. Soon. But I want to taste this monster, first." I ran my hands along the length of him, Jamie groaning through my touches.

So smooth, those beautiful veins, full of life. I opened my mouth and he slid in past my tongue. His body shivered and once he seated himself fully down the back of my throat, he eased out.

Stepping back, he ground out, "I can't..."

My heart pounded, thinking he would pull the plug on this whole thing. "You can't..."

"I won't last. Not now. Not with *you*."

Nodding, I stood up and lifted the dress over my head. Thanks to the cups sewn in, I'd skipped a bra.

Jamie breathed heavily looking at me. "I'm such a fucking moron. I could have had you. Had all of you."

"Now you can. I admit, seven years ago I still carried some baby fat. You're getting a much better version of me." I gripped the ends of my thong.

"No, let me." He sank to the carpet and while kneeling, he pressed his nose into my stomach. Jamie just breathed me in for a few seconds, his face against my belly.

Was he thinking...about Layla? "Jamie, did you get to watch Layla grow with your child?"

"No," his voice choked up.

"I'm sorry," I whispered, fingering the soft strands of his jet-black hair. "No matter when and no matter who your next child is with, that won't happen again. I'm sure of it."

He lifted his chin and our stares collided. A wave of blurry premonitions passed through my vision. Me with his baby.

Whoa, intense.

"My turn," he said with a sly grin as he slid my thong down.

"The one good thing about being a woman is, I can come apart over and over and it won't bring things to…" I gasped feeling a warm tongue on my center. All thoughts melted away, and I just…felt.

"Lift your leg," he ground out.

Next, I faced the bed, Jamie crouched down, his back against the edge. With my leg lifted, he had access to all of me. Every cell in my body hummed to life. Sizzled under his tongue, as Jamie tasted me. My nipples hardened to painful peaks. The pleasure storming through me wrecked me and I pulsed in seconds, climaxing in his mouth.

"God, you taste so good. That's right, come for me, Harper. Come in my mouth."

Everything inside me ached. Desire overwhelming me, heat pooled under my skin, my body warming to a fever. I held Jamie's hands and gently rocked against his mouth, his tongue. The air around me tasted different, potent, and sweet.

Feeling like my bones were rubber, I clasped on to Jamie as he lifted me up. "Good, darlin'?"

"Who am I? Where am I?" I joked, catching my breath.

"That's how I want my woman. Mindless." He kissed me and laid me on the bed.

The stitching of his quilt felt rough against my back. Better than a satin comforter, I joked to myself. Jamie was a good ole country boy from Texas. Like me. Different parts, sure. But the man's downhome nature made him more attractive.

"I have to get something," he whispered.

Protection.

All single men carried protection. It meant they were responsible. Plus, when a man *didn't* have any, a woman might worry her man had been going through twenty-packs like a maniac.

Jamie came back to the bed with a condom wrapper and tore it open with his teeth. I kissed his long neck, the whoosh of his blood so strong there.

"Open wider for me." His fingers slid in and out of my heat as my hips moved in synch. "Show me all of you. *Tonight*, you're mine."

I shivered when I realized how many thoughts Jamie had crept into over the years. A summer's worth of memories had filled me with sorrow and regret for not being more open with him. I should have let him know I'd been falling for him that summer. I should have taken a chance.

This was *my* second chance. Was I brave enough?

Jamie sat up on his knees, deep in the V of my legs, my thighs, and just kept brushing his fingers along my entrance. Taking his time. God, he'd destroy me, wouldn't he?

One finger, then two, then three entered me. I felt so full. Complete. And just with fingers. "You're so tight," Jamie whispered and then collided his gaze with mine.

"I'm gonna lose control."

"Good. It's me, Jamie."

He lowered his lips to my belly and again just kissed me. Like some phantom, some shadow of a baby to come one day was inside me. Or maybe he was pretending. Projecting. His lips trailed up my stomach, stopped at my breasts and next his tongue sank so damn deep into my mouth.

At the same time, his cock buried inside me. Stars popped out behind my eyes, beautiful sparkles that heated my chest. He gripped my bottom, bringing us even closer as he roughly claimed me. I didn't care. He'd been right, I could handle him.

It felt amazing, better than anything I'd imagined.

Then he slowed, control returning to him. He slipped out and then slid back in, inch by torturous inch.

"This is too damn good." He snuggled his head in the crook of my shoulder. "You're too damn good for me, Harper."

I held him tight as I was sure demons were attacking him. All the guilt he'd felt bubbling to the surface because I'd worn down the veneer as lust stripped him bare.

Wrapping my legs around his waist, his one hand found the back of my thigh, locking me against him.

"Yeah, right there," he groaned.

His body went rigid, his hips jerking. He kissed me like the only air in the room came from my lungs. Like he needed me. Like he'd die if our lips weren't touching. His arms tightened around my waist as he shattered.

"Say something." His breath was hot in my ear.

The warmth crawled up and got inside my soul. I'd never felt so complete. His mouth closed around my jugular, like it helped the blood rush through me.

A pang settled in the back of my throat as I wondered what the hell to say. *I think I love you*, would ruin the mood.

"How about that drink now?" I cuddled against him.

"I have a better idea." He kissed my forehead.

"Better than whiskey?"

"I'll show you." He stood and strode naked to his dresser.

From a lower drawer, he took out a pair of sweats and one of his concert tee-shirts. "Sorry that I don't have any women's clothes for you to put on. But here, slip into these."

"Thanks."

After he put on a pair of terrycloth shorts and nothing else, we walked quietly down the steps and into the kitchen. Jamie snipped the bright red casing of a new bottle of *Elijah Craig*, and I smirked, but my attention focused on the knife in his hand as it danced dangerously close to his fingers.

"Do you want me to do that?" I asked worriedly. It didn't matter if I lost a finger.

"No, no, I got it." He gracefully twisted the cork and it slid smoothly out of the bottle. *Pop.*

He poured two generous fingers-worth into cut crystal glasses and ceremoniously tapped one against mine.

"Truth or dare?" He put down his glass.

"Oooo." I took a sip. "I'm guessing any dare would make some noise. So, truth. I have nothing to hide from you."

"Do you *really* want to be stuffed away in an office every day?"

I froze, the glass stopping before my lips. He'd been paying attention about my job. "Yes. No. I don't know," I whined. "I don't know anything. Two weeks ago, I knew where my life was headed and now..."

"Now, I'm back in your life."

"Darn it." I pointed my glass at him. "Am I that transparent?"

"Sometimes." Jamie took my glass and swallowed a sip.

I stared at his mouth again, my blatant gape catching his attention.

"I assume that was an invitation for me to kiss you again." He swept his mouth across my lips. "Man, I can't get enough of you. But I need to catch my breath."

I curled against him. "Me, too."

"Since the guitar lesson is for Chloe, can I get something else from you tonight?" he asked, softly.

My breath hitched. "You just did."

"I want more than that."

"What more can I give you, Jamie Miller?"

"Sing for me."

Chapter Eleven

Harper

My throat tightened up. "Sing what?"

"One of those songs you've written and tossed aside."

"Why?"

"I missed your voice. Hearing it all summer when we worked on my song... You see…you got to hear me all these years. I didn't get that same pleasure. It…did something to me. Your voice."

I was too choked up to respond. No one had ever said that. In all the butt-kissing comments about my songwriting, and even demos I cut, no one wanted just the pleasure of my voice the way Jamie did.

"Okay." I leaned against his counter. "Here?"

"No. I have a music room, too." He took my hand and brought me into his basement.

When the lights hit Jamie's shoulders, the familiar aura around him overwhelmed me. He was just like me. His talent matched mine. Who was I kidding? He exceeded my abilities. It was a shame it didn't always come through on the charts or award shows. As far as I was concerned, everything Jamie touched turned to gold.

"Guitar or piano?" I loved the charming arrangement of instruments, the low ceiling, and cushiony carpet.

"A cappella," he demanded with his arms crossed over his luscious bare chest. "Just your voice."

I wasn't sure what he expected me to sing. Something hidden in my wicker basket would be easy, but that was on the other side of town.

The song I wrote for him seven years ago? Sung in my key, but not in the timing I'd intended? I copied the mood he'd upended with his bad boy singing style.

By the last line, Jamie was red faced and stared at me with a lustful gaze. Wiping his eyes, he reached for me. "That was amazing, darlin', I got chills because it reminded me of when I listened to that CD you burned for me. Hearing your voice sing my song, I felt like you were mine. That *song* was mine. But you were, too."

"Yeah," I whispered. I always felt like I belonged to Jamie because when he left Austin that summer, he took a piece of me with him. I never felt the same.

"Can I ask you a question?" When I nodded, he cocked his head to the side. "So, if you get promoted to CEO, who's gonna get all those songs sitting in your basket?"

I thought he'd hit me with something more personal. "Honestly, those songs were just for me. To make the pain go away."

"What pain?"

"When all the material builds up and you feel like you're going to explode."

"I know what you mean." He exhaled. "I have the same disease, Harper."

We were so alike it scared me. It's what drew my mother and father together once upon a time. Two obsessed kids who loved music. Look how *that* had turned out?

*

Back in Jamie's bed, I cried out again. I didn't remember the last time I'd spent all night making love. Oh right…never. That time of year, a glow peeked over the mountains early, I whimpered through another moment of bliss just as the sun sparkled against the horizon wiping away the darkness.

"What time does Chloe wake up?" I asked quietly and rested my head against Jamie's chest as I watched the sky go from pink to fire-engine red as the Nashville sun started to blaze.

Jamie lifted his right arm to check his Gear watch, and I wondered how bumping and grinding registered on that thing. "In about an hour. If you give me a few minutes, I'll be ready to go again."

I chuckled. "Let's not push this to the limit." I stretched, the sheet slipping down, and Jamie growled catching one of my nipples in his mouth. Hell's bells. "I should get going."

"I'm already going," he said, pushing the sheet away.

"I'm serious." Something told me Jamie wouldn't let me just walk out of his life again. The genie got let out of the bottle and he wasn't a man to just go back to handshakes. "Are you going to tell your daughter what we're doing?"

"What are we doing?" He sat up.

"We're enjoying each other until you go on tour."

"That's what you want me to tell her?"

"I don't know how to translate that for an eleven-year-old." I curled up against him. "What I meant was, if you want to tell your daughter, we're together right now, I'm okay with that. I just don't want her to find out while I'm doing the walk of shame down your driveway. Can I have that bit of dignity?"

"I can do dignity." He got out of bed and stretched facing me.

Would the view of him ever stop stunning me? Tall, lean, solid muscle. Chiseled abs and sculpted thighs. And I was…his for the next month or so. A feeling of ease spread through me. I could enjoy Jamie and hopefully, it would make the loneliness when he left not sting as much.

Even when he slipped into ratty house sweats, he looked hot. Jamie killed it in the country genre because he brought a piece of L.A. glam to the table.

Meanwhile, I faced a fashion emergency. I had no choice but to put the dress back on. For some reason, I'd rather slink home in that than an oversized pair of sweats and tee-shirt. The dress did look amazing on me. Even the morning after.

After Jamie zipped the back for me, kissing away every inch of skin he covered, which wasn't much, he took my mouth, hard and good. "We're gonna just do this until I leave?"

"Not just this. We have a song to finish. To record. We have meetings." I locked my wrists around his neck.

He kissed me a few more times, but I eased away or I'd never leave.

Walking down the stairs quietly in my six-inch heels I loved because I stood as tall as Jamie in them, I felt like Zeus's mistress sneaking away from Olympus.

"Do you want to have dinner tonight with me and Clo?" Jamie asked me at his door.

"I would love that." I kissed his nose.

"I'll figure out how to explain this to her. Explain about us before you get here." Jamie held me and kissed me against the back of the door.

The man looked so sexy, shirtless, with his broad chest and crinkled muscular shoulders.

Even I knew that was going to be a tricky conversation. "Well, at least you have a few hours to figure out what to say."

"Thank God," Jamie exhaled, but his jaw quirked and

he turned around quickly.

Chloe lumbered into the foyer after coming down from the stairs. Her dark hair stood up in all directions and she rubbed her eyes, adorably oblivious.

When I gasped, though, Chloe opened her eyes. Wide. Staring at me in an evening dress. Jamie shirtless in sweatpants. Both our hair just as messed up.

Oops…

Jamie

"We'll talk about it when you get home from school." I futzed with Chloe's hair in the downstairs bathroom hours after Harper sprung out of here, flushed and gasping with embarrassment.

"But, Daddy—"

"We'll *talk* about it when you get home from school." The argument went back and forth while Chloe got ready for school.

When Marta arrived, the woman walked into a war zone, looking surprised at all the tension because every other day the house was whisper quiet. "What's going on?" she said, watching Chloe stomp to her room with only one braid done.

I rolled my eyes. How goddamn embarrassing. I was in unchartered territory. And so was Chloe. As far as I knew, Layla never dated anyone and if she had, she kept it way on the down-low, that Cam didn't even know.

Marta had signed a non-disclosure agreement, so why not spill my troubles? "I had an overnight guest." I turned away to pour coffee in a to-go mug wishing I could add some whiskey to it.

Marta burst out laughing.

"It's not funny." I breathed into the cup and took a

sip. "My daughter may be traumatized."

"Oh God, she didn't see anything did she?"

"No." My stomach flipped, thankful for small mercies. Facing the nanny, I admitted, "I was escorting the lady out and Chloe saw us. Fully clothed, well…her."

"Was this *her*, Harper Montgomery by any chance?" Marta asked, smirking.

Dear God. Figuring I had nothing to lose, I nodded. "And how would you know that?"

"Chloe lights up when she talks about her. She was thrilled to meet her at your contract signing. To go swimming in her pool. And did she really meet Gigi, too?"

"Marta, with all due respect, focus." I pushed down my sudden jolt of anger. "Why didn't you say anything to me about Chloe mooning over Harper?"

"Do you want a report of every conversation I have with your daughter?"

"Of course not." In my selfish mind, Chloe was happy, and had everything an eleven-year-old could want, except a mother. Chloe missing Layla had never seemed as glaring since meeting Harper. She'd opened up a wound I never noticed had been gushing blood under the surface. "Anything else I should know?"

"Just how pretty she thinks Harper is. And how excited she is that Harper is writing another song for you. I didn't see it as anything different from the other artists you've worked with."

Made sense.

Marta straightened her back. "Will Miss Montgomery be spending the night here again?" When I shot her a look, she held up a finger. "Because if yes, you need to address with Chloe what's going on."

"How do I do that?"

Marta arched her eyebrows. "It's most important to state your intentions with Miss Montgomery."

I collapsed in a kitchen chair. I had no intentions. Except to have sex with her for the next month. Harper was on the same page. But somehow, even the G-rated version of that wasn't something Chloe would understand. Damn, what an awkward age. Too young to understand that adults had needs. And too old to be patronized. That's where I got stuck. How could I explain to Chloe what Harper and I were doing, if I had no idea what *I* was looking for?

"I'll go finish her hair and you can talk to her on the drive to school." Marta disappeared up the stairs and ambled to Chloe's wing on the second floor.

I nodded, but cursed under my breath. Like I wanted to talk about Harper and me being friends with benefits for a month while driving.

*

Chloe was unusually quiet in the car after a morning of temper tantrums. With her head buried in a book, she chose to now ignore me. What was the right move here? Send her to school with images of Harper strutting away from the house at the crack of dawn? Let those images plague Chloe's mind and affect her concentration or lay it on the line?

Parents made mistakes. Single parents made big ones, I'd heard. Not Layla, though. Man, she had kept her shit together. Sure, she had her parents and her twin sister, Sierra, all huddled in a support system. I had Cam on the road with me. He always walked a fine line between being my friend, even when his father railroaded me. It must have warred with his instincts to stand with his own family. I knew Cam would come up empty helping me figure this Harper thing out.

I had been running interference to keep any kind of awkward scenes from Chloe. Living like a monk for months on end, and then letting loose while she was tucked away on Renner Ranch. Damn, I'd isolated her from anything major happening to me, relationship-wise. She had no scar tissue from something like that morning's awkward encounter.

When I pulled over a block before the school, Chloe finally looked up from her book. "Why did we stop?"

"Clo, Harper and I are friends."

"Adult friends don't sleep over," she answered with a mouthful of snark.

I squeezed the steering wheel. "I want her as a friend who sleeps over." When Chloe just looked at me like I was crazy, I said, "She's someone I want to spend some time with before I go on tour."

"Then what?"

"What do you mean?"

"You…you won't see her when you're on tour?"

"No. I'll be away. On tour." I watched my daughter through the mirror, but finally turned around, realizing that wasn't a conversation to have through a narrow reflection. "Clo, you know I go away every summer. That's how I support us."

"Right." She looked down, my words confusing her obviously.

"Clo, Harper and I just want to spend some time together before I leave. That's all. We're friends. And yes, sometimes she may sleep over. Are you okay with that?"

The eyes staring back at me went glassy. Damn it. I

undid my seatbelt, got out of the car, and opened her door. "Chloe, I loved your mother very much. But she didn't want to live with me. She didn't like that I traveled for my music."

"I know," she said, nodding. "She loved you, too, Daddy."

Now I wanted to scream. Why had Layla and I been so damn stubborn? We had a kid for Pete's sake. We should have worked harder to figure out a compromise. We *were* in love once.

Except, now Layla was gone and I couldn't change the past.

"Harper is going to teach you how to play guitar. No matter what happens, you and she will always be able to do that." Meaning, if I screwed up and broke her heart.

Who's though? Harper's or Chloe's?

Chapter Twelve

Harper

I braced myself for what I felt would be an interrogation's worth of questions from Chloe about why I was in her daddy's house at the crack of dawn in an evening gown, high heels, and with sex hair. Jamie had assured me in a text he and his daughter had talked. Explained to Chloe how we were just spending time together before Jamie left for his tour.

When Chloe answered the door, fear scraped my insides further, except the bright smile on the precious angel's face immediately relaxed me. Jamie strutted up behind Chloe. The possession in his eyes and his swagger with his daughter near filled a place in my heart that had been empty for…forever. That powerful protectiveness I never felt from my own father. Because he was never around.

"You made it." Whatever Jamie had wanted or didn't want at one time, this was his life now and he was doing an amazing job balancing family and work. Could it really be not too late to repair a relationship with my own dad? Or should I just move on and be part of *this* daddy-daughter lovefest in Jamie's house? Let Jamie adore me. Let Chloe worship me. It seemed so easy, so right.

"I did. And I take it these are yours?" From my bag, I took out a pair of pink flip-flops with plastic flamingos on the tops.

"Oh cool." Chloe took them. "I wondered where I left them."

Jamie scooted his daughter out of the way so I could step into the foyer. "What do you say, Clo?"

Now wasn't that a loaded question?

"Thank you, Harper."

If we all went off script, all kinds of questions would come ripping out of everyone's mouth. I wasn't into temporary flings.

"Something smells good," I remarked and felt Jamie's hand hit my waist when Chloe skipped ahead in the house.

"No kidding," he said and leaned in to kiss my cheek.

"I'm sure I don't smell like sweet onions." I tugged on his plaid shirt. "If so, I have some perfume to return."

"Daddy made his famous chili," Chloe announced, climbing up on a stool to sit at the breakfast bar separating the kitchen and the dining room. Her legs swung happily as her attention fell to a laptop.

No questions. At all. Whew.

"Is the chili famous because you're famous?" I asked Jamie, following him in the kitchen.

"It's my mom's recipe," he said, stirring chili inside what looked like a lobster pot.

He'd never mentioned his mother before, and the faint bite in his tone had me curious. Chloe stayed focused on her computer and Jamie made no attempt to elaborate on *Mom*. Gigi was a handful enough for me to worry about.

"I didn't know what to bring, so I stopped at the bakery on Elm and grabbed some red velvet cupcakes for dessert." I took out the plastic holder with four ginormous dark red cupcakes, and cream cheese icing.

"Chloe loves red velvet." Jamie took the packaging and laid a gentle kiss on my lips.

I held my breath along with him, both of us waiting for some kind of eruption from the countertop. Our eyes slid sideways at the same time. Chloe bopped in her seat holding a pencil and writing in a notebook.

"Hi," Jamie said in a low seductive drawl, more man, than dad.

He'd not had to balance those two sides of himself before, had he? If no other woman had been in the house, and he'd not had a girlfriend, why me? And why would he put his and Chloe's hearts on the line now? For me?

"Hey, back," I answered him, and right there in his eyes, I got my answer.

I was the link that crashed us both together. I was the side of his music world that took a backseat most of the year so he could be a good dad.

Was I dragging out a side of him that he didn't want Chloe to see?

Or was I the ingredient to tame that beast so he didn't have to keep those lines divided anymore?

While Jamie finished with the chili, I sat with Chloe at the breakfast bar asking about school. After a string of clipped, one-word answers, Jamie breathed into the back of my neck. "That's normal."

Instead of an awkward staring contest at a formal dining table with me on one end, Jamie on the other, and poor Chloe at the center spot, everyone silent, awkwardly slurping up chili, dinner turned into a casual, *grab your bowl and some cornbread and let's sit in the living room.*

No television, though, just some music. Rock, of all things. But Jamie's music always had that strong edge.

"Daddy, let's play the game," Chloe said after swallowing a mouthful of chili.

"Game?" I asked, digging into my bowl because it was goddamn delicious. I hoped I didn't need my hands because I wasn't putting down this food.

"Chloe sings my songs, but there's always a lyric she doesn't like. So I have to make up a new version of the song," Jamie said, narrowing his eyes.

"Not your song, Harper," Chloe said and then licked her spoon. "*That* song was perfect."

"It was my song, too, brat." Jamie flicked a cornbread crumb at her.

"Okay, Daddy." She picked up the crumb and put it in her bowl, an air of snooty and adorable derision in her tone.

These two were hysterical.

"Can we do it to my songs?" I asked.

Jamie cleared his throat. "I don't know if Clo knows your other songs."

I thought about that. "Let's test that." I felt no hesitation about singing in front of Jamie, the man with the velvet voice. I crooned, "If you're gonna say goodbye, just say it. And if you're gonna wait…" I stopped.

Chloe's eyes bulged. "If you're gonna wait so long, I'll break you," she sang back. "*That's* your song?"

"It sure is," Jamie said, grumbling into his bowl.

"Very good, Chloe."

"That song is everywhere, that's hardly a challenge."

"It sure is everywhere," Jamie said and put his bowl down.

Good one, Harper.

Jamie stood and looked out into his yard. No matter how successful an artist was, fierce competition made even award-winning artists question themselves. And no matter how many awards someone went home with, someone else always went home with more. I never wanted to live like that.

121

Seeing what it did to my mother made me respect Jamie so much more. My mother wrecked her own life *and* my childhood chasing that brass ring. Jamie seemed content with his career and I didn't think he'd take Chloe down with him if it all fell apart.

"Does it help to say that song got turned down by four other artists before Kayla Munson picked it up? And I heard she had to be convinced."

Jamie swung around with his dark eyebrows cinched together. "You're kidding me? Have people in this town lost their minds?"

I relaxed my shoulders. "No. There's a lot of competition." I kept out how unfair it could be to artists, too. No need to scare the little girl into thinking her father couldn't make enough money to feed her. "But you know what? Singing on a stage is just so utterly amazing. A lot of people can write a song, Chloe. There're plenty of songwriters out there. But not everyone can stand on a stage and sing like a god."

Jamie watched me as each word came out of my mouth. Managing artists was my life. The life on stage was the hardest. Because it went beyond singing. It was a presence. A magic to capture each and every damn time.

"Daddy really is the *best* singer, isn't he?"

"He sure is, Chloe. He sure is."

Jamie

"Please stay over. Please." I kissed Harper against the refrigerator an hour later. Her rich floral scent reminded me of the wildflower fields in Wild Heart, Texas.

Chloe was taking her shower, my ears balancing

between listening to the water and my own beating heart.

"I can't. I mean, I shouldn't." Harper's drenching kisses blew my mind, our mouths locked together.

"You can't call me a god in front of my kid again. I can't take it."

"Just being honest. I didn't have to tell her though, did I?" She pushed her fingers into the back of my hair.

For ten months out of the year, I shut down this side of myself. Ignored these needs to give my daughter a happy life. I had believed for years my music destroyed relationships. I'd lost the first love of my life because of my need to be on stage. That addiction to the cheering and the lights drove me and Layla never understood me.

Harper would understand. Not make me feel like a piece of shit for loving something as much as... I choked. I couldn't possibly love Harper, although any woman who called me a god, kissed me into a heart attack, was worth keeping close to my heart. And my daughter was crazy about her. Jeez, when would that combination come along again?

Hearing footsteps down the carpeted stairs, I lurched back and set my body back to Daddy mode.

"Can I have my cupcake now?" Chloe asked, shuffling back into the kitchen.

"Okay. They're kind of big." I took a plate from an upper cabinet and snagged a cake cutter. "How about you start with half?"

"We can share one. All of us," Chloe said, looking from me to Harper.

That's what it would come to, wouldn't it? Sharing. Everything. Only, that didn't sound awful. But could I live a sane life on the road? Not having to parent sent the real world packing every summer. I just needed to be present enough for a phone call every night before I went on stage. Chloe blessedly sank right into the Renner Ranch lifestyle every summer. Filled with activities such as paddle boating down the river, riding her bike along the easement that stretched from the main road past all the cottages on the property including her Uncle Cam's house, and of course, she loved her horse.

I miss Sweet Bell…

It'd been easy to keep my daughter off the horse, and Layla's parents had been traumatized into that submission. The only thing we'd all agreed on. But Chloe was older now. More stubborn. Hell, she got a double dose of that trait from both me and Layla. Poor kid.

With Chloe in a red velvet coma, she licked the last of the icing off her fork and then climbed down from her stool. Hugging Harper, she said, "Are you coming back tomorrow?"

My daughter voiced my unasked question. Now I worried the two of us would overwhelm and smother the poor woman.

"I don't want you guys getting sick of me." She held Chloe's chin. "But your dad and I have to finish the song. So, we'll figure out a schedule."

Chloe shrugged and then fell into me. "Night, Daddy." She droned on to me, where Harper got cheery and excitement.

She was tired of me, wasn't she? Same ole, same ole, since September. Harper was new blood. Shiny. Exciting.

No shit.

"Get going," I said with a kiss on my daughter's forehead. "Brush your teeth. I'll be up in a minute to say goodnight after I walk Harper to her car."

"Oh guys, get a room." She hooted with laughter as she slogged up the stairs and headed to her wing.

I have a room... Jesus fucking Christ. I was so not prepared to play this balance game.

Harper pulled me out of the house, holding my hand. "You okay? Breathe."

"Does it show?" I rested my hands on my thighs and bent over.

"I wish I could help you. Maybe you need..." She took a harsh breath.

"Maybe I need what?" I faced her, alarmed at her shaky voice.

"Maybe you need to date a single mother. I'm just as lost with this one, Jamie."

"No," fired from my mouth. "We'll figure this out. Together. You and me, you're who I want, Harper. Even without you all these years, I refused to fumble my inability to manage my personal life and being a father in front of some expert single mother."

Harper scoffed. "You think single mothers are experts? I was raised by one. I assure you—"

I stopped her with my mouth. "That's not what I meant. I don't care if you have no kids or ten kids, I want *you*, Harper."

Now Harper laughed. "I'm not sure you'd want me if I had ten kids. I'm guessing I'd look a little more run down."

I laughed with her and held her. Just held on. Every breath and every move were a mixture of scary as hell and oh so comfortable. Even if it were temporary because I was going on the road soon.

"What time do you go to work in the morning?" I

asked, brushing the hair from her face.

She answered with narrowing eyes. "I'm usually on the road around seven a.m. Why?"

"Just curious," I answered and kissed her into oblivion to make her forget her own name.

Chapter Thirteen

Harper

I woke to the roar of a motorcycle. Sitting up in bed and rubbing my eyes, I heard my gate opening. What the heck? I scrambled from my bed and watched a mysterious stranger in a black helmet, dark brown leather jacket, and jeans roll into my courtyard.

Then a blast of floral print and long blonde hair sashayed into the courtyard to meet the biker. Great, was Gigi meeting strange men in *my* house? The span of those shoulders racked me with a shot of familiar. The helmet came off and a warm gooey feeling of just plain giddiness came over me.

Jamie.

I dashed into my closet, pulled on a pair of short shorts, a tank top, and slipped on calf-high cowboy boots.

"I'll get you coffee, Jamie-pie," Gigi said to him in the foyer below.

Damn, I hoped that woman had a book to keep her occupied. Jamie in a leather jacket, all windblown from a Harley sent sweet shivers licking up my spine.

"Is this why you asked me what time I go to work?" I asked, leaning over my railing on the second floor.

Jamie looked up and the connection between our eyes made my throat tighten. "Guilty."

I flitted down the stairs, and at the bottom step, Jamie grabbed me and kissed me, deeper and deeper, sending warm tingles through me.

"I was gonna ask if you want sugar, but it looks like you found some," Gigi cooed, holding a mug of coffee.

Jamie took a breath, his head hovering over mine.

This was just damn fun. Living for these moments. Caught up. Heart pounding. Waiting. Waiting to have great sex again.

"Is there coffee for me, too?" I asked Gigi.

Gigi lifted a mug and said, "This is my only drug, right now, so I keep a pot going at all hours."

Jamie slurped from his mug while I poured my own cup from the carafe in the kitchen. Mid-pour, I spun around. "Where's Chloe?"

"School," Jamie answered. "Wanna call out of work today?"

My eyes lit up, then I glanced at Gigi.

"I'll be in my pool house cave. Listening to music. Loudly." My mother winked.

I smiled then put down my coffee cup. "Okay. You heard the woman. Upstairs with ya."

"That's not what I had in mind," Jamie said behind his mug, sounding serious and…put off.

I froze. That feeling when Jamie said no to me seven years ago rocketed through me, eating away my confidence. I grabbed my middle and fought for a response. No doubt, the first words out of my mouth should be an apology as his music label executive for making an unwanted advance at him, *my artist*.

"I'm very sorry." I folded my arms across my chest to hide blossoming nipples screaming from inside my top. *Look at us!* "That was inappropriate of me to suggest."

He stormed up to me. "I'm not turning you down," he said, gripping my arms. "That's not what I meant. Don't do that. Don't retreat on me. This is not Austin. We're different people now. I'm not that same guy."

"I wasn't…"

"Bullshit."

Getting my breathing in check, I turned my back to him and said, "So what can I do for you, Jamie? Why are you here?"

"Turn around."

"I—"

"Look at me!"

Startled, I faced him. His jaw had slacked like mine.

"I felt worthless. As a man. Okay, not a man. As any kind of partner, a woman would want. I gave Layla no choice. Because what woman could love *me* enough to walk away from money and live on the road with me and eat Ramen Noodles? With a baby no less. I didn't think I had anything to offer anyone. Except my cock for a long time. I liked you. I liked *us*. I liked what we had seven years ago. And sleeping with you would have exposed the fraud I was in the relationship department. I knew you weren't a one-night-stand girl."

I took in his words. All of them. Fraud, ringing the loudest. "The road to success in our business cuts through a lot of graveyards. Families. Kids." I looked over my shoulder and out at the pool house. "I'm mostly sorry you didn't get the chance to show Layla what an amazing father you could be. I hope she knows that…wherever she is."

He gathered me in his arms and crushed me against his chest. "You see it? Don't you?"

I held him, then took his face between my hands. "I saw it in two minutes, Jamie. That day when you signed your contract. The room was thick with the amazing relationship you have with Chloe. I've seen a lot of collateral damage in this business, starting with spouses and kids. Your daughter is not one of them, do you understand me?"

"God, I hope that's true." He drew a sharp breath. "Every summer when I have to leave her, the same anguish starts all over again. The doubt. The shame."

I thought about that. "Can I ask why she has to go with her grandparents? She's an incredibly mature responsible young lady. The right nanny—"

"I can't take her with me. Her grandparents sued me for custody when Layla died. It was a mess, Harper. This was the compromise. Summers and holidays and any other time they want her. I have to send her to them, no questions asked. I'm lucky they haven't abused it. I never intended to keep her from them. But she's *mine*, damn it."

I knew how he felt. I started to feel that way about him, and it was going to get me into a whole boatload of trouble.

After a moment of no one saying anything, Jamie nodded and said, "I didn't want to *just* fuck you then. I don't want to just fuck you now. Even if I have to leave. I want…"

"Okay," I answered, shrugging. I didn't really care what came after that.

He smiled. "Let's take a ride. There's a place on the river we can get food, too."

"On that thing?" I pointed to his motorcycle from the front floor-to-ceiling windows.

"You don't trust me?"

"I trust you. I don't trust some idiot going ninety miles an hour trying to take a picture of us."

"I must have given you the impression I'm a much bigger deal than I actually am."

"I see you as a big deal."

"I love that. I love how you see me. And I also really like that it's not crazy with people following me around. Or Chloe. I'm very lucky. I drop her off at school and I pick her up. No one says a word to me."

"That makes me feel relieved, to be honest. No one reacts well when a camera is shoved in their kids' faces. Bad press is so toxic these days."

"Hey now, you sound like my label exec and not the woman I want to make come on a picnic blanket listening to the Cumberland River wash against the shore."

"Can I shower first?"

"Can I join you?"

*

An hour later, from a saddlebag hanging off the back of a silver and black Harley Davidson, Jamie removed two helmets. He planted one on his own head first, adding a few inches to his already towering height.

Settling the spare helmet on my head, Jamie moved a few stray hairs from my eyes that got caught in a warm breeze. The way he took charge of securing my helmet with possession in his eyes, tightened my throat. Despite his tough exterior, amplified by the HOG, there was an unnerving gentleness in his touch when he tugged my chin strap so delicately in place.

He was such an amazing father, my mind screamed as I fought tears whenever thoughts like that dared to creep in. I had no relationship with my dad. I'd love to give a little girl a great daddy one day.

Jamie swung one of his long legs across the seat. In a low, yet powerful baritone voice, he said, "Get on, darlin'."

I tugged at the hem of the denim dress I put on and lifted my leg. My hands skated forward under Jamie's leather jacket and sunk into the waistband of his jeans. A warm hand covered one of mine briefly, squeezing approvingly of my placement.

Jamie throttled the engine in a few quick blasts, making me jump and turning me the hell on. When the thundering roar lessened, he turned his head. "Hold on. Do *not* let go, do you understand me?"

I nodded, silently asking him the same exact thing.

Jamie

For a singer, words were everything to me. Usually. Harper's touch spoke volumes. Having her arms around my waist as we buzzed along Route 66 to go back into the heart of downtown Nashville felt better than those truths I'd spilled in her house earlier. I'd been on one hell of a roll and had to stop.

A doubt lingered in me and I worried I'd said too much to her. Opened too wide to let her see the downside to who I really was and what I had to offer.

Nothing.

When I got on the road, it was unfathomable that being on stage wouldn't inject me with the same adrenaline as always. That I'd stop wanting that adoration from women's bodies. Early on, the measure of how great I was on stage had been how many women wanted to sleep with me after the show.

I wouldn't make any promises to Harper, not knowing what I could keep and what I couldn't. Should I even ask her to wait for me? Knowing the wreck I was on the other side of the summer.

Running through the last few years in my head while I drove, I realized, I'd calmed down *a lot* having to face Chloe every September. The shit that used to happen on the road before that? Jeez, it was a wonder I had any respect for myself at all.

Maybe. Maybe I could do it.

One whole summer. No sex.

The difference this time, I was going in sated. Satisfied from a woman I cared about. Who knew what a month with Harper could do to me? Look what a couple of damn weeks had done?

*

The morning was perfect for a picnic at the Arboretum. With a few people walking around, though, any hope of sexy time on a blanket was squashed. No one stared at us, though, and I didn't mind skipping the physical parts. Harper and I walked through the grounds, holding hands like we were on a…date.

I liked it.

When we got closer to the river, I laid out a blanket and just plopped down. Enjoyed the spring sunshine before it got all scorching from the cruel Nashville sun. Even though Harper was my music label exec, I wasn't the country music star right now. I was just a cowboy far from home holding a woman I was crazy about. Harper easily rested her back against my chest. It'd been one of the best non-music adult days I'd had in…years.

Harper reached back and pulled my head down. I thought I would get a sizzling kiss, instead she said, "What time does Clo get home?"

I kissed her first, then said, "Not until five today, she has a painting project due."

Harper twisted around. "Painting? Can she draw?"

I nodded. "Some." Chloe's interests diverged more than the freeway system in Nashville. Whatever it was, though, I supported it.

"What does she like to draw?"

I stilled, and cursed under my breath. "Horses, mostly."

"And that makes you angry?" Harper asked, laying a warm palm over my hand.

"Her mother was thrown from a horse. That's how Layla died," I gritted out.

Harper's mouth tipped open. "Oh, sweet Jesus. I had no idea. I'm so…sorry."

"Chloe had been riding since she was young. It was something they did together. Layla did tournaments. I'd only ever seen her completely in control of those damn horses. I know she taught Chloe the safe way to ride and do…tricks, too. Since the accident though…" I stopped and put my head down.

"What?" She fingered my chin to meet her eyes.

"Chloe's not allowed on a horse."

"At all?" Harper sat back on her knees. "You said it yourself, what happened to Layla was an accident. If she were killed in a car, would you forbid Chloe from driving?"

I glared at her. Living with Chloe and Harper would mean being ganged up on. I was getting a taste of that, and wasn't sure I liked it very much. "It's different. She doesn't need to be on a horse."

It didn't matter that Layla and I weren't in a relationship when she died. A piece of me went to the grave with her. Because that same piece came from Chloe's heart, too. Her grieving was my grieving. I'd trade places with Layla if Chloe could have one more ounce of happiness than she did today.

Harper took a moment to respond, watching me. "Clearly, this isn't my business." She flicked some leftover crumbs on the blanket.

I grabbed her wrist. "Don't do that. Don't shut down because we disagree."

Harper blinked and then blinked again. "Chloe's your daughter and so of course you have the final say. And I trust your judgement, you've done a great job. It's not like I'll be around to make a difference." She stood and turned away, the air between us suddenly thick and tense.

Did she want to be around to make a difference?

How in the world could this work out with Harper? I left every summer for punishing, day after day tours. She had a real job, she was my label exec. Nothing to sneeze at. Without her, there'd be no label for me. And she wanted to be... Oh Christ, she expected Gregory to name her CEO.

So, what the hell was I doing?

Chapter Fourteen

Harper

"Are you hungry?" Jamie asked. As a dad, he probably knew food was a great diversion.

"Starved." I gave him a smile. We had the whole day together and didn't want to add friction.

"They have food trucks over there." He pointed.

While my stomach growled, seeing so many people waiting in line and sitting at tables gave me pause. Then the bad memories of being out with my mother crept in. Gigi getting swarmed by fans. Me overlooked, overshadowed, pushed aside. Sometimes literally.

"Harper?" Jamie called out to me. "Girl, you're shaking."

I swallowed. "I'm fine. Do you think that's a good idea?"

"Tacos are always a good idea."

That got a smile. "I mean to be around so many people. You can be recognized."

He shrugged. "So? I've been recognized before. I know how to handle it."

"And did you have Chloe with you?"

He stared. "No."

"A...woman?"

He bit his lip. "I kept my affairs on the road discreet. So, no. I never got spotted with a woman."

"I'm your label exec, Jamie. I can't be seen with you like this." I played the conversation in my head with Michael. Fessing up the headache I used as an excuse to take the day off was bull crap. "We've really gone up to the edge. The kiss at the gala. The auction."

He nodded and from his knapsack, he took out a

baseball cap. With his shades back on, he said, "Can you tell it's me?"

"I can." I leaned against his chest. "I can spot you a mile away."

He bent down and kissed me. Picking up our blanket, he said, "People over there are hungry. They want food. They're not expecting some musician to be standing in line behind them."

I barked a laugh. "*Some* musician." Jamie Miller was a music god.

"Come on. Trust me?"

"Your album will be out soon. You have a lot to prove. Being involved with your label exec would cause a frenzy that will only have people looking to drag both of us down." Smacking the rim of his cap, I added, "This is your time to shine. Your album is going to be phenomenal. I don't want to ruin it for you."

"If it's gonna get ruined, I can't imagine anyone I'd like to be ruined over more than you."

"You have an answer for everything, don't you?"

"I learned that from being a dad."

Only getting caught having a fling with Jamie would jeopardize my chance at the CEO job. Then a fantasy flashed in my mind. *The CEO and the country music star.* Nashville's power couple. Adrenalin rushed through my body. I needed to be named CEO first. Deal with any fallout second.

After glancing more closely at the trucks, I saw what Jamie saw. People in their own worlds. On their phones. Looking at menus. Ordering food. Eating food.

Hunger got the better of me. "Okay, let's give this a try."

Jamie snagged my hand. He'd stand out more

swaggering in the food truck line by himself. Locked arms with a woman would be a great deflection.

To my relief, no one gave us a second glance, only to acknowledge some kind of man candy wanted to eat, too. Jamie was so tall and broad. But with all that jet-black hair up in a cap and his signature green eyes behind mirrored shades, short attention spans quickly went back to TikTok, Snapchat, and Instagram.

Carrying six tacos, four for Jamie, two for me in a box while I juggled a large bottle of water, we sat at a picnic table at the start of a hill down to the river. Jamie initially snuggled up next to me on the same side, but I eventually kicked him over to the opposite bench.

"Please, your hand on my thigh will make me blow our cover."

Grumbling, he slogged to the other side. My eyes followed several people walking by carrying food and showing no sign of recognizing the Nashville star. Something my PR department wouldn't appreciate, of course. I sighed and picked up a fish taco, happy to eat in peace.

A park person came by to take away empty plates and gazed at Jamie's hat with suspicion. He'd left it on because I told him he looked irresistible in it.

Jamie opened his mouth to say something else, but his cell whined. He gave the phone a curious gape. "It's Chloe's school. Maybe the paint class was canceled. I'll…be right back."

"I'm not going anywhere." I winked.

"Better not." He pulled his long legs from the picnic table and said, "Hello," into his phone. He gave my shoulder a squeeze before he walked a few steps closer to the river.

I cleaned up the rest of the empty taco wrappers. That good ole boy could eat. I set out the last taco, folded his napkin, and waited patiently for him to return.

Jamie sauntered back up the hill toward the table with a strange look on his face.

Worry?

No. *Terror*.

Chloe.

I stood up and rushed up to him. "What's the matter? Is Chloe okay?"

"Yeah," he said, but his breath clipped. "She…got into a fight."

"What?" I chirped. "That's impossible."

"I didn't get the whole story. They told me to get up there. Now."

My heart pounded at how Jamie spun around, looking wrecked.

"Do you… Are we done?"

"Jamie." I took his head in my hands, a feat since he towered over me. "I don't know how to drive a motorcycle. You need to get it together if we're riding out of here on your bike."

"Right. Right." He snagged my hand and steered me back to the parking lot.

This was why people shouldn't drive motorcycles.

Chloe was in trouble. And we were miles away.

"Jamie, can Cam send a car for you?"

"Me?" He jerked around. "You think I'd leave you here?"

"Your daughter needs you. I would expect you to leave me somewhere if it meant…"

"Stop. I'm not leaving you. She's not hurt. But the other parent is on her way."

"What happened?"

"I don't know."

Now I upset him even more. Breathing heavily, I said, "Can you…teach me to drive? Can you get the bike started and do the gears from behind me?"

"No. That would be more dangerous." He leaned forward with his hands on his thighs taking deep breaths. "Okay. I'm fine."

"Cam. Can you send Cam to the school for you? Just to be there with Chloe?" My voice cracked, thinking of her sitting in school all alone, afraid, upset.

Been there. Done that.

"Fuckin'-a. I didn't think of that. Darlin', this is why I need you." He pulled out his phone.

"I'll talk to him." I snagged it from him. "Get the bike revved up and put your helmet on." I heard Cam's voice. "J? What's up?"

"It's Harper. I—"

"Uh oh. What'd he do?"

"Nothing. Chloe's in trouble at school. We're in the Arboretum at Cumberland River. Jamie rode his bike. I don't want him driving one hundred miles an hour. He's…" I eyed him. "The call upset him. Please get to the school. We're on our way."

"Got it. Drive safe. Do I need to know why you're with him?"

"Nope. Not your business. Chloe is though."

"I'm on my way." When the phone went dead, I handed it back to Jamie. "Call the school back. Tell them you're on your way, but her uncle will be there first and he has permission to make decisions on your behalf."

Jamie nodded and dialed the school back. "How did you know to think that?"

"I was raised by aunts and uncles. I found out the hard way how not having proper authorizations from a parent can mess things up."

Missed school trips. No medical treatment for falls on the playground. And the days my lunch account dropped to zero. Thank goodness, schools didn't let children go hungry. Even ones with rich parents.

Jamie's voice sounded strong talking to the school and I secured my own helmet. When he tucked the phone back in his jacket, he slammed his lips against mine. "I'm sorry."

"For what?"

"Falling apart."

"It's your daughter, you have permission to be a hysterical puddle."

He snorted a laugh. "I think I have it together more than that. Did your mother turn into a—"

"Puddle?" I held Jamie's shoulders as he lifted me on the bike. "Yeah."

I left out the time she showed up at school drunk. Jamie maybe had some love-drunk going on. I squeezed his waist the entire trip to keep him together. Only a few times did he take his hand off one of the throttles to squeeze back. With two hands, I gripped his chest, his abs, but I kept my touch more loving than sexual. With his daughter in trouble, I would never make Jamie war with himself.

I breathed a sigh of relief seeing the school's blue and gold sign from several blocks away. Jamie rolled his HOG right up to the front steps. As he hopped off, I said, "I assume you don't bring Chloe to school on your bike?"

"No. My Range Rover." He looked around and

realized he attracted attention.

"Jamie," Cam called out from the school's front door, spinning him around.

I assumed Cam showed up in a car and if Chloe had to leave school, her uncle could drive her. I felt so helpless.

Nodding to Jamie, I said, "Go."

After shoving his helmet in the saddlebag, he jogged to the stairs and climbed them two at a time. Leather jacket, tight jeans, windblown jet-black hair. The teachers were gonna have heart attacks.

I removed my helmet and tucked it in the other saddlebag. Staring at the school, curiosity burned through me. As well as a pull I couldn't explain. Was Chloe okay? And why did I think maybe the little girl needed a woman right now, too?

I released a shaky breath. If Jamie needed me, he'd have asked me to go in. Only...he hadn't been concerned with how I'd get home. Did he expect me to wait?

Nodding, I stepped away from the bike and took out my phone. Dialing, I counted the rings to my assistant and lost my breath when the convertible Corvette pulled up in front of the school.

Michael.

What the heck?

Good lord. This wasn't going to end well for me.

The cool label exec in a dress shirt, trousers, and shades, looking like he should have been on an album cover, lifted out of his seat. "Harper."

Shaking my head, I ambled quickly to the curb. "What are you doing here?"

"Cam called me."

"Why?"

"He figured you'd need a ride."

I folded my arms. "You're the A&R VP at our label. You're not my chauffeur. What—" My throat went tight. "You're not here to give me a ride. You drove all this way to get me out of here."

"Chloe got into a fight with someone because of you, Harper."

"Me?"

Michael got out of the car and I backed up, thinking he planned to haul me off my feet. "Where did you get that information?"

"Cam called the school. They explained to him what happened." Michael crept toward me, but I stepped back.

If Chloe got in trouble for me, I had a right to be there. Settle whatever wild misunderstanding had occurred. "What happened?"

Michael gripped my forearms keeping me in place. "Chloe's been telling people you're Jamie's girlfriend. You've been sleeping over?" He scoffed his question and it didn't sound like he thought Chloe was lying.

"That's none of your business." I tried to get out of Michael's hold, but he practically dragged me to the car. "Is Jamie the *only* single parent in the school? Do no other kids' single mom or dad go on dates?"

"Those parents aren't megastars, Harper. What the fuck is wrong with you?"

Now, I pushed him away. "How dare you talk to me like that," I said through gritted teeth.

"I'm sorry." He grabbed me again. Michael wasn't as tall as Jamie, but at six-two he got a powerful hold on me and pulled me into his chest again. His hand cupped the back of my head. "I'm sorry. I'm sorry."

My mind spun in all directions. Finally, I realized we

were standing in front of Chloe's school. Jamie's *girlfriend*, being held by another man.

"I have to go in there." I nudged away. "If this has to do with me, I'm going inside."

"I'll wait for you," Michael said on an exhale and stepped back.

"You don't have to do that, I'm—"

"I want to make sure my *artist* is okay."

His artist. Jamie was Michael's artist. That tested his allegiance. Because Michael always looked out for me, too.

"Fine." I spun around and climbed those same steps up to the school's entrance.

I expected to smell lead paint, a memory from all the small-town rural schools in Texas I bounced around in. Or the public schools in Nashville where I'd made presentations to music students after being invited by music teachers. The lobby of Chloe's school looked more like a five-star hotel. Of course, this was a private school.

That meant the other children there were from rich privileged parents. Music wasn't the only industry in Nashville, though. Jamie might not find common ground with a parent who wasn't also an artist. Someone who'd understand the strange nuance of fame.

Fame. Like my mother.

"Can I help you?" A security guard held his arm out preventing me from going further inside.

"I'm with Jamie Miller." I held my head high.

If the guard had been standing there the whole time, he'd have seen me ride up on the back of his bike. Huffing, he took out his radio. "Name?"

"Harper. Harper Montgomery."

He blinked. "Gigi's daughter?" Music may not have been the only game in town, but everyone in Nashville knew Gigi. "Down the hall, to the right. They're in the principal's office."

"Thank you. Is Chloe all right? Is the other…girl okay, too?" I assumed the fight was with another little girl and not a boy.

"Both girls are fine. Just some pushing and shoving."

"Thank you." I reached out and squeezed the man's arm.

I turned the corner in the corridor like the guard had said and saw Jamie standing outside the office, Chloe tucked against him. Cam stood there, too, his arms folded.

"Harper!" Chloe spotted me and broke away from Jamie.

The adults all stared at me as Chloe dove into my arms. Not all of them looked happy. Especially Jamie.

"I just wanted to see if you're okay." I smoothed Chloe's forehead and fingered her glossy dark braid.

She was dressed in a blue and gray tartan vest, white shirt, and matching skirt. "I'm fine."

A shadow fanned out and I looked up to find Jamie staring down at us. His expression unreadable.

"I couldn't just leave," I said firmly.

Jamie rubbed his forehead. "Shoot, I left you out there, didn't I?"

"Michael's outside with his car. Cam called him."

"Great." Jamie nodded and brushed a hand down the front of his face. "Clo, go to Uncle Cam."

"But Harper came to see me. I want to show her my desk, my—"

"*Clo!*"

My breath hitched. "Jamie."

His eyes narrowed into slits, but he breathed. "Chloe, honey, you can show Harper another time. You pushed Taylor into the mud. You don't get to show Harper around *today*."

"Okay, Daddy." Chloe lowered her head and slogged off. She stood next to Cam who put his arm around her. My stomach unclenched when I saw Cam smile down at Chloe. Aunts and uncles got to be nice guys. Parents had to be bad ones.

Poor Jamie.

He walked down the hall, and I followed him, noticing he hadn't touched me. It made me feel cold and empty. But we were at Chloe's school.

"I didn't mean to cause a problem." I held my middle. "I couldn't leave without knowing—"

"I slept with Taylor's mother," Jamie deadpanned.

I felt my eyes twitch. "Okay. Recently?"

"A few months ago. *Once.* It was…a mistake. The loneliness…broke me."

"Please tell me Taylor's mom is single," I asked with my label executive brain.

He gave me a rough glare. "You think I would screw another man's wife?"

"Of course not. I didn't mean…. I don't know what I mean." I took a deep breath and walking away, I said, "I wanted to make sure Chloe was okay."

"That's it? I told you I slept with someone else and you don't care?"

"A few months ago, I wasn't in the picture." Except I did care. Because that mother would be at drop off and pick up every day. At every school play, every event. I felt dizzy. "Why did you tell me that? What did that—"

My breath hitched.

Chloe's been telling people you're Jamie's girlfriend.

Oh, hell's bells. Hell hath no fury like a woman scorned.

"I'm gonna take Chloe home." Jamie kept his eyes on me. "I'm probably gonna pull her out of school."

My stomach twisted. Chloe wanted to show me the school. She looked so happy doing her homework. "Please don't do that. The school year is almost over. This will all blow over."

Jamie stared at me.

"What did Taylor say to Chloe that made her push the little girl?"

Jamie didn't answer.

"I already know it was something about me."

"I didn't get the specifics and I don't care what was said. They're just kids. But yeah, it was about you." Jamie's head lowered, his face flushed with embarrassment.

Because we were dating. Wait, were we dating?

I straightened my back. "Well, if this Taylor girl said something untoward about me, Chloe had the right to defend me."

"Just not push someone. That tells me…" Jamie wiped his mouth. "She's even more crazy about you than I thought." He snuck a look at me through his dark lashes.

The sound of heels clicking, echoing off the lockers and a blast of perfume turned the corner before one of the most elegant, beautiful women I'd ever seen came into view. Even behind clunky Dolce & Gabbana sunglasses.

Long blonde hair, perfectly straightened sat on slender shoulders.

My mama had golden hair like you, Gigi.

Jamie preferred blondes.

Got it. All those discreet affairs on the road sharpened in my mind. A parade of women just like the one standing right there. *I was lonely…*

"Mr. Miller." Taylor's mom lowered her shades to take a long look at him and then let her eyes drift to me while I braced for some kind of snide comment. Nothing.

The woman looked past me in my old cowboy boots, rough and tumble denim zip-up dress, and windswept dark curls that no doubt had bugs caught in them from clinging to a bad boy musician on a motorcycle. Not my usual look. I'd strutted up and down the Blue Rock corridors in expensive high-powered suits and dresses. My hair and makeup perfect. My head held high.

Blue Rock…

If this situation got out, Kravet and his PR minions would have a field day with me. Hell's bells. Little girls fighting in a schoolyard because Jamie wanted me. Yeah, that would sell lots of albums. *Not.*

"Ms. Warner." Jamie nodded to the woman. "Please send me the bill for Taylor's uniform."

"And shoes, I was told." The woman held up a tote bag. A change of clothes for poor Taylor. The little girl must have been sitting in a dirty uniform and wet shoes this whole time. Kids were just kids. They said stupid things sometimes. Adults said stupid things sometimes.

I took a step back because this situation ran deeper beyond two little girls fighting over a swing. And because I wasn't Jamie's girlfriend, we were *nothing*, this had *nothing* to do with me.

"I'll get going," I said, tiptoeing backward.

"I'll call you later," Jamie said, but didn't touch me. Kept his distance.

Ms. Warner stood there, shoulder to shoulder with Jamie. Yeah, this problem concerned their daughters. That meant I had no place.

Nodding, I said, "Tell Chloe I said goodbye."

Without looking back, I spun around and next I was nearly slipping down the steps in front of the school. I had no memory of the short walk down the other corridor or saying goodbye to the guard.

At the bottom step, I felt hands around my waist. "Whoa, Poppy, I got you." Michael put his arm around me and steered me to his car.

He waited. Michael waited. And called me Poppy. "You never call me Poppy."

"I see the look on your face when your mother calls you that. I figured any other time, you'd punch me." He opened the passenger door to his Vette.

"You figured I wouldn't punch you now?"

"You practically fell down an entire flight of concrete steps. So, no."

I looked back at the school. Had I almost fallen? Where was my head? Oh right. Jamie. Chloe. Alone. With…Ms. Warner, who I would bet held the Miss Tennessee title, or some other beauty queen designation.

Michael got me in the front seat of his car and even did my seatbelt because I was still out of it thinking of Jamie standing there with a beautiful woman he'd already succumbed to.

"How long, Harper?" Michael swung the car away from the curve. "If you want me to help you with Gregory when he finds out, I need to know all the details."

"A few weeks," I didn't bother lying. "But—"

"There's a *but*?"

Had I hurt him somehow? Beyond the possible fallout from a label exec getting busy with an artist?

"We're just getting it out of our system, Michael. He's going on the road in a few weeks and that'll be it."

He barked a laugh. "Whose idea was that?"

I opened my mouth to answer, but realized I couldn't recall who made that decision, only it was mutually agreed upon. "Mine," I said to save face. To make it seem like I'd steeled my heart to more.

And in no way was bullied into letting a music god use me for a few weeks.

I was lonely…

"I made a mistake." I pinched the hem of my dress, not wanting Michael to see my legs. Legs I'd wrapped around Jamie's waist while he made me come undone earlier in the shower. Cried out his name as I fell apart in his arms.

My breath whooshed out. Had that blonde mom been in Jamie's bed?

I've not had a girlfriend.

No other women's been in my house.

"Do you love him?" Michael asked, still staring at the road.

"Why does that matter to you?" My breath hitched. "Michael, you're my best friend. You've never given me—"

"And I never will. You're…"

"I'm what?" I clutched my throat, afraid of how that sentence ended. "What?"

"You're too good for me. I'm just some failed

musician schlepping to clubs making other good ole boys' dreams come true. You're frickin' royalty."

"I'm not too good for anyone. I chose to do this kind of work. After what I saw my parents go through."

"Exactly." Michael now faced me. "Why would you want a life exactly the same as the childhood that nearly wrecked you?"

That's what I got for shooting whiskey with this cowboy and spilling bad childhood memories. But I believed a life with Jamie would not be the neglect-fest my parents inflicted on me. If Jamie managed to balance his career for his daughter, certainly he'd do the same for his wife. My brain went fuzzy. No, I wasn't going to be Jamie's wife. Our fling was temporary. That was it.

"I don't want that life. Which is why we agreed this was temporary."

Michael roared with laughter. "I've met some stupid sumbitches in this business. Jamie is *not* dumb. There is no way he's just taking what he can get from you to then *walk* away."

"I think there's a compliment in there somewhere. So, thank you."

When he made the turn at my block, the idea of walking in my house alone shattered me. That morning I woke to the sound of Jamie's motorcycle. Made love to him in my shower and until an hour ago, I knew unless the earth exploded, I'd be in his bed that night.

That's hope for ya. Dare to dream and you'll be destroyed.

"If it were just you and Jamie, I would say, go ahead and keep things quiet. But there's a little girl involved. And a whole school. Parents. Parents buy records."

"You think dating me will hurt his record sales?"

Michael shrugged. "Who knows what moves the needle these days. What upsets the algorithms. He's leaving in a few weeks and you said this was just for fun. He's got a launch to rehearse for. And then he's got to promote the record. Let him do all of that with a clear head."

Clear head? He already had to give Chloe up. He'll be messed up enough. Perhaps at that exact moment, Jamie's train of thought was chugging behind Michael's.

"You haven't lived under a rock, Harper. You know what he is. It's the reason you didn't want to sign him. Let him go, now." Michael stared at me. "I know guys like that. Jamie will never change. He didn't change for the mother of his child. Why would he change for you?"

"Why are you being so harsh?"

"You came out of that school white. Pale. Looking ready to throw up. I can't handle seeing you like that."

"I'm fine. I'll be fine. I mean... It'll be fine." Another vision of Jamie sitting there with Ms. Warner made my stomach flip. Would he go back to her place and bang her again to make up for Chloe's mistake?

"Are we in agreement, Harper?"

"Mmmm." To say yes would feel like glass going down my throat.

"I'm always here if you want to talk or just need to drown yourself in some whiskey."

I nodded and opened my gate with my phone app. Once Michael swung around my fountain, he said, "I'll get your door."

"I got it." I didn't expect that type of A-list treatment. Sure, Michael was a southern gentleman, but we were both VP's with equal power at the label. "I'll see you tomorrow." I opened my own goddamn door.

Chapter Fifteen

Jamie

After Chloe went to bed, a text came in from Harper.

Have to see you.

I worried that shit show at the school with Melody Warner would fuck up my applecart. My smooth sailing with Harper until I left. She had calmed Chloe and me, made us forget our looming separation. That wasn't something I was about to give up.

After a soft knocking on my door, I found a woman on my doorstep who looked more wrecked than I felt. "Hi."

Gripping her hand, I brought her into my house and leaned her up against the back of the door. "I'm sorry."

"You don't have anything to be sorry for."

"I've been an idiot. Acting like some damn clean slate who could start all over again with you."

"Are we…starting over?" She breathed. "I thought we were just having fun. When you're just having fun, eventually that's gonna end."

"What if I don't want it to end?"

"You're leaving. It will end."

I stepped back and swore under my breath. "Why? I've been in this business for seven years. Guys have girlfriends. Guys have wives. Guys have kids and get on the road. I thought you…" I had to stop when I saw her chest heaving. "It's because of your parents, isn't it?"

She swallowed. "That would mean I'm harboring years of pain and sorrow that's preventing me from…falling in love," she said that last part so damn low and haunting, my brain fuzzed out.

"I'm drowning in pain, too, Poppy."

"I'm not that little girl anymore." She covered her eyes.

"Talk to me. Trust me, I'll let you analyze me next."

She sniffed and looked up at me. "Should two damaged souls try to make a go of it? I mean, Chloe deserves a shot with something better. That Ms.—"

"Don't," I gritted out.

"She looked mighty put together, Jamie. Solid. Beautiful. I mean, what was wrong with her?"

"Nothing." I stepped away.

I'd been telling myself for years Chloe deserved all of me during the school year when she was with me. Maybe that'd been an epic flawed philosophy.

"Did Chloe know?"

"Know about what?"

"That you and Ms.—"

"Her name is Melody." I wiped my mouth. "And Chloe found out. The girls were at a sleepover. Taylor told Chloe a few days later. After, I'd told Melody it was a mistake. And that it wouldn't happen again."

"What did Chloe say about it? You and Melody?"

"She wasn't happy about it. Said…"

"What?"

I laughed and crossed my arms. "Said Melody wasn't right for me. Honestly, I thought maybe she just wasn't ready for me to date. I figured with the tour coming up, it was best to just bury any further talks about me and Melody as quickly as they started."

"So, why am I here?"

"You're my surprise. You're the spark I didn't see coming. Clearly, whatever Chloe's objections were to

Melody, that doesn't apply to you."

"Why?"

"I don't know." I took a breath. "And I don't care."

"I don't know if I can hold on while you're away. I'm just being honest."

I nodded. "I understand. Can we...try?"

"Trying is the part that will hurt the most. Maybe if Chloe were—"

"Maybe if she were what?"

"All those guys you mentioned who go on the road, they leave their kids behind with their mamas. Their mamas have a piece of them while they're gone."

My legs weakened and I had to grip a nearby chair. "That wasn't enough for Layla."

"I've got triggers from Gigi and Billy. You're still dealing with guilt about Layla. I'd say we're toxic together. Chloe deserves better than that."

I stared at her, feeling my eyes well up. "But we can't change the past, Poppy. All we can do is move forward. Pay it forward. I've been trying every damn day with Chloe."

"I've told you, you're amazing with her. She's loved and well cared for." She looked away, and thumbed her chin.

"What is it?"

"What happens when you...get married and have more children? Will Chloe still have to spend the summers back home in Texas?"

Her calling Texas home spread warmth through my heart. We came from the same place. Our roots were tangled together under the ground somehow. What could grow from it?

"I don't know. I meant what I said that I would never

keep her from Layla's parents. But if my situation changed." I blew out a breath. "If I got married and had more kids, that'd be one hell of a *situation* change." My vision blurred, a shock going through my body imagining it.

"Can I ask a question that's been haunting me?"

This should be good. But I'd bared my soul as to why I didn't sleep with her seven years ago. "I'd rather not answer questions about Melody. That was one and done." I moved closer to her, feeling her softening to me.

"It's not that, although, of course it bothers me since you'll see her again." Harper straightened now, looking stronger. "But Jamie, you've lived in Nashville for a few years now. With Chloe. Why haven't you tried to get in touch with me?"

I coughed a laugh. "That's not obvious? I was terrified to be in the same room with you to sign my contract. I thought you hated me."

"Hated you?"

"For not, giving you what you wanted that night." And I never felt at home here in Nashville, always felt like I didn't belong.

"I was humiliated more than anything."

"I'm sorry. I hope I cleared that up the night I kissed you in the rain." I watched as a shiver passed through her. "Come here, Poppy. Kiss me like that again. Let's finish what we started this morning. We have busy lives. You're gonna run a record music label one day. I have to make music and take care of Chloe. We have to figure out how to pause shit. And get right back to it." I brushed my hand across her cheek.

"Was Chloe all right when you brought her home?"

"Yes and no. She's a kid. Kids melt down and then

out of nowhere get happy again."

Harper smiled. "I feel terrible that fight was about me."

"I love that it was about you." I kissed her and held her again. "That she was defending you. I don't think she'd defend me like that."

"I think you're very wrong. If she were defending me, she defended you…us."

"Us…" My voice cracked. I'd never been an us, except with Chloe. "What do you want, Harper? Right now?"

"You."

"Good, because I want that, too." I wanted Harper more than anything at that moment.

I wanted to bring her back to that place she was that morning in the shower. Out of control and mindless. This time, I wanted her in my music room. I steered her down the carpeted steps to my finished basement.

Behind the second door to my studio, I gently laid her down on the sofa, unzipped my jeans then slipped off her boots. "I got what you need, right here, darlin'."

She sat up and slid her lightweight leather jacket down her tan shoulders. "I was already wired driving over here."

"I can see that. Take me. Take all of me. I'm yours."

Her eyes flashed open at my statement and crinkled in the corners. Next, she laughed hysterically, lifting that same denim dress over her head. "That's from our song, sweet talker." Her curves gently shifted when I undid the hooks to remove her bra.

My mouth closed around the pointed tips of Harper's firm breasts, alternating between my tongue and my lips. The more she arched her back, the more my excitement strained against the heat between her legs causing my own soft cry of agony.

Her fingers slipped below the waistband of my jeans, but I grasped her hand and moved it over her head. "No," I whispered. "Let me please you, Harper."

"You are, let me show you how much." She tugged my fingers inside her panties.

The heated and damp skin damn near made me explode. She slid her panties down toned legs and kicked them away from her ankles. I reached into my pocket for my wallet. With Harper back in my life, I figured I had to be prepared for anything.

Harper lifted her shoulders and gasped, her eyes fixated on what she had done to me. I watched her with steady scrutiny while I pushed my jeans down.

"Like what you see?" I sliced through the condom wrapper.

"Oh yes." She sat up and took the condom from my hand, shocking me further. "Let me do that."

There was something strangely pure but erotic having another set of fingers slide on a condom. "That's so good, Harper," I bit out.

Once she sheathed my cock, a fury ignited within me. I lifted her right leg over my shoulder and moved my hips forward. Even though she was slick to the touch, the pressure from her tightness and my size always took me by surprise. "You're killing me, woman."

"Jamie," she cried out in desperate agonizing pants.

"That's me, I'm not going anywhere," I said, stroking her cheek. The words, '*I love you Harper,*' nearly slipped from my trembling lips.

My body joined with hers felt like love, but I was still too frightened to cross that line. But it was coming. I had the wherewithal during mind-blowing sex to stop myself because I was in complete control with a woman under me. It was outside in the real world where I would find myself on my knees somewhere crying to her, begging her to forgive me for being an idiot seven years ago.

Yeah, I was in love with her and that just fucked things up worse. Made it all the more complicated and scarier, because now losing her would destroy me.

Harper cried out in tiny soul shattering moans.

Damn, she was close already. I ate it up since I just entered her. Fuck-all, I loved how her crumbling tolerance stroked my ego.

"Man, I love how you transform when we're alone. Call me an egomaniac, but it gets me hard to feel how you melt in my arms."

"I'm melting all right. Can't you feel it?" She took my hand and slid it between her legs. "In case that annoying rubber didn't let you know how you make me feel."

"Oh, I feel it." Jeez, did I ever.

"How about this." She pushed forward to get on top of me.

Her breasts pressed against my damp chest as her hips moved in a rhythm she deviously figured out drove me crazy.

Crazy. Yeah, that's how I felt at the moment, so filled with lunacy. The throbbing started deep within Harper. Her head tipped back, her nipples expanded, every inch of that skin, reddened and pulsed.

A wicked jolt shot up the length of my cock, ripping a deeper cry from her. She felt it. Together we rocked, in sync. Perfect. Nothing could ruin that moment.

Harper

Jamie Miller had the power to blow me apart again, just when I'd found some peace in my life. Even if that peace also made me feel dull, boring, and lonely.

I needed to know something before my heart took the last lap. Set this 'fling' back on the course it needed to be on because in the dark scary cobwebbed corner of my mind, I knew once Jamie left for his tour, poof. That would be it.

Perhaps it was best to put an end to everything right now because it was too much.

Looking him dead in the eye, I asked, "Are you gonna sleep with women this summer again?"

The glow Jamie had those last few minutes disappeared. Fast. "Ouch." He rubbed his chest like I'd delivered a blow.

The pale, troubled look on his face made me want to snap the words back in my mouth. "Well then..."

His worried expression had deep and critical written all over it. Like my question had just put our little fling on life support and I was standing there holding the plug.

"Never mind." I yanked my dress back on not bothering with the bra. It was best we had this conversation when I had some clothes on.

One-boot hobbling away from the sofa, I opened a door that led to the lower grade portion of his yard. It had a small concrete pad and a few chairs to sit on. To distract from the scary question I just asked, I stared at the sky.

Jamie burst outside, barely dressed. The strength in his hold when he gripped my arm was just as alarming as the frightened look in his eyes. Was he falling for me?

"Harper, Christ. Stop running away from me the minute you think you're gonna get an answer you don't like."

Be the good muse, Harper, a faint voice whispered. *Don't drag him down into the dungeon of your emotional baggage.* Jamie had an album to launch. To wrap this into emotional payback would send it spiraling downward.

Love. Did I love Jamie? Whatever I told myself I felt seven years ago couldn't hold a candle to what my heart was doing now. Every aching need I had for the man was met and soothed. Daily.

For years I felt like I'd been on a roundabout, going in circles. A month ago, I couldn't see a path to happiness. Then I got a flat tire and was forced off one of the entry lanes.

Voilà. There I was.

"Okay. What am I then? *Am* I your girlfriend?" I asked. "Where did Chloe get all of that from?"

Jamie

I studied Harper. Talk about a 'come-to-Jesus' moment. The last woman I considered my girlfriend was Layla. Look where that got her. Yet another brave woman, beautiful, sophisticated, sweet, and kind, wanted to walk beside me. And there I was letting her.

The feeling of love I'd stuffed away earlier walloped me. A rush of heat through my heart and a tight throat. Yeah, this *was* love. So much that I was scared to death for her. Protect her at all costs.

Taking Harper's hand, I led her back into the house. I grabbed the closest bottle of whiskey. Pouring two shots, I said, "I need to warn you about something."

"Ominous. Okay." She sank into a chair at the bar I'd set up in my studio.

"I only loved one woman, Chloe's mom." *And* Chloe, of course, but that was different. "But I wasn't capable of sacrificing my need to keep playing music."

"I'm not asking you to stop playing *music*." Her back stiffened.

I cleared my throat. "I never had to behave on the road." I took a sip of my drink, swirled the spiciness on my tongue, and let it burn down my throat to keep my focus. "I have no blueprint or idea how to handle this."

"I'm not asking you to give up partying and having a good time." Her hand slipped into mine. "You can do this, Jamie. I see something so different in you." My heart ached. Man, she really believed in me.

"I want to try," I whispered. "I'm just so afraid of messing up." I had almost fifteen years to look back on and dissect what I'd done wrong with Layla. Now, the hours I spent with Chloe, I was a different man. A man I liked. A man a little girl looked up to with large green eyes, *my eyes* and called me Daddy. Those moments saved me.

Harper brought that man into the relationship realm. Something I hadn't expected. But I was still scared I'd break her heart. "This is the promise I'm willing to make. Even if I…" My stomach cramped. "If I do something stupid, or even if I come to the ridiculous conclusion that I don't want this, I won't just vanish. I will tell you. To your face. I promise."

I'd face that firing squad for Harper. If it made me ending our relationship easier for her. Give her the answers and the closure I denied her years ago.

"Okay."

"Okay?" I was amazed. "You're quite brave to take me on."

"I'll take my chances." She kissed me gently on the mouth." You and Chloe are worth it."

Chapter Sixteen

Harper

I jammed diamond-encrusted hoop earrings into my lobes for Jamie's album launch party a week later. His lovemaking at night had grown serious and intense. Especially the night after he recorded our song. Jamie had held me with the kind of possession in his touch, I'd only read about in BDSM novels.

Yeah, I read those, so what?

With every sunset, though, Jamie's eyes also held a look of terror that I was sure had to do with the months ahead of him on tour. He'd be losing both me and Chloe.

Only my departure would be permanent if Michael got his way. Sitting in his Corvette on the way to the Grand Ole Opry, I squeezed my phone debating whether to text Jamie and ask how he was doing. Launches were terrifying, even to seasoned artists. I had to hand it to Kravet and his team, kicking off Jamie's tour at the flippin' Opry was genius.

Inside the historic venue, Michael kept his hand on my waist and steered me to Blue Rock's VIP corner behind red velvet ropes. As the co-author of the opening song, the media vultures would rush to me for a comment. Then hopefully forget I existed once Jamie appeared at the reception later on.

All the secrecy had been easy behind closed doors. Soon I'd be thrust into the same room with Jamie and had to act professionally distant. I woke that morning in his bed, his hands all over me, tangled up. Then ate breakfast with Chloe before going to work. It felt so normal and now we were being thrown to the wolves.

Michael marched through the Opry's lobby in his

A&R VP glory. Jamie was *his* artist, the humongous risk he took to sign. Michael deserved to take credit for Jamie's success and gloat all night how he'd been right.

And I, the lone voice of dissension, had been wrong. Dead wrong.

Good work.

My eyes searched to find a non-threatening familiar face, but I didn't see the hand that came out of nowhere grab my wrist. If the skin hadn't been ice-cold and dainty, I'd have thought it was Jamie.

"I have a bone to pick with you, lady!" Sugar Anne Harris, publicist extraordinaire found me and looked ready to lay into me.

"Me?" I shoved a finger in my chest, reminding me my heart was still pounding.

"I lost my access to your building." She folded her arms. "How do you reckon I scope out new clients?"

"Who pulled your pass?" I asked her.

"Your assistant Maisy said Kravet did."

"He's in finance, what does that have to do with…" My throat closed up. *Gregory gave me license to direct marketing dollars to Jamie however I want.* Kravet had gotten to my boss somehow. What else had Kravet convinced the CEO of Blue Rock Records to do? Why had Gregory given so much power to the guy?

Blue Rock was in trouble, that I knew. Same ole, same ole wasn't the strategy for Jamie, apparently. Good lord.

"I'm sorry," I apologized to Sugar Anne. "I probably should have given you the heads-up that the bastard of Blue Rock was on a warpath."

"Things are getting tough, Harper." The pain in Sugar Anne's voice seeped through her ordinarily over-the-top, cheery, southern-bell deportment. "Too many artists are going Indy and trying to do this themselves."

"That was always Gregory's vision. Be small enough and not get in our own way." I grew up in a different world and saw what my parents had gone through with their big record label.

"I need a drink, how about you?" Sugar Anne said, looking around with hopelessness in her eyes.

"You have no idea." I looped my arm with Sugar Anne as we strutted through the lobby in search of southern comfort.

"One gimlet and a Jim Beam, rocks please," she said to the bartender, uncrumpling a twenty.

I exhaled and reached for my wallet. "I got this."

Waiting for the drinks, I examined the grandeur and majesty of the Opry. High ceilings, the lights, all the painted portraits. The place was Olympus to country music gods and goddesses. Of all the options Sam Riley, Kravet's second-in-command had floated past me, this one got my highest recommendation. Based on Kravet's initial ideas for Jamie, I worried his launch would take place in a strip club.

The bartender handed over my amber goodness. "Thank you." I gently tapped the rim of my thick crystal glass against Sugar Anne's martini and swallowed a much-needed icy gulp.

"Well, we know what's on her mind," she said, pointing.

A beautiful young girl glided through the crowd. Her short skirt and tight low-cut top ensured *she* wasn't going home alone.

"If country music keeps signing bad boys, rockstars are gonna have themselves some real groupie competition," I replied.

Sugar Anne leaned in. "Your handsome BFF is getting a lot of attention tonight."

"Good for him." I found Michael holding a glass of whiskey talking to producers, looking a little too sexy for his own good.

Then I noticed what Sugar Anne had zeroed in on, as only a good publicist would. Low-cut Woman slinked up to Michael and hung shamefully on his arm. A small chuckle rumbled in my chest when I saw him place a hand on that woman's lower back, touching skin. One more occupied bimbo meant one less groupie clawing at Jamie. He, he.

I started to turn around when Michael and Low-cut Woman broke off from the crowd. I could read that girl's dirty mind from across the room. Oh gross, a stairwell quickie? "Michael, come on, cowboy. You can do better that, you deserve—"

My words died in my throat when I realized Michael was taking Low-cut Woman to the…the backstage door.

The thought of girls like *that* being brought to Jamie made me feel like I was slipping into anaphylactic shock.

Not today.

"I'll be right back," I said, shoving my drink in Sugar Anne's hand.

A fireball of possessiveness rolled through my body so hot, so fast, I was surprised the carpet didn't light up under my feet as I barreled toward the same door. Michael had cut a path back into the crowd or I'd have dragged him with me. I was about to look like a complete lunatic and could use a little cover when I exploded.

The bourbon had worked enough magic to give me the courage to go backstage and face what the hell was going on in Jamie's dressing room. Better to get it over with early, than stress about it all night. There wasn't enough Jim Beam in the city of Nashville to calm my nerves if I had to wait for hours.

A man dressed in a black tee-shirt that read 'Security' in bright white letters scanned my full access badge and said, "Third door on the left, Miss Montgomery."

Slowly, I moved through the dark narrow corridor to Jamie's dressing room. Music *thump-thump-thumped* from behind that damn third door. I breathed a sigh of relief that the thing was closed, giving me an extra minute to steady myself.

I pushed the door and it flew open so fast I stepped back. The whack of sound and the crush of people startled me. I'd been in that dressing room before. Twenty people, tops, made it feel crowded. There had to be a hundred guests in that thing now.

All women.

In short skirts and V-neck tops showing plenty of inappropriate cleavage. High heels. Long hair. Blondes. Perfume. Everywhere. Was I out of touch? Had Blue Rock really become uptight and too proper, encouraging artists to focus *only* on the music?

Clutching my throat, I had no clue where to begin to look for Jamie. For this type of guest list, the PR whack-job who put this together should have made him sit in the corner on a throne and let his subjects come to him. Looking at both back walls, I saw nothing. Just more girls.

I stopped. Raw possessiveness clawed at my insides. Did I not trust Jamie? Would he take this 'surprise' visit as me checking up on him? My business card still read,

Blue Rock Records, Vice President. I had every right to be there, even though Michael and I gave our artists space before performances.

But Jamie wasn't just my artist, he was my lover. I knew a moment of truth was upon me. The look on Jamie's face when he saw me would tell me everything. His facial expression would *show* me if what he'd *told* me about being done with all the women nonsense on the road rang true.

But where the heck was he?

A small dose of relief crept in. Jamie wasn't in that crowded room. All these girls were out here, waiting for him. Ready for him. My breath caught when a shock of jet-black hair grabbed my brain. His incredible height sent him soaring above the crowd. His head leaned left and a coif of golden hair next to him came into view.

Cam Renner.

Oh, thank heavens.

A female moved out of the way for just a second giving me a wide shot of Jamie's stunning tall figure...as he zipped up his fly.

Jamie

I stormed out of the junket room with Cam's voice calling out behind me.

"I can't believe you showed your hip tattoo to that jerk," my best friend grumbled.

"He thought it wasn't real. What moron examines pictures of me and accuses me of having a fake tatt?"

"Morons." Cam put his hand on my back. "I appreciate you kept your cool, though."

I stopped. "Have I really been that much of an asshole in the past?"

"Yes?" Cam scrunched his face. "But…this thing with Harper really has had a good effect on you."

Our magic happened all over again, I couldn't deny that. There I was preparing to leave again. Leave *her*…

Looking around, I was amazed at how packed the dressing room had become since I'd been doing my interviews. I thought about my very first launch, nothing more than a coat closet filled with friends and relatives, if a cousin from Cleveland counted.

I didn't recognize a single face. All the sofas were overflowing with bodies. Female bodies. Sexy. Lots of legs. Ugh. If I'd had my choice, it would be the coat closet with just Harper and Chloe. They were all I wanted right now. And from the looks of it, I wasn't getting what I wanted.

If there was something to lose my cool over, it was not openly loving the woman in my life. "You know, Cameron, if you're trying to keep me from doing something really stupid, you could have cut this guest list from my pregame. The interviews were enough."

"I didn't do this."

I rolled my eyes and gripped Cam's shoulder. "I've known you almost your whole life. If you accepted me after what happened with Layla, how could you think I wouldn't accept a few missteps from you?"

Cam shrugged out of the hold. "I don't know what you're talking about, J."

"Where the heck did all these girls come from?" Burning tension filled my chest.

Christ, what would Harper say if she saw all this?

"You're welcome," a voice croaked out from behind me.

I spun around and was jarred at the crunchy old man

who contrasted poorly with the tall, beauties all around me. "Mr. Kravet."

"Good party, huh?" the man's creepy voice sputtered.

I looked around and then back at Cam who shook his head, pissed to be overstepped. *Don't mess with Texas…* "You invited all these people?" I asked Kravet.

"My PR people did."

"Harper never mentioned—" I bit down on my lip.

"Harper? As in Harper Montgomery?"

"And Michael Bradley. They briefed me on this whole thing. I have to go on stage in a few minutes, sir. I can't have all these distractions."

"Yes, beautiful women are quite distracting." He glanced around, too, and gave a heavy sigh.

"No. The noise. The crush of people. And where is my band? I have a routine right before a show."

Kravet smirked at Cam. "So dedicated. He wants his band. Do you know what I want?"

Uh oh. "No."

"For you to stop pretending." Kravet tugged me by the arm and sneered at Cam when he tried to follow.

"It's fine," I grunted back to Cam and let myself be dragged down the hallway by Kravet. At least it was quiet there. When we got to the dead end, I pulled out of the man's grimy hands. "What am I pretending?"

"That you're prepared to be a good little boy and that you're through with all that." He pointed to the sea of women.

I shook my head.

"Do you know how many people would kill for *that*? To have just one of those beautiful women?"

All I saw was that Harper and Chloe were missing.

I'd had my fair share of all that nonsense. Chloe kept my ass home at night and Harper made me never want a woman's hand on my body again.

"Sir, I have a daughter. She lives with me now. Sure, I made a lot of bad decisions in the past. I can't lose another contract. I'm thirty-two. That was all bullshit. The music matters, now."

"Sales matter to me." His eyes scanned my body. "And the fantasy will only make more women buy your records."

"Fantasy?"

"Female listeners will see you with lots of pretty girls, and think, hey, why not me?"

Oh, great.

"That makes them go to shows," Kravet added. "You're a smart man. You know that's where the real money is. People can pirate your music, listen for free on the radio. Twenty thousand women aren't getting into an arena for free."

My *360 Contract* meant the label took a cut of my concerts. The deal sounded great at the time since it meant they'd promote me beyond just the launch. Only, *this* wasn't supposed to be part of the payment. Kravet was pimping me out. I hadn't read the terms word for word, but I trusted Cam wouldn't have agreed to anything that said I was supposed to put-out.

A man in a headset rushed toward us.

"Mr. Miller, there you are." The stage manager was a welcomed distraction. "It's time, sir."

"There're more out in the audience. Now give those people what they came for." Kravet winked and sank back into the crowd of women.

Cam sauntered up to me shaking his head. "Come on,

I'll say a few words for you, after you leave." My best friend steered me around all the hungry eyes and lips being licked.

I should have been gracious and thanked everyone for coming myself, except I didn't invite anyone. And I was relieved to get the hell out of there.

I met the stage manager out in the corridor and froze. The lingering scent of perfume sharply overwhelmed me. Harper's floral scent… Oh, for fuck's sake. I spun around with a hand on my head.

Harper *had* been back there and she must have stormed away mad. If I'd gone to her dressing room and saw nothing but skin and six-pack abs, I'd be furious, too.

I followed the stage manager on unsteady feet. *What the fuck am I going to tell her about that circus?* Her not finding me suggested she took one look at the piles of women and had taken off. There would be hell to pay.

My comeback tour was getting off to a shitty start.

Harper

I wished I could melt into the wall. I hid behind other executives with my eyes closed, willing away tears. If I'd simply refused Jamie and stood my ground that it was inappropriate for us to be in a relationship, none of this would be happening. Then I'd be front and center, tall and proud of the most talented singer country music had to offer.

Michael's introduction of Jamie was excited and heartfelt. Even if his words sounded a *little* overused and canned.

Jamie stepped onto the stage to deafening applause and cheers. Fans who'd been waiting patiently in the sweltering heat, then poured into the Opry, and filled every seat. Blue Rock had delivered their god, wearing black pants laced up the side seams and an iridescent sheer top that made my blood pulse hot in my throat. His devilish stage smirk made girls cheer more as he squinted into the crowd and tossed random waves here and there.

The opening music to the song we wrote, *Time and Place* began with a small hand signal by Jamie. I may have been dying inside, but I couldn't deny Jamie's performance was a shining example of flawless perfection.

After the song, when the crowd finally calmed down, Jamie stood frozen for a moment. He held the microphone tight in his grasp, his other hand gripping the neck of the guitar. He brought his lips to the mic and opened his mouth. Without music playing behind him, he looked like he was debating whether to give a speech.

He had asked if I minded a mention thrown my way and a thank you for my work on the song. I couldn't have said no any faster than I did. While it was perfectly acceptable to thank a co-songwriter, I knew he'd get mushy and maybe throw caution to the wind. Make some kind of declaration.

Jamie only released a small breath and said, "Thank you," in the lowest, sexiest goddamn drawl I ever heard.

The rest of his set sailed by and a roar of angry boo's erupted in the auditorium when the house lights came on. I had never seen an audience demand more at a launch. Everyone was addicted to Jamie's voice.

I was addicted to every other part of his body.

My heart ached. How could he have betrayed me already? Cam's smiling face had perplexed the hell out of me. Had he been watching? Were they…sharing a woman? I wasn't naïve. I knew what went on with music gods and their groupies.

"Hell's bells, that was magnificent," Sugar Anne cooed next to me.

I jumped. I'd disappeared inside my own head and when I dragged myself back to reality, my surroundings startled me. "I reckon I can't pay you a large sum of money to turn around and forget you saw me walk out the door early?"

"This is *your* night as well. You wrote one of the songs. Why are you standing here alone while the other writers and executives are in the VIP box?"

I might have had every right to be in the center of other proud Blue Rock execs, but people really didn't want to make conversation with a woman on the edge of a breakdown.

Chapter Seventeen

Jamie

The crowd's reaction when I left the stage forced me to accept this was going to be my life for the next two months.

The boo's bothered me. I would have happily sung more songs. I was a performer, first and foremost. Even if I nearly choked early on. It had been years since the evil bitch known as stage fright came to blow me before a show. Knowing Harper was watching me with *god-knows-what* awful thoughts in her head had nearly crippled me.

After the show, assistants and handlers quickly shuffled me backstage. The dressing room had mercifully emptied out. Now flowers and gift baskets, each with letters of congratulations were all over the place.

Rory and my other band members joined me, making me feel slightly better. They huddled together and I told each and every one of them what a great job *they* did.

"Are you ready to see everyone, Jamie?" Cam broke in to move the evening along.

"I'm ready," I said.

Was I ready to face Harper?

What I was not prepared for, however, were all the women from backstage now waiting for me at the reception. In the lobby, a sea of blonde hair and short skirts made my stomach queasy and I had trouble speaking at times.

All I could manage were handshakes and humble, *Thank-you's* to the repeated comments such as *Good job!*, *You're incredible!*, and *That was amazing!*

"I have a table over here," Cam said, leading me to the back corner of the room. "We'll let everyone come to us."

"Nonsense." Kravet appeared and steered me toward the center of the room. "The boy should mingle," he said over his shoulder to Cam who suddenly got swallowed up by reporters asking him questions and couldn't rescue me from this asshole.

"Last I checked, sir, I'm a man," I argued bitterly, keeping myself in check because he was still a VP with my label. One thing I learned after losing three contracts: don't argue with the people responsible for my livelihood.

"Yes, you are. Now go act like a man who loves women." He gave me a hard shove.

Getting physical meant all bets were off. "Dickhead, I can walk. If you touch me again…"

"Let me put my cards on the table." Kravet stopped me from hanging myself with a threat against an exec at my label. "I was in charge of vetting you for your contract. Quite the info I found out about your early days, the drinking, the women. And then having a child you never saw."

My gut burned, but it didn't pay to argue. My breath shallowed out. I needed to find Harper. This was all bullshit. When did it no longer matter what I wanted? What was the point of all the sacrifices if I had to give up my heart?

"I wanted you with Blue Rock. Those idiots at the large labels with crazy deep pockets held you back because they were afraid you'd get them big fat embarrassing lawsuits from scorned women. Good thing Blue Rock has virtually no cash. That's where *you* come in. You get out there and be the stud these women want. I want you to mingle, flirt, let all those women touch you." He brushed against my silk shirt. "Open this up more, man. Give women a taste of that fantasy we talked about. Let them think you'll go off in a dark corner, or that song you sang on stage, will be your last song. Because there's one thing country music fans hate, it's a deadbeat dad."

I was ready to throw up. Kravet knew about Layla. He threatened to expose what happened years back. Hang our dirty laundry out for everyone to see. We'd both look bad. A woman keeping her baby from the daddy. A daddy not giving up *everything* to be a daddy. We were young and we both let Layla's father control us. Who knew how our past mistakes would look eleven years later? And with Layla not around to defend herself. Chloe having to listen to trash talk about her mother.

If a mountain could be moved for Chloe, I would do it. If Kravet's price to keep Layla and her memory out of this so long as I played along and acted like a whore, that's what I had to do.

"Now go put on the show I fucking paid for." Kravet spun away taking his gross smell with him.

There was no time to think about the consequences of my actions, or fight back, not with my past hanging over me like a noose. Seven years ago, I left Harper to sign my first contract and live my dream. Now I had to hurt her again to *keep* the damn thing.

Forgive me, Harper…

Harper

I struggled to breathe, struggled to stand, but most of all I struggled to hear Jamie. His appearance triggered a frenzy in the main reception room, but his velvet voice was drowned in a monotonous pool of blurred sounds. Oh, how I wanted to be in the middle of it all. Except, it would feel like rolling around in barbed wire, I suspected.

A mass of people moved along like a cloud and I assumed Jamie was floating in the center. My heart pounded and I had to get my mind on something else. After spotting Gregory talking to someone who ran a bank in Memphis, I decided to make sure I was still in his good graces.

"I'm going to go talk to Gregory." I inched away from Sugar Anne.

"Get my badge reactivated, please."

I smiled, my eyes staying on Sugar Anne while I absently took a step forward. The collision would have startled me regardless of who it was. A familiar musky scent and the *I'd know that body anywhere* feeling registered.

A set of familiar hands steadied me from falling on my face, but when I confirmed who it was, those hands left my body. Quickly.

Jamie's sexy stage clothes were gone, replaced with a pair of dress slacks and a black silk button-down shirt. God, he had gotten better looking since that morning. This wasn't the same Jamie trudging around his bedroom picking dirty clothes off his floor, or braiding Chloe's hair. This man was different. Mr. Music God had arrived.

The crushing weight of how much I wanted him seized my body. Could I forgive his indiscretions if he came home to me every September? If he could admit he loved me, the way I knew I loved him? Did I have that in me?

The way Jamie had held me last night, tighter and tighter with each breath had made me feel more secure than I ever thought possible.

After the cloud of lust filtered out, I noticed the harem gathered around him. Low Cut Woman and several clones. All blonde. *My mama had golden hair*. Apparently, that was Jamie's preference. Like Melody Warner.

"Oh, Jamie, you sweet thang," Sugar Anne jumped in, blissfully unaware of the mountain of tension that had just crumbled upon us. "You were brilliant tonight."

I cleared my throat. "This is Sugar Anne Harris, a publicist."

"Nice to meet you," Jamie said all monotone and ruthless. He had a room full of women to conquer.

Sex sells, Kravet had said.

Sugar Anne leaned in. "If you're ever not happy with your current representation, sweet thang, Harper knows where to find me." She winked.

"Thank you, Sugar Anne," Jamie said, but he gazed at me with empty eyes.

"Are you all right?" Sugar Anne asked while I glared at Jamie. "You're looking pale, dearie."

The evening could not have gone any more wrong for me. "I'm fine."

"Harper, tell your boy here, how great he was." Sugar Anne nudged me.

An enormous surge of guilt had been eating away at me all night for allowing this personal turmoil to get in the way of my professional responsibility.

I moved my eyes back to Jamie. "It's late and I'm leaving."

When Jamie's face blanked out, I turned away

stifling a moan of sorrow. God, what had I gotten myself into?

"Harper!"

The sound of Jamie's voice and the hint of desperate vulnerability brought me to a halt instantly. It was so loud, everyone had stopped and looked around.

Oh, great.

Kravet leaned against a bistro table several yards away sipping a drink and watched me and Jamie with anger in his eyes.

For everyone's sake, I had to make sure there was no question about my relationship status. "You did very nicely tonight, Mr. Miller. I have to be in the office early tomorrow morning, so get the hell out of my way."

I stormed off, but only got a few feet from the main doors before I got grabbed.

"Nice try, come with me." Jamie tugged me down a hallway, the heat coming off his body made me dizzy.

"What are you doing? Are you insane?" I clawed my way free, but it was no use.

"Apparently." He leaned me against the wall. "Those women were invited by Kravet. He wants a bad boy to show off. I'm giving the CFO of my label what he wants, Poppy. How could you not know Kravet would pull something like this?"

Sure, parading music gods with women was nothing new. For *show*. He wasn't supposed to sleep with them in his dressing room! "I saw you."

"You saw me," Jamie repeated. "Where? When?"

"Your dressing room. You were pulling up your pants." When he opened his mouth, I poked his chest, his shirt barely buttoned. "I've been around musicians my whole life. I know what that means. Just own it." My

181

pride screamed for me to play it cool. My anger told me to lash out. My insecurity kicked them both in the shins. "Tell me you had a moment of weakness and you're sorry," I managed, holding back sobs.

My heart pounded as I looked at a man I had fallen hard for. Again. Only this time, it was real. This time, Jamie gave back. Everything I felt, he was there, sharing it all with me. The idea he'd just throw it away so soon wrecked me. Made me question my judgement. My sanity even.

Jamie stared at me, his expression unreadable. "Wait here," he said low, drips of anger in his tone. "Do *not* move."

He briskly walked down the hall while I leaned against a column. Its marble surface cooled my heated skin.

Jamie burst through the cloud of people, dragging Cam by the arm, both of them looking pissed off. Jamie drew his manager up close to him, his fist closed around the guy's tie. "Did I say anything to you on the way over here?"

"Did you ignore my 'what the fuck are you doing?' question? Yeah, you didn't say anything."

Jamie sneered at him. "Don't curse like that in front of her, man." Looking back at me, he said in controlled anger, "Tell him what you saw, Harper."

His wingman was his alibi. Perfect.

"Before the show, in the dressing room, I saw you and Jamie leaving a meeting room. Jamie was zipping his fly."

Without a look between them, Cam spilled out, "He was showing some idiot his hip tattoo."

"*Who* was I showing it to?"

"Oh, Kurt Styler from Tunes.com."

"I didn't think he'd call a girl an idiot," I murmured.

"Now, you can go." Jamie released Cam, who stomped away shaking his head.

I opened my mouth to speak, but he laid his fingers across my lips. "I need you to have a little more faith in me, darlin'. Not a lot. I deserve none of it. So, I'm starting slow here. Did you think I'd *screw* someone the night of my launch? Backstage?"

"I was startled by what I saw. Stuff's gonna happen, Jamie. I'm not sure you can count on me to be open-minded and trusting."

"Why not?"

"I have to leave." I felt small compared to Jamie's tall powerful body.

"Nope. Not happening."

My stomach flipped as he moved closer. "What are you doing?"

"What I should have done five minutes ago." Jamie pulled me in against his body.

In an instant, his mouth was hot and wet on mine. It had only been a few hours, but I was aching to feel his lips. I was ready to sink deep into his kiss. Slide up my dress. Let him have me. I didn't care. Didn't care who saw. Didn't care who heard me yell, the way I wanted to scream when he was inside me.

Jamie drew my face closer, holding my chin. "I didn't sleep with or go near any girl in that dressing room," he declared, his eyes drilled into mine. "There're plenty of women out there. I know that. You know that. They're all gorgeous and sexy. But there's one thing about them, I hate."

Despite my head spinning from the kiss, I asked,

"What's that?"

"They're not *you*. I don't want a groupie. Trust me, there've been plenty. You and your suits and your dresses, you've ruined me for all of that, Harper." He leaned into my forehead, his breath hot, coming off his lips in fast pants. "You made me rethink everything I thought I knew about myself. What's possible for me. How to balance all this madness. That I can be that false god out there with all those women and *still only want you*. I only want you, Poppy. And goddamn, I don't think I mean until I leave. We… Chloe and I need you."

My eyes settled hungrily on Jamie's mouth.

Game changer.

"Home. Now," he said, gripping my waist.

"Uh, I hate to break up your little make-up party over here." Cam snuck up behind us. "Michael's looking for you."

"Looking for who?" Jamie answered, his voice rough and harsh.

"Both of you," Cam answered.

"Great," Jamie grunted, but dutifully followed his manager, holding my hand.

Tight.

The crowd had thinned out considerably and the air felt breathable again. Cool from the air conditioners and not stuffy from the body heat that boiled up the place into the ninety-degree range. And the moisture from all the tongues dangling for Jamie were blessedly gone.

Let 'em crave the man.

He was mine.

This was real. Now things were serious.

In a small meeting room off the lobby, Michael sat with a laptop and Cam looked over his shoulder. They were both smiling. Stupidly.

Kravet's absence made me smile. The dog must have limped home with his tail between his leg since Jamie, the Blue Rock alpha bested him by refusing to play his game.

Michael glanced up. "Oh good, you're here. Have a seat. I have a few things to say. Ronny asked me to do the release briefing. He had to leave."

Holy Mary Mother of Jesus. Michael was sucking up to Ronny Kravet. Why? How had so much power shifted in such a short amount of time? Was Michael fixing to make Kravet and all his money-making ideas his *consigliere* to make a play for the CEO slot? I'd objected to signing Jamie. The singer who just blew thousands of people away.

You were overruled on this one, by a landslide.

That CEO job was mine!

After a calming breath, I motioned Jamie to sit on the other side of the meeting table next to Cam while I situated myself on the far end.

Alone. This was war.

"Sales emailed me some numbers already," Michael began. "As of midnight, pre-orders for album and digital downloads of singles have already exceeded expectations. We should have the actual numbers in a few hours." The ecstatic grin on his face was a double-edged sword. This was his win. And my loss because I'd opposed it. "It looks like we're already off to a good start. Based on these numbers, there's no reason why we, I mean Jamie, shouldn't debut in the top ten."

The buzz about the album's anticipated position on the charts gave me an extra minute to get myself together. Jamie shook Michael's hand and he and Cam exchanged high-fives.

"I also wanted to tell you that we're gonna handle you a little differently, Jamie," Michael continued. "Gregory and Ronny want A&R to have more of a long-term relationship with the artists we bring in. As you know from your other labels, the A&R department usually manages the relationship with signed artists and that the development directors, for those who even *have* those departments, they merely support A&R. I admit I agree with that approach."

Gregory had so often praised my team for the amazing job we did managing the label's artists. There was Michael dismissing my efforts, and worse, agreeing with Kravet.

"Personally…" Michael continued. "I feel the more we're invested with the artists we bring in, the better focused we'll be." He leaned forward, his passion about this subject quite evident. "I, I mean *we,* want to consider an artist's sustainability before we offer them contracts." He stopped and shot me one last look. *Oh, dear God. Here it comes.* "So, you won't be assigned a director from Harper's department. You'll work directly with me." Michael finished with his eyes squarely on Jamie. "Any questions?"

I caught my breath and gripped the edge of the table. Processing. *The more artists we bring in…* Jamie wasn't just a once-off, hotter than hell artist who needed extra resources. Gregory and Ronny were…restructuring. I was about to lose my job.

Jamie looked like he was struggling to process what he was being told.

I stood, glaring at Michael. "You boys seem to have everything under control." I briskly walked out of the meeting room without waiting for a response or even saying goodbye to anyone.

In the lobby, I read a text from Jamie:

DO NOT LEAVE

I stopped for a moment to consider what to do. Helplessness suffocated me. There I was on the sidewalk in a sparkly dress all alone with no ride home. All the options sucked.

Wait for Jamie and be so pissed off I might possibly lash out at him.

Suck up to Michael and take a ride home with him.

Call Gigi and ask my mama to get out of bed to pick me up.

Ugh.

My phone beeped again with another message from Jamie:

Where are you?

I swallowed warm tears and called the only person I could stand to be alone with at the moment.

"Sugar Anne! I need a ride home."

Chapter Eighteen

Harper

In my yard, I sat by the glass fire pit. The sparkling beads released flames that danced and wiggled with all kinds of juicy fruit colors. Just not much heat.

I sipped from a bottle of liquid gold bourbon that warmed me up a whole heck of a lot more than this fraud of a fire. I'd wrapped myself up in a blanket with a bottle of hooch between my legs.

Gigi padded over from the pool house and frowned down at me. "No glass?" My mother folded her arms across a satin floral maxi dress. "Good lord, this should be good."

"Want some?" I held the bottle of Maker's Mark to Gigi.

"Nah." My mother took a seat next to me. I wanted so much to praise Gigi's temporary break from drinking, but we'd been down that road before. Still, I felt like a shit for not even providing any encouragement. I opened my mouth to fix that, but my mother was more concerned about me, apparently. "You and lover boy have a fight?"

I quickly uttered, "If you're referring to Jamie, he's not a boy. He's thirty-two. He's a man."

"Yes, he is. He's an adult and so are you. You're what? Twenty-nine now?"

"Close. Thirty-three." Not that I'd received a birthday card or a text most years. "And no, we didn't have a fight. Things at the label are a little dicey right now and Jamie's getting ready to go out on the road so…" I took a deep gulp. "I've got a lot on my mind at the moment."

"I have to say, this whole thing with Jamie is

surprising. You don't do casual affairs, Poppy. Never have. That *man* means something to you."

"Of course, he does. Do you think I would spend time with his daughter if—"

"Do you love him?" Gigi leaned over to draw my chin up to face her. "And don't you dare tell me it's none of my business. This relationship became a two-way street when you turned eighteen."

"All right." I made yet another attempt to close the distance between me and Gigi. "I'm in love with him."

"Does *he* know that?"

I pressed my lips against the bottle again, but couldn't take a sip. "He's under a lot of pressure. You of all people should know the sacrifices needed to make it in this business."

"Poppy—" Gigi exhaled sharply at the dig. "Do you think I enjoyed leaving you behind? Do you think I was able to appreciate my success when I was heartbroken and my arms ached to hold you when…"

"What?" I was surprised Gigi didn't finish her typical long-winded justification on the subject.

"It just occurred to me that you'll never understand until you become a mother."

A determined look of, *Yeah, I said it,* passed between us.

I puffed my chest forward. "If you haven't noticed, I'm not in a position to be a mother right now." When Chloe crashed into my mind, my breathing came up short. Poor little girl didn't have a mother. Whoever Jamie…married would be it. Everything. The weight of that responsibility crushed my chest, fearing I couldn't live up to it. Loving Jamie through the music madness would be hard enough. Although, I wouldn't be alone.

"Position?" Gigi sat back and crossed her legs. "You have a man who loves you. Did *you* notice I asked if you loved him? That was the only part of this story I wasn't sure about. I know he loves you. It radiates from him. And that little girl of his. You've got them both wrapped around your pinky."

"But he's still gotta be out there making music, Mama." I choked on my answer. "You've had your day, Daddy's had his. I'm not fixing to trap him with my insecurities or with a baby, if that's what you meant. He needs to tour for his album. Period. We both knew this was coming."

Except he was accepting it better than me. The look on his face at the briefing, he was all music god. The boyfriend had left the building.

"Jamie *was* quite frank that he liked his life on the road." Gigi adjusted her long skirt to cover her legs against the damp evening air.

The reality of my life with Jamie, country music's bad boy, had been screaming at me for weeks. I had drowned in my struggle to decide what side of that life I wanted to be on. With him on the road? Waiting at home for him with Chloe? Living between his world and mine? It was the last option that frightened me the most—none of the above.

The familiar roar of the motorcycle sent a chill through me. The Harley revved angrily from the courtyard like Jamie was sending warning shots across the bow.

Looking all fired up, he marched across the backyard. I could have changed my gate code if I really wanted to be alone. Except, I suspected he'd just climb the fence given the crazed look on his face.

Gigi whispered in my ear, "Honey, that boy don't need to be trapped by you."

Jamie gave Gigi a smile, but turned sad eyes to me. My leaving…hurt him.

"Who's with Chloe?" I asked and glanced at my phone.

"Marta's staying over tonight," Jamie answered, sounding miffed. "She doesn't do it often, but I made it worth her while."

We'd planned for me to sleep over just like I'd been doing the last few weeks. My running home left Jamie with a choice. Go home to Chloe, or make it rain all over his nanny to be with me. "I would have understood if you didn't come chasing after me."

"Chloe's asleep," he said firmly.

"Time for me to leave." Gigi gripped the handles of her chair and stood up. "And not just this after-party. I'm moving out."

"What?" A bolt of alarm rushed through me. "No, you don't have to."

"Yes, I do, my Poppy. I was asked to provide music for a documentary. The producer is in New York. It's best I go live there for a while." Gigi folded her arms.

"That's really cool," Jamie responded, his hand straying to my mother's shoulder.

Damn him for beating me to the encouragement part. His grace was even more massive since *he* just came from screaming fans and faced a top ten position on the billboard charts.

I managed to get to my feet. After a slight wobble, my hips settled nicely in Jamie's magic hands.

"Mama, seriously, don't go anywhere. And I want to hear all about this documentary." I knew better than anyone how projects were lifesavers.

Gigi nodded. "We'll talk tomorrow. Why don't you kids go inside, it smells like rain." She sauntered back to the pool house with a perfect sober gait.

Meanwhile, I was ready to fall over if Jamie wasn't holding me.

He lifted up the bottle I had set on the ground. "Pulled out the Mark?" He took a good swig and stretched his lips. "No glass, even?"

"I thought a glass would slow me down."

He mouthed 'wow' as he hiked inside the house then came out with two sparkling crystal tumblers with ice. "You seem hell-bent on rehabilitating me. I prefer my woman to not drink straight from the bottle." He divided the rest of the bourbon into the two short glasses and handed me one.

"I'm sorry I left," I muttered into my glass.

"I drove here furious, I ain't gonna lie. Then I realized you'd had quite a night. It's hard to think straight sometimes when it's all about you. Know what I mean?"

"Yep." I slid more bourbon into my mouth, knowing it would taste better on Jamie's lips. But he was pissed at me.

"The hardest part of us making this work, I suspect, will be getting used to the fact that no matter what, you're gonna have your own career. And there will be ups and downs for you that have nothing to do with me. I'd be an asshole to ignore that. This is me, *not* ignoring it." He folded his massive body in the wicker chair across from my loveseat. "What's going on with your job?"

It was smart of him to put a roaring fire in between us. I was buzzed enough to tackle him, preferring an earth-shattering orgasm to feel better.

A deep gulp of my drink allowed me to softly profess, "Kravet's playing some kind of game. He suddenly has Gregory's ultimate favor. If they want to shut down my department, I have nothing to fight with. And with Michael in agreement—" My head fell forward as the defeat of losing my ally hit me.

"That must have burned you to hear him say that. Are you angry with him?"

I swallowed another tangy sip. "He was just being honest. I know that man. *And* that's how most other labels are run, so I have no right to demand Blue Rock keep Talent Relations going." That job gave me a place in a vicious world that had expected me to assume the empty throne my parents had kicked over and lit on fire when they walked away from music.

"I don't get Kravet's anger toward you." Jamie shook his head and then a dark shadow took over his features. "Did something happen between you and that guy? Did he ever *touch* you or anything?"

I snickered. "No. He's not that stupid."

Jamie wiped his mouth. "Good thing. Not sure how I would explain to Cam I lost another contract because I punched the CFO in the mouth."

I was rocked by his words. "You would do that?" A lightheaded feeling swamped me.

"I'm a typical Texas gentleman. I protect my woman from assholes." His deep voice poured over me.

"Just take care of Chloe."

"You don't need taking care of?" He stared for a moment. "Of course, not. No one took care of you, did they, Harper?"

"I did all right. I had wonderful relatives who were

really good at pretending they didn't mind a sullen teenager sleeping on their sofa."

Jamie rubbed his hands across his face. "Jesus flippin' Christ. I want to like that woman." He pointed across the pool. "But it's—"

"It's done. And you're not doing that to Chloe. That's what's important. And my parents weren't the only ones who dumped kids to go on the road. You're part of a new generation of musician dads, Jamie. Own it and take credit for it." I raised my glass to him.

"Thank you, darlin'. And you're really good at changing the subject. Back to Kravet. I'm serious. I'm part of the label. I need to know how to work with that…"

"What?"

He shook his head. "Nothing."

Jamie surrounded by scantily-clad women had been orchestrated by Kravet. Only, that wasn't anything earthshattering in my business. It just kicked me in the gut because it was *my* man, damn it.

Swallowing, I said, "I truly don't know what Kravet's beef is. It could just be he doesn't accept women in high-ranking positions."

"I *love* my women in high-ranking positions," he joked.

The launch had come and gone. Tonight, I was supposed to set Jamie free. Kravet had more of those women-filled meet and greets in store for him. I was helpless to fight against it. But Jamie made some kind of declaration to me, and the fight to untangle myself would be harder. Everyone at the label would be head over boots happy with his album, working like mad to promote him. I had a couple more weeks until he went on the road.

We just had to lay low until then. "There is something I agree with Kravet on."

"This should be good." Jamie sat up, a look of concern crossing his face.

"I hate that I agree with the misogynist PR approach that says music gods need to be single to be a hit."

"If I was just starting out, I would agree with you." He gripped his glass, swirling the few remaining drops. "There's more right?"

"Plenty."

"I'm not gonna Monday-morning quarterback my career and assume because I was single and couldn't keep it in my pants that's what made me a success."

"If your music was shit, I would say, perhaps." I tilted my smile at him.

Jamie's expression changed. "Don't give me those little dangerous smirks, darlin'." He rounded the firepit and kissed me wildly. "You'll find yourself hauled off your feet next."

"Okay, I'll practice my pouting." I looked at my Adonis. "You're a sex symbol, take it or leave it. We're not just selling your music, we're selling the idea of you. We're selling a fantasy."

He grunted, "That's what Kravet said."

"He is right about this."

"You don't mind millions of women fantasizing about me?"

"Millions? That's optimistic."

"Answer the question, Harper."

"They can have the fantasy. Chloe gets the reality. Because you're really a great dad."

Jamie was silent. His eyes looked more stormy-gray

than green as they followed mine. "Come here."

"Oh, and just so you know," I said, climbing into his lap, "you may like my demure dresses and skirts. But I can be your fantasy, too. I can be all over you the way you want and beg you to take me. I'm still a woman and I'm no different from those girls tonight."

"No, there is a difference." He gathered me closer. "They're not you."

After he laid another scorching hot kiss that felt like velvet fire in my mouth, I said, "*Now*, did you say something about hauling me off my feet?"

Jamie

By the third step on Harper's staircase, it hit me. I was about to lay down a woman I was pretty sure I was in love with for the first time in over a decade.

Whoa, my inner voice said.

It felt so much better like this instead of mindless hookups. Harper was more beautiful, sexy, and ferocious than anyone I'd been with. I could do things to her, test the limits, all in the confines of a safe and consensual relationship. Gah, I'd really just been a stranger's fantasy. None of those women cared about me.

I could have all my fantasies with Harper.

As she was about to slip into her closet to transform from sexy siren into a soft feather of a naked woman, I grabbed her and pushed her down on the bed. "You got to put this dress on. Let me take it off." I pressed my mouth against hers, drinking in slow deep kisses as my hands pulled her in by the waist.

"You feel quite ready, Mr. Miller," she said, squirming against me.

"I can wait." But she had a point, so I took the time

to cradle her head gently while I kissed her softly.

Her little moans deepened with every kiss, igniting me like a stick of dynamite. The more she opened her mouth, the more I swept my tongue inside, never getting enough. It would never be enough. Keeping my hands above the waist for control, I reached into her dark waves and tugged on the ends.

"God, I love that."

"I know," I growled. "Okay. Clothes come off. Now."

"Yes, sir." Harper sat up and let me shimmy her out of the tight sparkly dress.

My eyes bulged. "That's the tiniest thong I've ever seen."

"I was hoping maybe you'd want a quickie before you went on stage."

I froze. "You believe me that nothing happened, right?"

"I do. I was…" She held the dress briefly against her chest. "It was a knee-jerk thing. My rational brain kept telling me there had to be some other explanation."

I leaned forward and snatched the dress from her to look at her perfect body. "Come here. Please."

She did as I asked and wrapped her legs around me, straddling me. This woman trusted me and that honor and responsibility swelled me with emotion. With care and determination, I removed her bra then slid the nearly-nothing-thong off, until she was delectably naked. This was how I liked her. This was when she felt like mine the most because no one else got this. I wanted to give her that feeling as well, that no one else would have me. That I was just as much hers as she was mine.

Her bare breasts against my chest felt so damn good.

Her arms lazily draped across my shoulders. Her whole damn body was soft, while I was coiled up and ready to explode.

"This is too easy to pass up." I laid her back against the mattress. "I have to drink you in, all of you."

She dug her nails into my scalp. "Yes. Make me come. I need it so bad."

"You'll get it, I promise."

I started with a gentle kiss on her mouth. This felt like love. Sure, there was going to be some good, carnal fucking. Raw. Dirty. That's what made Harper so impossible to resist. She could satisfy every side of me.

My hands explored her body, every silky inch imprinting on my mind. There may be some hot sex with her in dark places just to get a quick fill and I needed to memorize all the places that made her breath hitch, starting with her nipples. My mouth closed around one peak; they puffed out when she was excited. Titty-hard-ons, I thought of them.

"You're still dressed," Harper reached for me, her hips squirming in heat.

"I have a woman to satisfy, darlin'."

My greedy mouth sucked and licked her nipples. I loved how her whole round petite breasts fit so nicely in my hands. It all clicked. How perfect she matched up with me.

I kissed the tender skin down her stomach until I reached my version of paradise. The lower I moved, the deeper, more guttural Harper's moans became. Oh yeah, she knew what was coming. I didn't want anything to be a foregone conclusion, though, so I roughly flipped her over and spread her legs. I took complete possession of her. Kissing every inch my tongue could reach.

Harper's little moans turned to cries and whimpers. "Please."

After I fingered her in a way I was sure no other man had, I turned her back over and sealed my mouth over her warm, wet, aching core. She tasted like honey and I wanted more, so I slid my tongue into the soft folds, ripping a scream from her.

Harper wasn't going to last too much longer, I could sense it, I could feel it, I could taste it. I roughly grabbed her thighs and spread her legs wider to start a series of mind-bending licks against her tight throbbing nub.

Harper squirmed and bucked like never before. I released one leg and fumbled with my zipper, releasing my hard cock. I sat up, shock ripping through me.

"Fuck me," I breathed out, thinking, panicking.

"I've been saying that." She kissed my neck.

"What?"

"I don't have protection with me." I hoped that also helped my argument that I hadn't planned on any action in my dressing room.

Harper bit her lip. "I have a confession."

My breath stilled. "Speak, woman."

"I'm on the pill." She took a breath. "I trust you, if you trust me."

"The first and last person who touched me without a condom was Layla. You can trust me." It made sense the next time I felt a woman wrapped around my bare cock would be Harper.

While my tongue laved her once again to a fever, I ground my hardon into the mattress praying I lasted long enough to satisfy her.

Harper

My mind slipped into a sweet haze and my body sizzled while Jamie's mouth brought me to a place I'd never known.

Ever.

I loved letting him take complete control over me. He relished it and was more passionate, taking me the way he wanted. As if he knew things about me I didn't. I didn't want to be anyone else. That pent-up, frustrated mess of a woman was done. This was the real me. Going mindless with pleasure by a man's mouth. No thoughts of anything or anyone. Just Jamie. Going down on me. Pleasing me. Not just what it felt like, but what it did to me.

It was more pleasure than I ever imagined. Each time with him felt better and better.

The moment of supreme bliss crashed on me. "Jamie, yes," I cried out, still pulling his hair.

My hips rocked against his mouth. I never wanted the ride to end. My breath went ragged when I felt him shift onto his knees.

He entered me with one hard thrust, seating himself deep inside. "Son of a bitch, you're still trembling. That feels so goddamn intense."

I loved having his mouth on mine again. His lips were wet and strong as he rocked into me. The give of the soft mattress allowed him to sink deep into me. As he continued to move, he settled his gaze on me, our foreheads touching.

"I wanted this so much. From the moment I saw you in Michael's office, I had to have you. Like this."

"Just like this?" I wrapped my legs tighter.

"All of this. Thank you," he groaned.

"For what?"

"Helping me find myself."

"Welcome home," I whispered, choked with emotion.

"Okay, enough sweet talk." Jamie sat up and threw one of my legs across his shoulder and settled into a rhythm of hard and forceful pumps. "God, I love fucking you. Shit, I can't hold on for long, I have no stamina for this."

"We'll just have to do this more," I cried out as my tensions quickly soared back to life.

"Are you close again?"

"Yeah."

"Just to be sure." He licked his thumb and rubbed my core in curling strokes. His eyes flickered with sinful thoughts. "It's *my* night, darlin' so I gotta have our usual round-two."

I bit my lip hard in anticipation. The Jamie Miller round-two was raw and intense. When he got his hands on my body, I'd give up nuclear secrets if I had any. "That's it, don't stop."

"Never." He tilted his head back. "Ever. I promise."

Chapter Nineteen

Harper

I woke up in my bed, wrapped in Jamie's arms from behind. The warmth and comfort were enough to keep me where I was, but the time seriously concerned me. As well as things like: did I shut off the fire pit? Were our whiskey glasses still lying on the ground outside? My foggy head, thanks to all the booze, failed to recall those details.

They had been unimportant last night, as Jamie took me again and again until we were both rode hard. Those memories, not fuzzy at all.

A text from Maisy popped in before I even checked my email.

Gregory is looking for you.

Startled, I typed: *On my way...*

I put my phone down and Jamie's hot breath brushed against my ear as he squeezed me tighter.

The soft, "Hey," he released was the familiar comfort I needed after a tumultuous night.

Twisting around, I put my head under his jaw and whispered back, "Good morning."

"Mmmm." The lazy response spoke volumes about Jamie's state of contentment at the moment.

Sleep was so important. I planned to be vigilant about his routine. A few extra hours of rest could make a world of difference. He would soon be back on that roller coaster. The drastic differences in life from being home and on the road were jarring.

I didn't want Jamie to think he needed to get up, but

I needed to get in the office and was curious about Chloe. I knew he did some light traveling for his music during the school year, but I felt guilty hogging him from his little girl so close to him leaving for his summer tour.

"Is Marta getting Chloe off to school?"

"Yeah," he whispered. "What time is it?"

"A little after nine. I have to go into the office. Gregory is looking for me."

Jamie grunted as I squirmed, but he eventually loosened his grip. He rolled over, his body covered in my blankets felt warm under my touch. I sighed in relief that he was there. For a couple of gut-wrenching hours the night before, I thought I lost him to a fever of easy women. Nope. He was in *my* bed.

I peeled myself away and Jamie's absence already created a dull ache, but the smell of coffee brewing downstairs made my body feel a little better. Wrapped up in a fluffy robe, I made my way down to the kitchen.

"Good morning." Gigi sounded chipper.

"Morning." I poured a hearty cup of joe and took a biting sip. Yum. "So, what's this documentary about?"

As Gigi spoke, I took in my mother. Plenty of early mornings, she'd slogged through hangovers with slurred speech. Gigi spoke sharply and precisely with bright focused eyes.

I was afraid to peek in the mirror, knowing I looked like a wrung-out mess. A little hungover, but mostly sex-drunk. "And do you have to work in New York?" I asked my mother.

Gigi's shoulders slumped. "Not unless I can build a studio in that glorified cabana."

"You're free to use mine."

Gigi put down her coffee cup. "What are we doing

here?"

"Who?"

"You. Me." She pointed. "Are we gonna make a go of this? Am I staying here?"

"Do you want to stay here?" I asked over the rim of my mug.

"Yes," Gigi rocket fired her answer, but turned away like she hadn't meant to sound so eager.

"How do you feel, Mama?"

"Fine." My mother certainly looked and sounded fine.

"When was the last drink you had?"

"Damn it, Poppy!" She slammed her mug down, breaking it in three pieces, black steaming silkiness flowing across my countertop.

"I got it. It's just a spill." I wadded up a paper towel and cleaned the mess.

My mother walked to the tall windows that overlooked the yard. "It was easy to ignore everything. You. You and me. What I'd given up." When I turned around, Gigi's face had fallen into a sad pout and her skin flushed red. "When I didn't have to see what kind of damage I'd done."

"I'm not damaged."

"Maybe not on the outside. Christ, you're tough as nails. You put on a good game face. Have everyone thinking you got it all together. But that man upstairs can melt you like butter on a hot skillet."

"Billy is more to blame for my issues with men."

"Billy Cross is a good man, young lady. He just…" Gigi kicked her heels. "I know he's stayed away from you because I came in that bargain. I have to start making my amends."

"Worry about yourself. Whatever you've been doing these last few weeks is working. You look great. You sound great. I'm proud of you, Mama." I felt warm and fuzzy about the new beginning for us.

My mother smirked. "I like you calling me Gigi better."

"That's what you told me to call you when I was five."

"I was so young and still calling my own mother Mama. It just felt weird."

"What's in a name, right?"

"Exactly."

"If Jamie and I were to ever have kids, I *will* insist they call you Mee-maw."

Gigi only looked stunned because a shadow stretched into the kitchen. Jamie's tall body lingered in the entryway. Thankfully, he'd put on the dress trousers he wore last night. And the silk shirt, but he didn't bother to button it up.

"Oh hey, that was just me goofing off. Don't worry, I don't even know if I want a child of my own, to be honest."

Jamie

I assessed one hell of a blast of information. Harper didn't know if she wanted kids? Did that mean *more* kids? Chloe? Too late, because I already had a kid.

I ran a hand across my face. That was way too much to unpack early in the morning. Without coffee.

"Seriously, I was kidding." She slid up to me.

I held her by the nape of the neck and kissed her deeply. "Kidding about what?"

"Exactly." She smiled, touching her lips. "Coffee's

made."

"Can I get it to go?" I plowed a hand through my hair, deeply massaging my scalp until all the hair stood up.

"Coming right up, honey," Gigi said.

"I, I was kidding." Harper turned pale and breathless.

"Darlin', I have a schedule, remember? I don't have it memorized, but I think Cam booked me an afternoon spot somewhere."

"Oh, right." She wrung her hands. "Here we go, I guess."

"Yes, here we go." I snapped the lid on the paper cup. "We *are* a 'we' now. You hitched your wagon to mine, darlin'."

Harper adorably impersonated a horse and kissed me by the door.

I cursed when I got into the courtyard. I'd forgotten I rode my bike. Kravet had insisted I take it to the launch. I downed the coffee and felt the hot sting on my lips the whole way from Oak Hill back to my house.

The morning air washed away any feeling of concern about what was coming. For the next couple of weeks, all the promos were local.

The transformation was setting in, though. I could feel the itch. Down-time in between albums, I was a different person. I felt different, different things mattered. I assumed I acted differently. Then there was touring Jamie.

Harper didn't know *that* Jamie. The asshole.

I revved the bike and pushed it faster as if I could outrun that guy.

I lost track of how many times my phone buzzed in my pocket. Parking the bike in my garage, I checked the messages and panicked when I saw all the calls were from Cam. Marta had sent me a text with a pic of Chloe eating breakfast, her usual zoned-out-before-school face. Unphased that I wasn't there. So, what had Cam's jockstrap in a fucking twist?

"Where've you been?" Cam practically shouted when I called back. "You know this is crunch time. When I call you man, you fucking pick up. I work twenty-four seven when you drop an album, I expect you to do the same."

I hated being yelled at, but Cam had a damn good point. "Yeah, I'm listening."

"Well sit down, too."

"What?" I stepped inside my kitchen. Screw that, I didn't need to sit.

"Did you see your email?"

"If I didn't pick up my phone, what makes you think I looked at an email?"

Cam cursed under her breath. "How you set on clothes?"

"What?" I spun around. "Why?"

"Pack up."

A tremor started in my fingers. "Huh? Why? *For what*?"

"That promo list I gave you a few days ago? Rip it up. You debuted at *number one*, you sumbitch! Blue Rock revised your schedule. We're headed out of town. Tonight. I already called my dad. He's sending the jet to pick up Chloe. There're only a few weeks left of school. You need to call them and officially take her out. My mom will make sure she finishes the school year back home. Get her a tutor if needed."

Now I saw red. Blinding fury. I'd had a few weeks left with my daughter and now it was all being ripped away from me. *That's* the price of being number one?

"Now, you wait one goddamn minute."

"James," Cam scolded me, using my full name. "Take a breath. We're a team. Me and you. You wanted this. You wanted to be a musician. My sister raised a kid by herself so you can have this dream. You don't get to pick and choose when the magic wagon comes along to scoop your ass up."

I found it hard to swallow. "Your sister lived in a house with servants and housekeepers. She wasn't slinging dirty diapers by herself. She was *single* because she told me to fuck off."

"Okay, man. I know. You're right. I knew this news was gonna blow you out of the water. Where are you now?"

"I'm home." Jesus, I only had a limited number of hours to pack and get Chloe situated. That included a really long goddamn talk about me leaving her early. When in the world could I say goodbye to Harper?

That's what I got for debuting at goddamn number one, losing the two girls I loved in one day.

Harper

I tiptoed into Blue Rock Records through a back door. The office buzzed with the usual frenzy of making music. The label had always been my safe space. The place I felt free. Warm smiles every morning from hard workers who loved music like I did.

Now, a dull hum came from the desks and cubicles I passed. And no one… No one looked me in the eye.

"What's all the fuss?" I asked Maisy, dropping off my purse and work bag on the girl's desk. "I had it in my schedule that I'd be in late today. We had a launch last night. Did Gregory say what's the matter?"

Maisy scooped up all my bags, tension rolling off her, too. "I don't know. But Harper, the board is here." She announced this with a flushed face and held her chest as if the wind had been knocked out of her.

"The board?" I adjusted my skirt, tightened my jacket, and smoothed back my hair.

"Yeah. I checked with Stacey. It wasn't in Gregory's schedule either. What's going on? We're not...closing, are we?"

All those whispers of Blue Rock's financial troubles hadn't been so hush-hush after all. No wonder everyone acted like zombies.

"Maisy," I assured her with a confident smile. "Jamie's album is set to debut in the top ten. No, we're not closing."

Except, *something* was wrong. Very wrong for the board to show up like this. In the elevator, I contemplated all the things that *could* possibly be wrong.

Passing the doors into the CEO's office which looked more like a penthouse villa than a business executive's suite, my eyes searched frantically for the man hoping to know what could be on his mind by the look on his face.

He was neither sitting at his desk, nor lounging on one of his sofas. In the back, left corner of his office, Gregory Blue stood behind his meeting table while several people perched in the leather club chairs.

The Blue Rock Board of Directors.

Michael sat in one of those chairs, but he was the only one not looking at me.

"Harper, have a seat," Gregory said from behind the one empty chair. "I have an announcement to make."

Pure elation zapped me in the chest. I did it! The

promotion was mine. My face curled into a smile and I bounded to the table, but Michael's soft head shake confirmed my worst suspicions. I halted, my throat closing, and I felt beads of sweat break out across my body.

No!

He kicked out the empty chair next to him, and exhaling I lowered into it. For someone getting named CEO, he hid his joy very well. My BFF was a good sport, but not enough to be miserable about a dream come true just because it would squash mine.

Well, crap.

"I want to thank everyone for coming on short notice." Gregory paced in front of a row of floor-to-ceiling windows. He drew a fist to his mouth then composed himself. "I thought now is as good a time as any to announce who will be taking my place."

My body shook and next a hand was in mine. Warm and familiar. Michael. When I turned to him, he lowered his eyes and shook his head.

Huh? He wasn't getting the job either?

My devastation turned to fury when a beaming Ronny Kravet ambled into the room.

"No. No. No!" I muttered dangerously under my breath and dug my fingernails into Michael's palm.

"Ronny Kravet has been keeping us in the black when a lot of other smaller labels would have crashed and burned," Gregory said, waving him over.

The man who stole my job strutted his way toward Gregory Blue and I needed a paper bag to breathe in and out of.

"Based on the success he's brought to this organization, I'm proud to announce that effective immediately, here is your new Blue Rock Records CEO."

The hand that had been in Michael's hand scraped away as I gripped the edge of the table. I felt like I had been blasted into a million little pieces.

Had the earth started spinning in the other direction? Sure felt that way as I lifted my chin and caught the dreadful glare of Ronny Kravet. Like I was a lamb going off to slaughter. My face numbed up like all the blood had drained away. I felt my cheeks flame with heat.

Blue Rock Record's new CEO delivered a quick speech. Thanking the board. Kravet didn't care to be a figurehead. It was the day-to-day work he was concerned about. He announced a plan to sit down with every VP and executive producer in the coming weeks to kick butts if anyone was behind schedule.

"I think now's a good time, Gregory," Kravet said, wrapping his hands behind his back.

Gregory nodded and dismissed the board. "Harper and Michael, please stay."

When the door closed and everyone else was gone, I let loose to Gregory. "Are you *kidding* me?"

The fire in Gregory's eyes suggested he expected me to challenge the decision. With his hands raised, he said, "I'm sorry, Poppy. The truth is I couldn't decide if either you or Michael should replace me."

Michael stifled a gasp and rubbed his forehead. Why did I think him not getting the job was my fault?

"Instead," Gregory admitted sadly, "I turned the decision over to the board. I had no idea they'd select someone else."

"So, why am I still here? Why is Michael still here? Are you making any organizational changes?" I asked.

What a friggin' neon-glowing-sign of a mistake it'd been to vote against signing Jamie Miller. Especially since the album I wanted nothing to do with was gonna debut so high on the charts. I heated up with embarrassment for being on the wrong side of that decision. No, I didn't deserve to be CEO.

My lungs emptied out. God, I'd put my personal feelings above what was best for the company.

The way Kravet looked at me with a steely hateful gaze, I didn't think I'd hold on to the Talent Relations VP position much longer now, either.

Son of a bitch, I may very well be out of a job altogether.

"No organizational changes yet," Kravet said and jostled an armful of folders. The man perpetually carried around papers, folders, receipts. He was a squirmy man. A record company should have a god at the top. Or goddess as I would have preferred. Anyone, but this nose-picking runt.

"Ronny brought some information to my attention," Gregory said, his tone ominous.

Michael squeezed my hand again. *Jamie.* And in a hiss, he whispered, "Told you."

Glossy prints slid down the conference table. Like air hockey pucks, they glided down one after the other, there were so many. I hadn't even *been* with Jamie that many times.

I picked them up and my heart fell into my stomach.

Jamie kissing me in the rain at the gala.

Jamie kissing me at the auction.

Jamie kissing me at the launch. *Last night.*

I looked at each of the photos, a photographer's watermark sat in the corner and across the pictures in faint script. Just not all, the one from the gala looked odd. The frame, the angle. "Why is this one different?"

"*That's* your response?" Michael mumbled to me.

I stood, and asked, "Where did this one come from?" I shuffled through the rest, many falling away, some down to the floor. I couldn't care less.

"That's what tipped me off," Kravet said, pointing. "Roger took that one and showed me. After that, I hired an investigator."

I turned a cold expression to Gregory. "You allowed him to expense a PI to investigate one of your VPs?" Everything I thought about the man had vanished.

"I paid for it with my own money," Kravet spit out.

"You *bought* yourself the CEO title." I folded my arms. "This is certainly a first. Good to know."

"For what it's worth, Harper," Gregory's voice lifted my eyes. "Ronny here went to the board behind my back. Bought himself the CEO title, isn't entirely accurate, but he sure stacked the deck in his favor."

"At what price?" I asked him.

"He threatened to use all these photos to shame us. Don't you see what you've done was wrong? And what kind of risk you were taking? You were a VP," Gregory chastised me and in that instance through his eyes, I agreed.

"*Were* a VP?" I staggered back into my seat.

"You're still a VP," Kravet said with a sneer. "It was the only way Gregory agreed to sanction my promotion without making this a proxy war. We would have had to put you on trial here. How many other VPs would have been in your corner? You heard Gregory, Jamie Miller is the key to our survival. Even if no one here gave a damn about you boning him—"

"Hey!" Michael finally spoke the frig up. "Watch how you talk to her."

Ronny needed Michael. Wiping out both senior VPs would cause an uproar in the ranks.

Kravet slithered toward me. "He's a rare find that Miller. He's been single since he started recording. Often said in interviews, relationships weren't for him. He's raw cookie dough to women on their periods everywhere. He's got the looks. He's got the height. He's got the dark brooding air about him."

"Sounds like *you* want to bone him." I sat back and crossed my arms, grateful I still had my job.

"If he asked me, I would," Kravet stated proudly, bragging how he'd let a man do him if it made him money.

"Harper, we've been dancing close to the fiscal edge for years." The sickening expression on Gregory's face did nothing to ease my tensions.

"Okay. But…" I had chosen to look the other way from the less than stellar numbers in the last few financial reports. "There's got to be something else we could do instead of selling our artists' souls."

"Who else has those photos?" Michael asked, turning the inquisition into a mitigation meeting.

"My guy gave me the disks." Kravet checked his nails.

I scoffed. "You know those can be copied right?"

"He came highly recommended."

"Glad you did your homework. Maybe if you put a little more thought into the proper way to market someone, rather than resort to blackmail and decades-old sex games."

"Shall I tell her, or shall you?" Kravet asked Michael

looking bored.

I spun toward my best friend. "Tell me what?"

"Why don't you bring Poppy down to your office," Gregory said to Michael and got on his phone.

"Oh, *Poppy*, just remember your contract expires at the end of this year," Kravet sneered at me.

"The renewals were always at my option unless—"

"Unless it could be proven to the board you were not doing your job. I think this more than counts." Kravet fisted some of the photos.

I swallowed hard. My job at Blue Rock was the reason I got out of bed. In an instant, everything I had held onto to stay sane in an insane world had been threatened.

Michael held his hand out to me, and guilt swamped me. Gregory hadn't been so sure about my ability to lead, so he turned over the CEO decision to a group of people who could be bought. When they picked Kravet, I had indirectly ruined Michael's chance to be CEO as well.

He steered me to my office, Maisy closing the door behind us. No questions asked. Inside, I straightened my suit jacket and sat on the sofa. It was too painful to sit at my desk since I felt like a fraud.

"Those photos of you and Jamie can't get out, Harper. They'll hurt *his* career. You know he's the ticket to us staying afloat."

I reluctantly nodded, my worst fear realized. What a sacrifice! Everyone's success and all the employees' livelihoods in exchange for my heartbreak.

"Kravet has bigger balls than I give him credit for." Michael shook his head.

With every breath I took, the same thoughts circled through my brain. How to make this work with Jamie while not ruining his career. But I didn't trust fans to be supportive of him settling down. Other CMT stars, sure. Not Jamie Miller, he was different. Female fans responded to him viscerally.

Shit, I was completely caddywonked. I held my arms tight across my chest. If I couldn't breathe, I couldn't cry.

Michael sat on the edge of my coffee table and gently patted my back. He leaned into my ear. "You don't need me to tell you that you can have anyone, Harper."

Anyone? "We can discuss the next man who's going to break my heart another time." My voice cracked.

Michael stared at me, his amber eyes soft and kind. I deserved none of it.

"I know this is completely inappropriate, but I'll tell Jamie." Michael looked as ruffled as I felt. "I'm not saying I don't trust you, but—"

"I wouldn't trust me." My unexpected humor earned me a small smile from Michael.

"I feel like I deserve to bear the brunt of his reaction. It's business. It's just how it is. An exec can't be sleeping with a signed artist. *My* signed artist. He's my responsibility." He drew a breath. "This is a rotten situation, huh?"

Rotten was a goddamn understatement.

"But it's my life. All of this marketing bullshit is stopping me from having the life I want. The life *he* wants."

"You're sure about that?" Michael asked coldly.

All he saw was Jamie the musician. The talent and drive. Jamie Miller was a package he had to promote.

"I am." Thanks to my keeping everything a secret, I couldn't open up about all the tender moments we'd shared. The hours with Chloe, where Jamie was a dad and not the stage god. "I got Kravet's message, okay. Loud and clear. There's a little girl involved, damn you. Give me time to—"

"Time?" Michael cocked his head at me. "Good lord, you don't know, do you?"

"Know what?"

"Jamie debuted at number one, Harper. Kravet's sending him out of town tonight. His summer starts now. It's done. He's leaving. End it now, or I will."

Number one... Jamie. My breathing clipped and my throat tightened. He did it. *We* did it. I made him number one again. Except, now the vicious promotion machine took over. The rushing sweep out of town shouldn't have rattled me the way it did. I'd been around artists my entire life. Last-minute gigs. Jam sessions. Recording. Interviews. Meetings. The whirlwind of uncertainty came with the package. Like living in tornado alley.

"You're sending him out to promote his album heartbroken from losing me *and* Chloe in the same damn day?"

Michael blinked then looked out at the skyline. "Tortured heart. Great songs."

"He's promoting an album, Michael. Not writing one."

Michael shook his head. Clearly, no one saw that Jamie and I weren't just *boning* each other. The wildcard I had up my sleeve was that Jamie and I might very well be in love. Something like that. Close to it.

Only, dishing that ace out would napalm this whole thing. They wanted to promote a single bad boy. Losing Jamie's convenient lay was an easy fix for Kravet. Ripping away someone he loved?

Without knowing what else to say, I got my strength going. "I won't destroy him tonight. You think once he gets on the road, he'll forget about me, right?"

Michael quirked a smile and leaned into me. I smelled his aftershave and the warm breath on my face stoked a long-buried desire. "I saw the way he looked at you. I don't believe that for a second," he whispered.

"Help me, Michael," I softly pleaded, but it was unfair to trade his stock with Kravet so I could have a boyfriend.

He swallowed, his Adams apple bobbing. "Why don't we let him leave and see what happens? I'll buy you time. I'll buy this damn situation time. But Harper, be prepared. His schedule is the sickest one I've seen in a long time. The guy's gonna be a frantic mess."

Love didn't always conquer all. In the music business, happily ever after with a red-hot number one musician was the exception. Not the rule.

Chapter Twenty

Jamie

Chloe wouldn't stop sobbing. Not wailing. Not screaming. Not throwing herself on the ground, pounding her fists, and bawling. Yeah, been there, done that. In stores. In front of people.

She just stifled choking sobs. Hiding her pain from me. That's how awful she felt. She'd grown up enough to know her breaking down would destroy me.

I'd much rather hear her scream. Collapse into my arms so I could calm her down.

Now she wouldn't let me touch her. I was dying from the inside out. I had to hand it to her, she knew there was no arguing this. She'd spoken to Cam and Sierra, Layla's twin sister. God bless the Renners for this one. Emergencies came up throughout the year, but Marta and Cam gave me cover whenever I asked. Picked up the slack when something unexpected kept me out late or dragged me out of town for a day or two.

The day to take that jet back home with her had only been moved up for two weeks, but those two weeks were precious as perfect diamonds to me. I'd had a shitload of plans with Chloe. Every summer got harder and harder for her to let go of me. Each year I needed a little more preparation. This felt like a bomb had gone off.

And thank heavens for Marta who stayed to help do some last-minute laundry and packing for Chloe.

I had my own shit to pack, but I wasn't adding bacon grease to this kitchen fire by making my daughter watch me pack up my clothes, too. I'd only banged out a few sentences in a text to Harper. That was a whole other world of hurt scraping the insides of my gut.

The Renner plane waited for us at the airport.

Heavy steps climbed my stairs and I turned to see Cam. My best friend. My manager. My daughter's uncle and godfather. So many times, I needed Cam to separate all that baggage. Now I needed the triple-pack combo because I couldn't handle this by myself.

"Car's ready, Clo," Cam said, striding up to her, stroking her hair. "Grandaddy's plane just landed at the airport." Cam knew how to be the bad guy. How to jump the line and be hated by Chloe when it gave me cover. "Aunt Sierra can't wait to see you. She's on the plane this time to ride home with you."

I didn't bother to say anything as I finished packing her clothes. Worry spread through me fearing many of her summer clothes wouldn't fit since she'd hit a growth spurt. But I knew her grandparents and Sierra would take care of that. Take care of anything she needed. They loved Chloe. And she loved them. After the Band-Aid got ripped off every summer, taking scarred tissue with it and stinging like hell, my daughter had simply settled in and accepted those two months every year without me.

"Daddy, where's Harper?" Chloe said, hiccupping.

Jesus Christ.

After a hard swallow, I sat back on my heels, so I was face to face with her. "She's working, Clo. There was some kind of emergency at the record label. A meeting she couldn't miss. No one knew I'd have to leave like this. And you, too. She'd want to be here." I hoped to hell that was true.

But Harper was dealing with her own upheaval.

I hadn't heard from her since that morning and my gut twisted reading the newsflash across my phone.

Ronny Kravet named new CEO of Blue Rock Records.

"Oh, Harper," I'd mumbled to myself waiting to pick Chloe up from school.

And there I was getting wrenched out of town like this the day she didn't get the promotion. This felt way more than a mere coincidence. This felt like a well-orchestrated hit. Kravet pushing me to flirt and flaunt my dirty side. In front of Harper. Then she loses the CEO job. Then I'm shoved out of town. Was my number one even goddamn real? Or were my numbers based on China click-farms, paid to download enough copies to push me to the top of the bestseller list so they could haul my ass out of town?

Now you're being paranoid...

That's what happened when you were ready to lose your mind.

"I'll give Harper Aunt Sierra's phone number, okay?" I said to Chloe while folding her little shirts. Frilly button-downs she started wearing because she'd outgrown those plaid jumpers she usually wore at home.

She bobbed her chin, tears tracking down her cheeks. I turned to Cam then Marta, who'd come into the bedroom to drop off more clean clothes. "Can I talk to Clo for a minute?" When the door clicked shut, I said, "Look at me, honey."

"I'm fine, Daddy." Her voice sounded strong all of a sudden and in a flash, I heard Layla.

It's fine, Jamie. Go. Leave. Go play that gee-tar you like better than me.

Jesus Fucking Christ.

"It's not fine. I'm torn up about this, too." I nudged

her arm. I wanted to grab her and crush her against me. I'd had to test her day by day to see how much affection she wanted as she grew older. She'd gone from jumping up and down begging to be held, to, well, now, sometimes she didn't want to be touched at all.

Yet, I still wanted to hug her like a five-year-old. That need to hold my baby hadn't gone away. Would it ever?

"You get a phone this summer. We can text. Trade pictures. All those selfies you take on my phone? Now you'll take them on yours and send them to me. You're old enough to read my schedule, Clo." Now I got firm with her because I wasn't going to take being ignored. "When I'm free, I'll be calling you. But you can check the schedule and see when I'm free and call me, too, okay. Please?" I willed away my tears. *If I fall apart, she'll fall apart.*

She said nothing.

"We've done this for five summers, Clo. This one is just starting a little sooner. Hey guess what?" I turned her body toward me. "Daddy's album is number one!"

Her little jaw dropped. "Really?"

I nodded, keeping it together. I'd waited all day to tell her.

"Because of Harper's song?" she asked, taking a breath and wiping the tears off her soft cheeks.

"That's my song, too, you know. I wrote it with her," I said to lighten the mood.

She scoffed, "Yeah, okay."

I let a breath of relief go, that somehow talking about Harper brought Chloe back and put a cork in the devastation. Stopped the bleeding. "The song isn't on the charts yet. Just the album. But will you watch it for me?

Keep track of the rankings and text me? Be my little personal assistant?"

She fell into my arms and then the tears gushed from me. How could a job be this important? I thought about Harper who didn't get *her* job. What the hell was she going through? And I couldn't be there for her because my own world had fallen apart. There was only so much of myself I could stretch out.

"Clo, Daddy's got a plane to catch, too," Cam called out from the downstairs foyer. The man was too good at his job. "Let's get on the road."

"Where are you going tonight, Daddy?" Chloe asked, pulling her monogrammed backpack on her slender shoulders. The night I brought her to Harper's house slammed into me, leveled me out. I couldn't breathe. That night was just a few weeks ago, but it felt like a year.

I grunted, "Clo, I don't even know."

Despite none of my shit being packed, I insisted on riding with my daughter to the airport, knowing Clo's meltdown might start all over again.

Cam drove my Range Rover, so I could sit in the back with Chloe. Hold her.

When the private airfield came into view, my throat tightened and I tasted bile rise up from my empty stomach. Forget Chloe melting down, I might beat her to it. Having Chloe ripped from me this time had a different meaning. I wasn't just slogging off to play my songs on a stage to make a living, I was also leaving a woman I'd fallen in love with.

Those familiar twists and turns to reach the hanger where Cord Renner's jet landed made me dizzy. Then there it was. The plane. The end of the line.

Holding it together, I unbuckled my and Chloe's seatbelts. Saying nothing, she got out on her side and trekked to the plane, her head held high. She would be a billionairess someday. But goddamn, she was still a little girl. When would this end?

I got out, cursing under my breath and snagged her suitcases from the back of the SUV. A few feet away, Sierra smoothly came down the airstairs and hugged Chloe.

It'll all blow over. It'll all blow over. She'll see Sweet Bell and forget all about me.

Sierra Renner still startled the hell out of me. To have an exact likeness of Layla walking around jarred me. But with Chloe looking so much like me, I loved how she got to look at her mother's identical twin and feel the love from her. Sierra was all Chloe had in that department for years.

Now…now there was Harper. Who looked more like both of us, with her glossy dark brown hair and blue eyes, instead of our green. On a cloudy day, everyone's eyes turned a little gray.

"Number One, killer," Sierra said, holding Chloe's hand near the bottom of the airstairs.

Celebrating my success stung, but it provided the legitimate excuse for all this madness. "Thank you, Sierra."

It'd been easy for her to celebrate my success as a professional artist, she had no skin in the game. Unlike her sister, who made me feel getting my first contract, my dream, wrecked any chance we'd have at a normal life. Raising our daughter together.

Cam loaded up the plane with Chloe's bags. Other years we'd made the trip with Chloe, both of us keeping the familiar wrapped around her like a blanket as much as possible. In a few hours, Cam and I would be getting on a different plane to I honestly had no fucking idea where.

With only minutes left before the takeoff window closed, I gave my daughter one more hug. This one I got in return felt strong. No more tears.

"Hey, guess what?" I said and then pinched her nose, bursting with my other surprise.

Giggling, she swiped my hand. "What?"

"Do you want to ride Sweet Bell this summer?"

Chloe went stock still, her face expressionless. "What?"

"If you want to ride her, I'll tell your granddaddy it's okay. I trust you to be careful. And you know who trusts you, too?"

She shook her head.

"Harper. She made me see this differently." She made me see so much differently. Mostly myself. That I wasn't worthless.

"Oh, Daddy." My daughter hugged me even harder this time.

I lifted off my knees and carried her in my arms. I wanted to put her in the plane, buckle her in the seat myself, but I didn't trust myself to leave the jet.

"Let's go, munchkin. Gran's getting supper on the table." Sierra stroked Chloe's dark braid. "Walker and Emma can't wait to see you, too."

"Aunt Sierra, did you hear? I can ride Sweet Bell, this summer." Clo twirled around.

"Seriously?" Sierra eyed me.

I nodded. "Tell your dad, I said it's okay."

"Your buddy, Logan, will watch out for her, for sure.

He'll do right by Clo, don't worry." Sierra didn't need to convince me my friend would watch my daughter like his life depended on it.

Layla dying took down everyone in this family.

I wanted Chloe to bring us all back up.

Harper

I knew Chloe had already flown back to Texas. It killed me that I didn't get a chance to say goodbye. Not so long, but goodbye. Because Michael's prediction Jamie and I fall apart was a bet a homeless person would make with all their spare change.

Debuting at number one meant Jamie was going to be dragged around by the fingernails this summer. No one squandered *that* marketing nugget of gold. Kravet would get his bad boy. Women would swoon and fall at his feet. No man, no single man without a commitment, was expected to be immune from such adoration.

"The door's open," Jamie's deep voice glided out of the intercom next to his door.

I hated how I'd already planted in my mind this would be the last time I'd see him. In a lover capacity. Jamie was now a Blue Rock Records Number One Selling artist. And I was a VP at that label. I'd have to see him again. And again. And again. Knowing I couldn't have him.

"Holy shit." I thought his living room looked like a twister had blown through, but his bedroom looked like the aftermath of a tsunami.

"I don't even know where to begin," he said with a shaky voice.

Black canvas cases lined up along the wall like mobilized soldiers. Luggage. I caught my breath, the trigger that always made leaving real. Like all those years seeing Gigi's Louis Vuittons lined up in the foyer in my grandmother's house and then watching her and my father leave.

"Except, I do know where to begin." All six-foot-four of Jamie was down on one knee.

My heart pounded in my chest. *No way.*

"I heard what happened at the label. You didn't get the CEO job." If this was his idea of a marriage proposal, it sort of sucked. "Talk to me, how do you feel about it?"

Considering he was the reason I didn't get it, he didn't want to know how I *really* felt about it. But I took responsibility. My actions were my own. Kravet wanted that spot and would have spilled anyone's blood to get it. "I won't lie, it sucks. But…"

"No buts, darlin'. I promise, you have my undivided attention. Go ahead, talk to me. Let it out. I'm here. It's the best I can do for now. Once the schedule gets finalized and you come visit me…"

The rest of his sentence drifted off in a blur. "Visit you?"

"Of course? You're not the CEO. That sucks, but don't you see the silver lining? I assume you have that thing called vacation time. A court ordered Chloe to stay on that damn ranch all summer. Ain't no court order keeping you from me."

"You'll be really busy."

He nodded. "Yep. And here's the best part. You know that world like the back of your hand. You can do this with me. *We* can do this."

"Jamie, I don't know what to say…"

"How about yes."

How about Kravet and Michael demanded I end

things so we can promote a bad boy. A fantasy. A god willing to share his body with whoever wants it.

"Um. How about we look at your schedule together when Kravet's minions finish chiseling it into the side of a mountain?"

"That sounds mighty hesitant of you." He stood and towered over me. "This changes nothing. Do you understand? You and me. Nothing's changed."

I sunk into a tight squeeze. "Jamie, you lost your daughter today. I lost a promotion today. I need to make it through to tomorrow before I can make any kind of plan for myself, okay?"

His face went still and his jaw jumped. "All right." He spun back around and the funnel cloud kicked up as he went back to packing.

I let my eyes drift across the mess. "Can I give you a hand with any of this?"

"After."

"After what?"

He kissed me long and deep. "After I make love to you."

Jamie

I thought I was a different person now, but I missed that Harper was different, too. It couldn't just have been the Talent Relations director in her who masterfully organized my clothes, set my guitar and travel keyboard in their cases. Every Garth Brooks concert tee-shirt she smoothed out and folded had a story and Harper wanted to hear it. Every plaid shirt she sniffed and then smiled because it smelled earthy like me, prompted a question about where I'd gotten them. She wanted to know how every tear in every pair of my jeans got there and I told her. Her fingers ran over every scuff on every pair of boots and I told her about some of the more harrowing rides on my motorcycle that made those marks.

It felt like all we did was talk, when we weren't making love. I was damn near hoarse, but didn't care if I couldn't sing for some stranger at a radio station. My voice was meant for Harper at the moment.

I lost track of how many times I came in those two hours, waiting for my world to be spun off in the wrong direction. With fifteen minutes to go, I lost it.

"What's wrong?" she asked, slipping her dress back on.

Smart, because I was ready to attack her again. I didn't deserve her, I thought sliding my jeans back on.

Every day it felt harder to keep my emotions a secret and I felt more damn ready than ever. But with my original promotion to stay in Nashville for several weeks out the window, my carefully constructed plan to tell Harper I loved her had fallen apart.

There was no goddamn way I could wait all summer. Gah! I had only twelve minutes left.

"Um, Harper?" My heart pounded so loudly in my ears that if I actually said those three little words, I might not hear myself. Or hear her say it back.

"Oh, she's here!" Harper sprang off the bed, the piles of clothes she'd made swaying like tall buildings in a fierce wind.

"Who?" I asked, but then blinked in amazement walking down my stairs. Gigi strolled into my living room. "I just wanted to say goodbye."

Harper retreated into the background and let Gigi have her moment with me. I hugged Gigi and her tiny body squeezed me back. A mom's hug. Something I hadn't felt in a very long time.

Breaking away from me, she spotted Billy's guitar. "You're leaving this behind?"

"It's quite valuable." I breathed. That decision whether or not to use Billy Cross's famous axe on stage nagged at me all over again.

Gigi brushed past me and scooped up the guitar. "I insist. Bring it back to life."

Even though I paid for it, it never really felt like mine. But Gigi and Harper trusted me with it and the confidence they had in me knocked the breath out of me.

My hands shook and my brain screamed, *No!* But my heart wanted it so bad. I was leaving Harper and I had nothing to give her, nothing to leave her with to make her mine. To prove this was real. Damn woman outmaneuvered me.

I nodded and forced my voice to say, "Thank you, Gigi. I'll take care of it. Guard it with my life, I promise."

"I don't doubt it for a minute. You go sell some more albums, sugar!"

After another hug, she left as quickly as she came in, Harper's Cadillac left running in my driveway.

"I don't call her Hurricane Gigi for nothing."

While Gigi had restored my faith in what trust was really all about, Harper had returned to her task of controlling this wreck of a situation.

When Harper finished packing up my clothes, each case was organized to hold different types of clothes, so I wouldn't be pawing through piles and messing everything up.

I had just met another side of Harper Montgomery. She had fire and determination in her. *And* mad organizational skills.

"Jamie, did you hear me?" She cupped my cheek.

"I, uh..."

Tell her. Just say it. Pour your heart out to her.

No, asshole. You don't drop a bomb like that and get on a plane.

Gah!

"I'm fine. Just freaked out."

"You should be." She zipped up the last case.

My cell phone buzzing sounded extra loud. Extra cruel. The limo was outside and ready to take me away. "I'll see you soon?"

"I'll call you tomorrow." Damn her for being brave and put together while I was falling apart.

In my driveway, I knew I couldn't stand there forever so I made my goodbye quick, even though I hated doing it that way. I grabbed her and laid a punishing kiss on her. Something long and drawn out meant goodbye and I refused to give her that impression. That I wasn't serious about wanting this to work out between us.

I let her go and despite the stars in her eyes, she managed, "Have a good flight."

I nodded and got in the limo, my voice gone. Which sucked since I needed to sing for the next two and half months.

Here we fucking go.

Chapter Twenty-One

Harper

The next two weeks passed by in a relentless painful blur. Schlepping to the office every day had been the chore of chores. Sitting at my desk at the label, staring at reports I just no longer gave a shit about, I detected a shadow at my office door.

Kravet glared at me with a blank expression then clomped toward my desk. Oh, how I loved when Gregory had popped into my office. I lit up just being around the man and would have gone to the ends of the earth to please him.

"When you have time, Harper," Kravet finally said, dropping a pile of clunky envelopes on my desk. "These were sent to me directly. I'm not signing anyone unsolicited. Just send them rejection letters."

"That's not my—" I started, but Kravet's icy stare stopped me from finishing my sentence.

When he turned to beat a path out of my office, I let the air out of my lungs. Except, he slammed the door.

Uh oh.

He opened his mouth, but grumbled when his phone rang. "No calls, Tracey," he barked into it.

"Her name is Stacey," I corrected him with contempt.

I knew working with Kravet would include saying as little as possible to the man, answer direct questions only. One minute the man was in my office, I was already under water.

"May I sit?" Kravet pointed to one of the striped wing chairs in front of my desk sounding a heck of a lot more cordial than I envisioned he would be with me. Especially behind closed doors.

"Of course."

"This is a nice office you have here." He gave it a creepy once-over.

He hadn't bothered redecorating Gregory's office. Ronny Kravet would stroll around in a dead man's suit if it saved a buck.

"What can I do for you?" I asked in a bland unemotional tone.

"I got a call from Roger in Publicity. It seems Jamie missed an interview last Friday night. My boy pulled a lot of strings to set that one up."

"The online rag that no one's heard of operated out of a basement. I seriously question Roger's skills if that was a hard one to pull off." I could have asked why that one change raised a red flag, but the answer was obvious.

"With Jamie's sales projections, the more saturation the better," Kravet countered smoothly. "You know that, Harper."

"I want our artists to be successful, Ronny. We can work together on this." I extended an olive branch in a last-ditch attempt to reason that he could have it both ways. Have Jamie appear to be single and…

"We *are* working together." He jutted forward in his seat. "You're sitting at that desk and I'm not bringing sexual harassment charges against you for the Jamie stunt." Ronny lit my olive branch on fire. "I've made myself clear. I don't want a tamed beast. I didn't push Gregory to sign him just to put him on a leash."

"I don't intend to put him on a leash." For a fraction of a second, I felt I may be able to argue my way out of this. "I agree that Jamie should appear to be single. Let his fans have that fantasy."

Country music didn't have many bad boys. Sure,

they all *sung* about getting loaded and hooking up, but most were good ole church-going boys with long-time girlfriends or wives. Jamie had operated outside the box since day one.

"That appearance change and any others you have in mind for Jamie will piss off the media and they won't include our artists in their programming." Kravet pointed at me. "That's the part you don't get. And why you could never do *this* job. You waved to the cameras and smiled when you picked up your awards. That's all you know how to do."

"I believe I earned those awards by writing some damn good songs."

"Now is not the time to—mess with me, Missy." He probably had to constantly remind himself that Blue Rock was a workplace with rules about using inappropriate language with a subordinate.

My destruction needed to be a clean kill.

Day after day, my life at Blue Rock had become unrecognizable. It was clear, I couldn't save it. So, I'd save myself and the relationship that had grown so utterly vital to me.

"Mr. Kravet…" I stood, even though my legs were shaking. "You'll have my resignation on your desk in an hour."

"I thought this job meant something to you, Harper?"

I closed my eyes. "You made it clear from the beginning you didn't see any value in my department." I looked back at him. "Isn't this a win/win for you?"

"Not if it means you're going to run off to be with Jamie."

"That's just the way your cookie is crumbling today, I'm afraid." I dug my purse out of the credenza cabinet and began packing up my desk. "Be careful what you wish, *Ronny.*"

Kravet smiled.

I smiled back. He had tried to humiliate me, but I was leaving Blue Rock with my dignity. Jamie and I were consenting adults. Kravet was the pervert who paid someone to spy on his own artist! Every moment that passed I felt light and free.

"Jamie didn't want his daughter, you know."

The words slammed into me, making me drop my bag. I looked up at him and cursed every breath out of my lungs for not even considering what might have gone down eleven years ago. I'd only seen the man Jamie was now with Chloe and how his daughter worshipped him.

Now.

Then? It never crossed my mind. It screamed back at me, fast and hot, that little tiny nugget of shame I kept hidden. My father didn't want me. Didn't want to marry Gigi. He was forced into it.

Struggling to speak, I said, "That's really low."

"Do you think I'm making this up?"

"I think you'll do anything and say anything at this point." My stomach turned at what had to be a vicious lie he was trying to force down my throat. "And where are you getting this information? That trusty PI of yours?"

"No. Gregory."

"What?" I went breathless.

"It was part of his vetting process. The raw digging you never saw. No, no one wanted you to be part of that shit show. Gregory wanted to hand you a shiny object to buff and put out on display."

"I don't believe you," I said, catching my breath, terror mounting with every inhale.

"Jamie challenged the paternity. Took a test to prove he wasn't the father." Kravet tapped his phone. "I have all the documents we got our hands on in a password protected file." He turned the screen toward me. "Here's her original birth certificate. No father listed."

I blinked not wanting to see it. Jamie had hinted here and there that Chloe's mother didn't want to marry him. *Wouldn't* marry him. Leaving him off the birth certificate actually supported his argument.

Maybe.

Then the name caught my eye. Chloe Renner.

She'd been given her mother's last name. Like me, because my father didn't want me.

"There could be a lot of reasons for this, Ronny." My fingers fidgeted to swipe right, swipe left, anything to get that off his screen. "Did you even ask him about it?"

"Michael wouldn't let us."

Michael. Jamie was his find. My BFF had a face to save. It made sense he'd have made Gregory overlook all of that. Because Chloe had been living with Jamie for five years and they looked frickin' adorable together.

"When the kid's mother died, he took the test, and got his name added to the records."

It'd taken that long? That part didn't make sense.

Kravet showed me the revised birth certificate. "See the issue date?"

"That was five years ago." I trusted Michael's judge of character. If he'd seen a different spin to all of this, I would, too.

"Do you know why he did it five years later?" Kravet asked, but it sounded like he knew the answer. He was tormenting me.

"The girl's mother died. He *wanted* custody." I

remembered him telling me how he had to fight to get her. That didn't sound like a man who didn't want his own child.

Billy never fought for me.

"Do you know *why* he wanted custody?"

I'd had enough of Ronny's games and smacked the phone out of his hand. "Because he *loved* her. Because she's his daughter. Because he's her father." By the end, I was screaming.

"Perhaps," Kravet answered, creeping back sensing my rage. "It's also because the Renners are wealthy. And I mean big Texas ranch wealthy. Cord Renner has had a heart condition for almost ten years. That daughter of Jamie's will be a wealthy little girl someday. Someone's gotta manage that money for her."

My head was spinning.

Kravet was right about the Renner wealth in Texas. It hadn't occurred to me that Jamie could be so manipulative. It went against everything I saw in him. And Cam… Cameron Renner was the presumptive heir to that throne. Surely, if he'd thought Jamie was up to something untoward, he wouldn't be representing the guy. Or his best friend.

"I have to talk to Jamie," I said, my breath shaky.

"Jamie has gone through extraordinary lengths to keep all of this a secret. I assume he'll keep lying. Even if it means he has to—"

"Dump me?" I had to sit down. "You don't know him very well."

"Neither do you, apparently."

Kravet was right about one thing, Jamie clearly never meant for that information about Chloe to come out. "And if I walk away?"

"I can't guarantee no one will ever find out about his duplicity. But let's not play with matches in a hay barn, Harper."

I put my head down, hiding my devastation. "I reckon you won't give me time to make this decision." Not to mention find Jamie and scream, *WTF?*

"No. If you go public with your relationship, it will hurt his sales. No one wants to listen to a lovesick fool mooning over his *label* executive. And when the media finds out it's *you*, Billy Cross and Gigi's princess? They will eat him alive. I'm not going to waste any more of my money promoting someone whose complete and utter public destruction is a slow-burning fuse. I may as well just pull and delete his album now."

I shot to my feet and flew at him. "Are you insane? Delete his album? Do you hear yourself?"

Every flash in my mind showed me a picture of Jamie refusing to hold Chloe. The way Billy refused to hold me. In the eyes of Jamie's fans that might very well be a career killer. Country music fans *won't* stand for that. Not now, anyway. Billy got away with it. It was a different time. He'd been forced to marry my mother because good ole boys in Texas weren't deadbeat dads. There was no social media back then. Jamie won't survive that kind of cancel-culture slaughter. There was no going back from charges of child neglect or abandonment. That *would* destroy him.

And Kravet just put the gun in my hand. Was I going to pull the trigger?

He picked up his phone and twirled it between his fingers. "Michael and I made it very clear, you can't have anything to do with Jamie. But you don't take direction very well. You've forced me to play dirty."

"I hope you're proud of yourself. You've turned this great label into your scorched earth playground."

"I take no pleasure in pointing out how this man has lied to you." Kravet came from the school of win at all costs. "It's your choice, Harper." He got up and waddled out of the office as quietly and eerily as he came in.

The assumption that Jamie would get swallowed up on his promo tour and forget about me had been dead wrong. He called me several times a day. Sent texts. Photos. Forwarded photos and messages from Chloe. It killed me because…he could do it. He *could* balance the madness that ripped an artist apart on the road and still keep what's important close to his heart.

Because he'd been doing it with Chloe. How could he not have had that kind of faith in himself?

If I started digging into his past now and forced him to answer questions, he'd be livid. And that…that could affect his performances. Kravet had him and me under a microscope. If his *bad boy* didn't bring home the gold, Kravet would blame me. Pull his album and fire me, since it wouldn't matter if we were together at that point. I'd be fine. I made enough in songwriting royalties, I didn't need this job salary-wise. Jamie had a daughter to support. He needed his career.

With his album sales through the roof, now was not the time to test what fans would and would not accept about Jamie's past. So, for his own good, I needed to cut him loose.

I'd get to keep my job and help other artists' dreams come true.

So long as I agreed to live with the nightmare of losing the only man I ever truly loved.

My heart pounding, I got on my phone.

"Yo," Michael answered.

"I need to take you up on that earlier offer."

Chapter Twenty-Two

Jamie

With half the day of promos in Houston over, I eyed my five-p.m. happy hour salvation like a tax refund check when the rent was two weeks late.

I checked my phone when I reached the hotel suite. Another day of no calls and only sketchy texts from Harper. She'd lost her promotion, me, *and* Chloe all in one damn day.

A loud knock on my door set me on my feet. That better be a near-naked Harper surprising me or a man with a bottle of whiskey. Anyone else risked getting slapped sideways.

My foul mood had my boots stomping against the thin printed carpet and I adjusted my hat itching for a fight. With anyone at this point.

A tall, sandy-blond man in the hallway set off a quick panic attack. I'd give my A&R guy a pass and wouldn't dare slap him. "What are *you* doing here?"

"We need to talk, Jamie." The hard line across Michael's lips confirmed my fears.

"Did something happen to Harper? Oh God, is she all right? She's barely talking to me."

"She's fine. But she's the reason I'm here." Michael folded his arms. "Can I come in?"

Michael's first of a thousand cuts took the shape of the horrifying details of what happened at the CEO announcement. All the pictures Kravet had taken of her and me. Good Christ. Why hadn't Harper mentioned *that*?

Oh, right. I was losing my daughter…again.

"You should know, too," Michael continued. "When

we were vetting you, we found some things in your past that, well, sort of bothered us."

I narrowed my eyes at Michael. "I'm a musician. I've been single for my entire career. What have I done on the road that no one else has?"

He shook his head. "Not that. I'm talking about what happened with your daughter when she was born. The issues you had with her mother."

"A woman refusing to marry me is an *issue*?"

Michael cocked his head. "What do you mean refused to marry you? You were forced to take a paternity test."

"Yeah, her father forced me to take one because he wouldn't let Layla name me as the father. Do you have any idea how many years it took to get my name on that damn thing?"

"Look, I believe Harper one hundred percent that you're a great father. Now."

"*Now?* I had no choice back then. They kept Chloe from me as much as they could. I did my best. I fought to get my name on the birth certificate so I could *see my daughter!*"

Michael paled and wandered further into my suite. "Got any whiskey?"

"Help yourself." I waved to the wet bar by the window. "That doesn't explain why Harper won't talk to me. What..." I stopped and needed to take a seat, my chest constricting. "She thinks I didn't want Chloe?"

Michael grabbed the bottle of Wild Turkey sitting on the wet bar and poured himself a glass. "For what it's worth, *I* didn't bring any of this up to her. As far as your Blue Rock contract, that was your past. And she didn't need to know any of it to manage you. And I figured..."

"You figured what?"

Michael slammed back a shot. Shrugging, he said, "You were young. People do dumb shit when they're young. My role is to make sure you come out unscathed."

"Me? And not Harper? The hell with Harper and what she wants?" My brain zapped. "Wait, you didn't tell her this. Who did? Kravet?"

Michael nodded taking another shot.

I took a deep breath. "How did Harper react?"

Michael rolled his eyes. "You have no idea about Harper and her father, do you?"

Confusion rolled through me. "I know they don't speak. I admit, I struggled with how to feel about that. I don't want anyone in her life who will upset her, but as a father, I'm kind of appalled that a man could walk away from his daughter. Because *I didn't do that*. I had everything against me and I fought."

Michael shook his head and put the bottle on the round table next to the window. "At the end of the day Jamie, you need to focus on your career right now. You have a number one album that's not budging, man." He poured another shot. "A relationship with Harper will only make people talk about you sleeping with your label executive. Your press will *stop* being about your music. Your crazy fucking talent. There's a whole operation out there looking to take people down over stuff like this. This is the kind of scandal right now that will bury you. There will be other women." Michael spread his hands out on the table. "You'll figure out—"

"Enough of that bullshit! I make my own goddamn decisions."

Michael narrowed his eyes and took a sip of his drink without answering.

Dude, that's still your A&R exec!

Forcing myself to be calm, I said, "I need to be with Harper now and tell her what really happened. My way. From my mouth. She's more important to me right now than promoting this album."

Overwhelmed with fury, I made a grab for the luggage I had yet to unpack.

"Listen to me." Michael cupped my shoulders. "Harper is not worth throwing away a number one album by putting your contract at risk. *No* woman is worth that. By leaving, you're in breach."

"Clearly you've never been in love." I had made the wrong choice twelve years ago, not fighting harder for Layla when she cast me aside. I made the wrong decision not trusting my instincts and going for it with Harper seven years ago when fate handed me a second chance at love. Harper and I could have been married by now and had kids of our own. Chloe would have had siblings and not felt so alone. Like me. Like Harper. I wasn't going to repeat my screwed-up history. The point of making mistakes, even horrific ones, was to learn and grow.

"If you walk out on this promo tour, this situation is out of my hands. I can't guarantee Kravet won't kill your contract, pull your album, sue you for breach, and make it so no other label would ever consider giving you a contract. Ever. Your career would be worse than dead."

The vertical mirror nailed to the wall gave me a full view of myself. In one blink, an old and haggard man appeared. Worn out and done. Another blink shot me back to when I was first starting out and I had no money. Defenseless against powerful people who took away my right to be a father.

That image sharpened. Losing my contract would set

me back. Fortunes vanished easily in this damn music business. I had Chloe now. I needed to support her. Damned, if I'll take a penny from the Renners. Any money they wanted to throw at me, to *control* me, went straight into Chloe's trust fund. That was *her* money.

The flip side to acting on my stupid pride, however, was even scarier. I had to sit. If I gave in, sucked it up, and agreed to be the single man-whore Kravet wanted, I'd be rewarded with the spoils of the man's devious plan. Did I want to bankroll Chloe's education with dirty money?

Even if I got past that, what kind of man would I be at that point?

Angry.

Filthy.

Alone.

Even broke, I could be a better man *with* Harper than without. I'd take my chances with the rest.

I stomped up to Michael feasting on my whiskey and pushed the bottle away, golden liquid spilling over the side. "Tell your buddy Kravet to take this contract and shove it up his ass."

"You're leaving to go be with Harper?" Michael asked.

"Yessiree." I stomped through the room gathering whatever wasn't nailed down.

"Uh, what'd I miss?" Cam said, standing in the doorway, the spare key card in his hand.

I knew *that* was a damn bad idea.

Michael strode up to Cam. "We all agreed at the label, Harper can't see him anymore. I came here to tell him, man to man." He glanced over his shoulder at me grabbing shit. "Keep him here, okay. It's what's best for all of us. I'll work on Harper."

"J, seriously," Cam pleaded. "The album is selling like mad. After every promo, there's this crazy spike of downloads. I don't know what kind of algorithms Kravet and his team have embedded on the sales platforms. You're going through the roof!" Cam got up close to me and grabbed me by the forearms. Whispering, he said, "Come on, man. Chloe's doing great back home. You spoke to her a little while ago. Let this thing with Harper settle down. Make that asshole Kravet think he's won. We've made them enough money to start signing other artists. Newbies they can boss around and forget about you. Have you heard from Harper?"

I grumbled and noticed Michael stuck around to hear the answer.

"No. Because those dickheads back in Nashville took a job away from her and threatened her with photographs."

Cam exhaled and tossed a look at Michael. "Pictures? *Really?*"

"You know it's best if he's single right now. Be that fantasy women want. Right. Now," Michael said to Cam.

My best friend stared at me, sending that *I know you'll do the right thing* look in my direction, instead of openly belittling me in front of a label exec. It's what I loved about him and why I kept *him,* a rancher's son as my manager and not some shark who'd push me to tour more and leave my daughter during the school year.

"Jamie and I need to get moving." Cam glanced at his phone. "We have that interview at W-KEG."

"Radio Kegger?" Michael asked, referencing the ongoing joke of the bizarre call letters to Houston's newest country radio station.

"Yeah, why?" Cam asked, checking my phone.

Michael let loose a snicker. "You'll find out."

*

On the ride over, I figured I would get interviewed by one giant asshole. Someone throwing me hard-as-fuck balls for questions. Drilling me on why my songs have more of a pop sound, than country. Yeah, those fuckers kept after me about that.

With the guitar case in my grasp, the check-in procedure at Houston's W-KEG was the same as the others and I flipped on my auto-pilot setting. Only thinking of how I'd talk to Harper and work everything out later. Maybe Cam was right. Let Kravet cool down. Get Harper off the asshole's radar.

Or get Harper another damn job. How about that? Then hire experts who knew how to promote an artist with good music *and* deal with my relationship status. There were married fucking artists who were killing it.

Married. Whoa...

"Will is ready for you," a production assistant said, peeking in the green room.

I removed the guitar Gigi made me bring from the beat-up case. Sure, it was a conversation piece if it came up. Let this radio announcer draw the conclusion where I got it from. After all, I had legitimately bought it in an auction.

I shuffled through the hallway, the glass wall of the radio booth on my right. A stocky man with super dark hair, but white at the temples wore a set of headphones and a Stetson the size of an SUV on his head. I tipped my own, feeling rather inadequate. Many of these disc jockeys were failed musicians. Resorting to scoffing up whatever kind of fame they could get on the backs of others.

"When the light goes green, you'll have three minutes of commercial time to get seated and talk briefly with Will."

Nodding, I wondered what Will was short for.

The light flickered and the PA opened the door. "Jamie Miller, Mr. Cross."

I froze. Cross. Will. William. Bill. Billy. *Billy Cross?*

"So, you're the hotshot, I hear so much about." The man stood and good Christ, he was taller than me. Six-six, at least. Yup, that was Harper's dad.

"Nice to meet you, sir. Thanks for having me here to—"

"Is that *my* gee-tar?" Billy glared at the axe in my hand.

"Actually, yes. I…I had no idea you were doing the interview. I kept hearing about a Will."

"Well, I don't want listeners tuning in because of who I am. I don't want to be a distraction. I love the music I'm playing."

"I'm surprised your boss doesn't want listeners at any cost." I was being pimped out, and misery loved company.

All tall glass of water of Billy Cross leaned into me. "Can you keep a secret? I *am* the boss. I own the radio station."

"Your secret's safe with me." I had my own skeletons to deal with.

"Sixty seconds, Will," a producer in the booth next to him announced.

"Copy." Billy took out his wallet. "Okay, what did you pay Gigi for my gee-tar? Five dollars, so she could buy a shot?"

I stifled a laugh out of respect for the good woman I'd met, the woman who'd shown decency and grace to my daughter. *Daughter.* "I won it in an auction. Harper donated it."

Billy changed in that moment. He turned around and ran an enormous hand through his hair. The darker strands as black and shiny as Harper's. "How much, then?"

"Ten grand, sir." I palmed the instrument that *was* rightfully mine.

"I don't have that much on me," he said, frowning and closed his wallet.

"Doesn't matter. It's not for sale."

"Twenty seconds, Will."

Will Cross bore no resemblance to the legendary singer Billy Cross. But he'd wanted it that way, hadn't he? Did none of these people here recognize him? "Have a seat, you and me have an interview to do." Billy lumbered back behind his desk, curved in a half-circle while a production assistant placed headphones on my head.

Billy stared longingly at the guitar while I played an unplugged version of *Time and Place*. Whether or not he looked the song up to know his own damn daughter, a woman he hadn't even acknowledged once, wrote it, I didn't know. His head bobbing to the beat, suggested even without looking it up, he'd recognized his daughter's talent. She'd gotten it from him. And Gigi.

When the interview was over and we cut to another commercial break, Billy returned, instead of Will, and said, "I'm signing off in ten minutes, can you wait in my office down the hall?"

Here it comes.

I blindly meandered down the hall and stepped inside Will's, Billy's office. For the owner of a radio station, he deserved something bigger than a closet. More cloak and dagger nonsense that I honestly didn't have time to deal with. I missed Chloe and wanted to speak to her.

Harper was a whole other world of hurt.

Billy came into the office and shuffled to his desk. "About my gee-tar—"

"You don't even want to know how your daughter is?" I asked and regretted it because Billy *instantly* caught on to why I had asked.

It struck me, one day I might be behind a desk looking at a man who'd… I couldn't even complete that thought without going breathless.

"Not a day goes by that I don't regret what happened there." Billy took off his hat and laid it on a small console behind him. "Her mother and me were young, you have no idea how—"

"I *do* know." I slammed my fist down on the desk. "*I* had a baby with my childhood sweetheart. Her mother wouldn't marry me, but that didn't give me permission to walk away. Even when she died."

Billy studied me, his eyes softening. "I'm sorry for your loss. What's your little girl's name?"

"Chloe."

"And where is she now?"

"With her grandparents while I tour. I'm out here giving it my all, so I can feed her the rest of the year. I tear myself away from her, so I can have all year long."

"How old?" He hauled what had to be size fourteen feet on his desk, his calves hanging off the side.

"Eleven."

Billy jiggled a finger at me. "See, you're better than

me. It's too late for me and Poppy."

"No. It's not. It's never too late, but…" I stepped back. I wasn't on any kind of footing with Harper and had no idea if she wanted Billy in her life since Michael kicked me out of hers. "Do you have any idea what's going on with her?"

"She's a VP at Blue Rock," he said, looking smug. "How *is* old Gregory Blue?"

"I don't know who's running your news division around here, but they need to be fired if you don't know that weeks ago Gregory Blue retired. Ronny Kravet is running the label now."

"*That* sniveling runt is the CEO?" Billy bristled. "Don't tell anyone I told you this, but you better start shopping for a new label. He nearly took down Sony Nashville ten years ago. Why Blue hired him, I'll never know."

Curiosity got the better of me. "What happened?"

"Kravet forced one of their artists to flirt with a groupie. The next day the girl claimed to have been raped."

I felt sick because he'd done the same to me. Only I didn't… "Which artist?"

"Vale Richards."

"Who?"

"Exactly."

The room grew quiet, and Billy turned pensive. "Did Poppy take it bad? Not getting the job? You think I don't know what's going on with her. But I knew she wanted that CEO spot." The man finally showed some empathy toward his daughter.

"You can say that. But we were there for her."

"We? You and your daughter?"

"I'm talking about Gigi."

Billy narrowed my eyes. "How did Gigi get her through it? She's in rehab."

I scoffed. "Not anymore. She busted out two months ago. Gigi is living with Harper now."

Billy whisked his feet off the desk taking half of the surface contents with them. "That woman is poison. I won't stand for her to take any more advantage of my…" He grabbed his Stetson and a jacket from a hook near the door. "I have to go. It was nice meeting you, son. And good luck. That album of yours is pure platinum."

Just like that, Billy Cross was gone.

I had to hold on to something as Harper's dad took most of the air with him. Something told me a freight train was now heading straight for Gigi. And it was all my fault. Me and my damn big mouth.

Great.

"J? You ready?" Cam's voice in the hall brought me back around.

"Yeah. I need a fucking drink." I never got my five-p.m. happy hour cocktail. Instead, I got handed a dose of heartbreak from a man drinking my whiskey.

"There's a bar across the street," Cam said, fingering his black cowboy hat. We got a few feet down the hall and then his phone rang. "Hey, Ma. What? Slow down. *What happened?*"

Harper

I closed my eyes and tapped my foot. Despite the computer's antiseptic interpretation of Gigi's genius chords and melody, I had a textured feel for the score my mother had created for the documentary.

"I think it's amazing." I took off the headset. "Have

you tried to play any of this at all on the piano?"

Gigi nervously shoved several blonde curls behind her ear. "A little."

"And?"

"It feels like it's coming back to me. Slowly."

I swelled with relief. One less thing to worry about. "That's great. So long as the sheet music is clear, you can pay studio musicians to cut your demo."

"Does that mean you'll give me access to my damn bank account?" My mother gathered the papers spread across the piano.

"We'll call the bank tomorrow and take off the holds."

"And how much do I have to pay *you* to get in the studio to work with me?"

My stomach tightened. "Let's take things one step at a time."

"You seem at peace, honey, considering things with Jamie didn't work out." Gigi tugged my waist and left the music room.

Peace? I must have gotten a Ph.D. in schooling my features.

I waited patiently for Gigi to go back to her cabana so I could break down in hysterics.

A beep from my security console near the front door drew my attention. The long stretch limo at the gate had me perplexed as hell until I studied the video monitor more closely.

The man staring into the camera made my heart pound. "Gigi, go to the pool house, okay?"

My mother came up behind me. "Who... Oh, lordy-bee."

"Exactly."

Gigi straightened. "No. I ain't afraid of him."

You should be, I kept that to myself, watching my father swagger out of a limo in my front yard and strut up to my front door. A part of me would have been elated for Billy to come visit me if Gigi weren't there. That meant my daddy wanted to see me. No, somehow, he must have gotten wind that Gigi left rehab. That *had* to be the reason Billy Cross was pounding on my front door.

"Hello, Daddy," I said when I opened the door. "What are you doing here?"

"Where is she?" He lumbered over the threshold.

"Come on in." I closed the door, watching Gigi hover behind the archway to my music room. So much for not being afraid. "Who are you looking for?"

"Okay, here it is." He put his hands on my shoulders. "I screwed up. I shouldn't have made you take care of her. No more. Just show me where she's hiding and I'll bring her back to that rehab place myself."

I didn't want Billy dragging my mother away, but I could have sworn I heard some kind of half-assed apology in there. He wasn't there to just deal with Gigi, he wanted to protect me. Only I didn't need protecting.

A gentle twang of piano keys floated out of my music room. Hearing my mother play piano again over the last couple of weeks had been the background noise that had filled my days.

Billy grunted, the sound meaning something different to him. "What the hell?"

He trudged through my foyer and straight into the music room.

"You're *playing*," he said, holding the door open.

"I sure am. Do you know what that means?" Gigi

asked from behind the piano.

He looked over his shoulder at me. "When did she drink last?"

"A couple of weeks ago, I think," I said, scurrying past him, to stand by my mother. Gigi and Billy's fights were legendary.

"No. I had a drink last night. One. One small shot. And that was enough. I wanted to stay sharp. I wanted…" She danced her hands across the keys, hitting every set of chords. "I wanted this." She pushed her hair back and grabbed my hand. "And I wanted *this*."

I felt my mother's lips on my skin and then…tears. I knelt down and let my mother cup my chin. "I'm here for you. I only sent you to those places to help you."

"I know, Poppy. But it's funny, huh? Being with you helped me most of all."

I gripped my mother's hand and kissed it back. Facing my father, I said, "You see. She's fine. She's working again. And I'm giving her access to her money."

Billy smiled. I wasn't sure when I'd seen *that* last. "I don't suppose I can get a drink. Sweet tea?"

Gigi quirked a smile. "Miss watching-her-weight over here wouldn't drink my famous sweet tea. Forced me to make that sun tea crap."

"Abomination." Billy cooed.

Oh, good lord. Were these two flirting?

"Come on, I'll make us a fresh pitcher." Gigi sashayed out of the music room, her long dress whooshing behind her. She then flipped her hair! "The sun is setting and it's so peaceful by the pool."

I watched in amazement as my parents stalked off together. Without screaming at each other. But to have some sweet tea by the sunset.

If my own love life wasn't such a mitigated disaster I would have been over the moon.

"Poppy, your phone's ringing, honey." Gigi returned to the music room, where I stayed frozen.

I followed her to the kitchen and answered the call. "Cam? What's up?"

"Chloe's in the hospital. She fell off her horse."

I went numb and sank to the porcelain tiles.

"Poppy, what the devil?" My father hit the floor next to me, his arms around my shoulders.

"Is she… Is she okay?"

"Broken arm and a bump on the head. She's in surgery now."

"Sur…surgery. Good, god, where's Jamie?"

"He's throwing up in the bathroom. He needs you, Harper. I'm worried he'll lose it."

I nodded. "Okay. Where?"

"Wild Heart, Texas." I recognized the name of his hometown. "My dad's sending the jet for us, it's only thirty-five minutes from Houston. I'll text you the address to the hospital."

The phone went dead and I held it against my forehead.

"Poppy, what's wrong?" Gigi asked me and next both my parents were holding me.

Yeah, *that's* never happened.

"Chloe. She had an accident." I stood and made my way to the stairs then spun around, realizing packing was a big ass waste of time. I needed to get to the airport. Get on a plane to Wild Heart, Texas. Was there even an airport there?

"Chloe? *Jamie's* daughter?" Billy asked.

"How do you know Jamie's daughter's name?" Gigi

256

asked.

"How do you know *Jamie*?" I asked.

"I interviewed him this afternoon on my radio show."

"This afternoon?" I asked, running through what I remembered of his schedule in my head. I wasn't managing him and Kravet kept his promotion schedule from me.

Billy nodded. "Where is this little girl hurt?"

"Texas. I have to book a flight."

"No, you don't." Billy took out his phone.

"Don't tell me what I—"

"I came here with my plane. I'll get you there," Billy grumbled into his phone. "Charlie. You know a town in Texas called Wild Heart? We need to get there now, instead of back to Houston. File a plan. I'm on my way to the hanger."

"When did you buy a plane?" Gigi asked.

"Ask me that when we're on it. Saddle up girls."

Chapter Twenty-Three

Jamie

I spotted Cam pacing in front of the airstairs putting his phone away. My stomach was still turning over and my eyes were blurry. "Any word on how the surgery went?"

"Not yet." Cam breathed, looking tense, reliving the horror when Layla fell off her horse.

I had always been nervous watching Layla at her shows, but I knew that girl inside and out. Watching her train and listening to her talk about technique. Without realizing it, she'd given me a sense of peace. I'd always thought, *she's got this.*

Everyone had agreed to keep Chloe off horses after the accident. It was just too raw to see her up there. Damn me for trying to make Chloe finish what Layla had started.

Cam led the march through the plane, but gave me my pick of seats on the smaller of the Renner jets.

"I'll get us a few shots of Beam." Cam took off his suit jacket and threw it on one of the sofa's seats. "Doubles."

I grabbed Cam by the shirt collar. "Are you crazy? I'm not showing up with alcohol on my breath. Chloe is goddamn coming home with me. Okay? She ain't staying there to recover. You work your magic with Blue Rock to get me out of this promo tour. I got a kid to take care of."

Cam calmly removed my hands from my shirt. "If hating me during this flight makes this easier, buddy, by all means."

I grunted. No, none of this was Cam's fault.

My stomach lurched when the plane took off, making everything I'd eaten in the last twenty-four hours jostle around my insides. Time to take stock. I had enough money to walk away from music for a while.

I grabbed Cam again, my heart racing, *Terminate my contract with Blue Rock*, burning my tongue. They were just words, they could be undone.

"J, what's up?"

My stomach heaved.

The words couldn't come out of my mouth. Twelve years since Layla told me she was pregnant, I was still stuck. I couldn't give music up. With my head hung low, I sunk further into my seat.

An awkward silence came over us as I painfully watched Cam's eyes wander all over his family jet. Sure, the thing came when he called for it. But Cam lived on the periphery of his father's horse ranch empire because he'd chosen to hitch his wagon to my music career.

Feeling guilty, I stood to get the feeling back in my legs. After walking up and down the center of the plane a few times, I said gruffly to Cam, "You going home after the hospital?"

Cam had a penthouse apartment in downtown Nashville as well as a classy brick colonial on his father's ranch compound. "Let's see how it goes."

I was the musical genius Cam's mother found to teach a rich boy the fundamentals about music and show Layla how to play piano when we were all teenagers. I strutted into the Renner mansion not realizing I'd walk out with a best friend and a sweet innocent girl I had to have.

"I play the dutiful son card when I have to," Cam continued. "But I never made it a secret I think what my father did after Layla died was despicable."

Cam had a crapload of money to inherit, though, and he was the only Renner son. No one was going to completely decimate their nose to spite their face. Cord Renner needed Cam, and vice versa. Everyone played the faction game on the surface to get what they wanted.

I knew solidly, Cam had my back. But if he were pushed by his father to make a choice, I expected Cam to go with his family. I was okay with that.

A son of a bitch of a rainstorm had grounded us in Houston for a couple torturous hours. It was close to eight p.m. by the time we made it to the hospital. After Cam had said a few words to the powers that be, we were let through.

The room numbers flashed by in the pediatric wing. Bright colors, tons of balloons, paper-mâché trees, and basketball stands were valiant attempts to make the place look less depressing.

Eyeing the doors on both sides I realized Chloe's room was in sight, and I let go of a long-held breath. Until I saw a man standing guard outside the room. Cord Renner hired a guard? Wait. No. That wasn't a guard. The dark hair, a shock of white at the temples. Towering height. Broad shoulders.

What the heck?

Billy Cross turned around.

What on heaven's plains was Billy Cross doing in a hospital *in Wild Heart Texas*?

It all slammed into me. Billy had taken off after talking about Harper.

Harper…

Billy lumbered up to me. "She's okay, son. Your little girl is okay. She's awake." He cupped my shoulder.

I turned to go inside the room and the small body in the bed under the covers filled my vision as I fought the tears.

"Daddy?" Chloe's little voice found me, but the woman sitting next to her hit me in the chest. "Harper's here."

"I see." I marched over and bent down to kiss my daughter. "Are you in pain?"

"A little."

"Her arm was broken in two places," Harper informed me.

"But they were clean breaks. She'll heal up nicely," Sierra added.

How did these two get so chummy, so quickly?

"And two tiny stitches on the back of her head. No concussion." Harper fingered Chloe's loose braid.

"Tell Daddy how you want to keep riding," Sierra said. "She's not afraid of anything, Jamie."

I smiled. "Just like your mother." Layla was the bravest of all because she put up with my bullshit. For years. Chloe... It never failed to amaze me what Layla and I did one crazy night when I was too charged up to go buy a box of condoms. We'd been broken up for months and I'd stopped carrying them in my wallet.

"They want to keep her overnight," Cord Renner said from the corner, being his usual cold self toward me.

Staying overnight made my head spin. That meant I was sleeping in a chair tonight. No problem. I'd sleep on the floor for Chloe.

"What happened?" I asked my daughter.

"It was my fault. I kicked up the speed too much. Logan warned me. But..." She was headstrong and stubborn like her mother. Plus, fearless like me. A bad combo.

"How did you fall?" I asked, bewildered because I knew my daughter could handle a horse at trotting speeds.

"When Sweet Bell stopped, I wasn't holding on right. I let go to…"

"If you tell me you had your phone with you…" I faced Cam's parents. "Who let her ride the horse with a phone?"

"They didn't know, Daddy."

"You're eleven. These people are responsible for you. Your *family*, not Logan."

"Jamie, don't yell at her grandparents in front of her," Harper whispered in my ear from behind.

I spun around. "And what are you doing here?"

"I called her," Cam said, standing next to his mother.

"You sent Michael to break up with me." My stomach twisted when Harper turned six shades of red.

Good going. Yell at the woman who flew six hundred miles to be with your daughter.

"I'm gonna get some coffee, Clo. I'll be back in a bit." After kissing my daughter's forehead, Harper stormed past me and sneered at Cam. "He needed me, huh?"

"Why were you yelling at Harper?" Chloe asked, pain in her voice.

My head was spinning. I sat down next to Chloe and held her hand. "You," I said to Cam. "You call Kravet, I want out of my contract."

"Jamie, now don't—" Cam argued.

"Don't…*don't* me."

"Daddy, what are you doing?" Chloe tried to sit up.

"I'm doing for you what I couldn't do for your

mother. I'm giving up music. You need me. This back and forth is crazy. There're other jobs I can get in that town that won't require me to tour. You're my daughter. You stay with me."

"Not according to our legal agreement," Cord huffed.

"Dad!" Cam snapped at his father because he knew the man could make me lose it. "Ma, help me out here."

"Cordero Renner." Faye Renner's strong voice turned the man around like a fire alarm. "Now is not the time to discuss the legal agreement."

"What legal agreement?" Billy Cross, who'd been hovering in the doorway, asked.

"What business is it of yours?" Cord asked, ready to throw down.

"Cord Renner?" Billy said. "Renner Ranch? The stables, the winery, and the B&B?"

"Yeah?" They tipped Stetson rims.

"Your company buys a lot of ads on my Houston radio station. I had a big mouth on stage, but that was only a couple of thousand people. Maybe a stadium's worth, here and there. Now my show's going national. I could let some things slip."

"Billy, thanks," I interjected. "I don't need you to fight this for me. She's my daughter. She belongs home with me."

Billy's eyes hit the floor. "You know what? You're right. That got me thinking."

He spun around, tipped his hat to Faye Renner, and left the room.

"I want to talk to a doctor. *Now,*" I said, eyeing Sierra.

Nodding, she shoved her hands in her pockets. "I agree." She gave her father dagger eyes on the way out.

263

"Can I be alone with my daughter, please?" I sniped to the people left in the room. I lost track.

After grumbling, everyone shuffled off.

"Daddy…"

I hushed Chloe with two fingers on her lips. "Are you really only in *a little* pain? Don't lie to me. Where does it really hurt?" I gently caressed my daughter's forehead.

"Here." She touched her chest. "It kills me. All this fighting over me."

"It's because we love you."

"I know." She let out a groan. "Daddy, don't stop making music."

"Right now, with you hurt, the music *is* gonna stop. I'm bringing you home to take care of you. Then we'll…we'll see, okay?"

"Okay," she said and curled against me.

Chloe felt so tiny, tucked into the covers. The heated blanket kept her warm. Her skin felt comfortable and not ice-cold, thank God. It'd been her against a goddamn horse!

I smiled seeing how her long dark braid sat on her shoulder. Her jet-black hair and green eyes… She was nearly an exact replica of me. Even though I'd been forced to take a paternity test, everyone knew the truth as soon as Chloe's face took form.

She was all mine.

"Daddy?"

"Yeah, honey?" I held her closer to me, watching out for her arm in a cast.

"Go make up with Harper."

I sighed. "The thing with Harper is complicated, honey. Her boss, the guy who runs my record label doesn't think she and I should be involved."

"What do you think?" She looked up at me.

"I think you need to not worry about me and Harper and just worry about yourself. You've got healing to do. I've broken both arms and my ankle." Falling off stage drunk, but I left that out. "You're gonna be in a cast for a while. But we'll get you through it."

"Am I really going home?"

At least she considered our house in Nashville her home. "Yeah. You like living there, right?"

She shrugged. "I like living here, too. My horse is here."

I couldn't mentally process what it would take to drag that dang horse across two states and half of Texas.

"Mr. Miller?" A doctor in a white coat and horn-rimmed glasses ambled in.

I stood up and shook the guy's hand. "Yeah, hi. What are we looking at here?"

The consultation didn't tell me anything I wasn't already told by...Harper. With a new round of meds to help Chloe get through the night, she grew sleepy. The less she moved around, the better.

I sang a few songs for my daughter and next she was asleep. I loved that I knew by the slack of her body, the tilt of her head, and the sound of her breathing. She *was* mine.

I scrubbed a hand down the side of my face and stood.

Cam had come by earlier to say he, Sierra, and his parents were leaving. I let them in to say goodnight. Everyone loved Chloe and had her best interests at heart. *Shit happens.* She'd taken tumbles, bumped her head, and scraped her knees at home and at school, too. Kids got hurt. It was a fact of life. Didn't make sense to start pointing fingers and handing out blame burgers.

I tiptoed to the door and peeked in the hallway. My heart jolted… There, sitting by herself in a plastic chair, short floral dress, cowboy boots, her head tipped back, eyes closed, dark hair falling all around her…Harper.

I'd been harsh with her earlier. She was due an apology.

Everyone wanted the best for *me*, too. My success was everyone's priority, even if at times, it wasn't mine.

I kneeled in front of her touching her bare knee.

Her eyes popped open, the blue overwhelming me against the short stretch of taupe wall behind her.

"How is she?" Harper asked me.

"She's asleep."

A stare stretched between us.

If I shit-canned my contract, she could be mine again. Only, I had a feeling she wouldn't let me do that. Like Chloe. Harper might even lose respect for me for caving. I didn't think I could win against those two ganging up on me.

And I kind of liked that.

"Why did Michael tell me it was over between us and not you?" I asked, still burned over that one.

"I'm not sure I would have been able to go through with it." She licked her lips.

"And that's it? You have nothing else to say to me?" I braced for an argument, even though I didn't know how much fight I had in me. It was ten p.m., I hadn't had any food in about eight hours and I needed a drink.

"Did you fight to get custody of Chloe for her family's money?" she whispered.

Of all the ways to drill down the funnel of shitty information. "No. She was my daughter. I wanted a life with her. Layla had made that difficult. But I decided a long time ago, not to speak ill of her. She's not here. She can't fight back and tell her side. The things that she never told me."

"Why weren't you on Chloe's birth certificate?"

"Her father didn't want me on it. He didn't want me to have anything to do with Layla, or Chloe after she was born. Everyone assumed when she said she wouldn't marry me, that I'd kick the dirt and go away. That's the impression I'd given everyone apparently. No one expected me to fight."

"You fought," Harper said quietly.

"For years." I slid into the seat next to her. "Even when I finally got myself listed as her father on the birth certificate, the courts wouldn't change her name."

Harper raised her chin. "What do you mean?"

I twisted to face her. "Chloe was two when I got my name put on, but the stupid cheap lawyer I hired didn't request her name be changed. That was a whole other set of hoops I had to jump through."

"So, Chloe's had how many changes to her birth certificate?"

"The original was amended twice. Ironically, the same year her name got changed, Layla died."

Harper's head fell forward. "Kravet showed me only two versions. Chloe's original and then the last one. He made it seem like you wanted Chloe to have your name so you could officially… Have something to do with her inheritance. God, I was so stupid to believe him. I'm sorry."

I scooped her hand in mine, loving how the warmth sparked heat in my own body when she squeezed it back.

My ace in the hole hadn't come out. But Harper had

been through the wringer, too. Seeing her so ragged and tired, the rest of the carnival ride came back to me. "Your dad was here. I met him at the radio station. What's going on with that?"

She took a moment to answer. "I won't cloud your mind up with that drama now."

"I kind of yelled at him."

"During the interview?" She brushed my knuckles and next our hands were tangled up.

"No. After. He took me to his office. I went to the station without any clue he was the DJ."

"Or ran the place."

"Or ran the place," I said with a low grumble of laugher. "I waltzed in there with his guitar."

"They kept your schedule from me. He also bought that station recently. I haven't had a chance to consider what that would mean for my artists." Hearing her still calling all the singers and songwriters signed to Blue Rock as her artists was a gut punch.

Harper loved her job.

I loved making music.

Well, crap.

"Where is Billy? And did I see your mom here, too?"

"Oh yeah." Harper adorably rolled her eyes. "That's a whole diverging road of trouble I won't drag you down, either." She took a breath. "Although, they were civil. Gigi's come a long way. I think she'll be okay. She played me some of that music for the documentary." She whistled. "The woman's still got it." Her hair spilled over her shoulders, the scent of wildflowers overwhelming me.

I kissed her, holding her face. Our mouths moved together, softly, sweetly. "I'm sorry I snapped at you, before."

"You were a daddy on the edge. You're forgiven." She kissed me again, slipping her body closer to mine.

Crap, I had to stay there in the hospital all night. "So, Gigi was playing again, huh?"

Her head laid against my chest. "It's all coming back to her."

I knew how that felt. With my fingers under Harper's chin, I looked in her eyes. Red and drooping. "Why don't you go get some sleep. Where are you staying?"

"I got a text from Gigi saying they got two rooms at a Holiday Inn." She studied me. "Where do you stay when you're here?"

"There's a guest house on the ranch I use. It's so I could be near Chloe. Cam's got a house there, too. Do you want me to call him to come collect you? Use my guest house?"

Her tired eyes answered my question and adrenaline kicked up in my system to tuck her away in the small slice of Wild Heart that I called mine. Even on enemy territory.

"Okay, I'll stay at your place," she said, lifting the strap of a tote bag over her shoulder. When she left Nashville to see Chloe, she'd planned to stay for a while, apparently.

"Then, we need to talk, Harper," I said, my voice shaky, knowing that conversation would change my life. Chloe's, too. I wanted this woman and wasn't letting go.

"Okay," she said and stiffened.

"Couples without kids can screw around with the on-again, off-again stuff. Chloe is…she's crazy about you. Today proved that more than ever. We need to figure this out. And I have things to consider, too."

"I agree." She sat up and stretched. "Tomorrow, then?"

It was wild to think the rest of my life, my future, Chloe's future was getting decided when the sun came up.

Nodding, I said, "Tomorrow."

Chapter Twenty-Four

Jamie

I woke up in the chair next to Chloe's bed feeling someone standing over me. The smell of cigarettes and leather set my boots firmly on the linoleum as I sat up.

"Morning," Cord said and tipped his hat to me. Leave it to that man to crawl in here early in the morning to rage his hate at me. "Here."

I took the stiff paper bag with a braided handle from him and looked inside. A toothbrush, toothpaste, a comb, and deodorant. "Thank you."

Cord kept his poker face on me for a moment, an improvement over the scowl I usually got. When a stir from Chloe sounded, his face changed to a smile. "Hey, munchkin."

"Hi, Grandpa," she said, sleep still in her eyes and voice.

I stood and Cord stepped back. After kissing her forehead which felt cool, I said, "How do you feel?"

"Hungry."

"That's a good sign, right there." Cord's scratchy southern drawl sounded pleased. "I'll go check with the nurse to see about some food."

For a moment I felt like I'd fallen into another dimension. Cord and I hadn't said a kind word to each other in…like…ever.

"How did you sleep?" I asked my daughter, fixing her braid.

"Ugh. I want to go home," she said and the lost look in her eyes felt familiar.

Where was home? For years it was there in Wild Heart. Now we lived in Nashville, but something always pulled me back to Texas.

Harper grew up in Texas as well.

Without addressing the painful question where was home, I said, "Soon. Let's talk to the doctor first." I stared down at the bag and ran my tongue along my teeth, cringing at the feeling in my mouth. "Clo, I'm gonna duck in the bathroom and brush my teeth."

I almost didn't want to look in the mirror, the voice in my head was having a field day with me over what to do about Chloe. What to do about Harper. All I wanted was a pleasant taste in my mouth. After a few swipes of the deodorant, whoever the hell it belonged to, I didn't care, I wet-combed my mop and left the bathroom.

"I heard someone's hungry." A nurse carrying a tray came into the room, Cord on her six.

"Munchkin, why don't we let Daddy go back to the ranch to get cleaned up while we wait for the doctors to come back." Cord shoved his hands in his pockets. "That's a good woman you have."

He'd seen the lights on in my guest house and knew I had Harper tucked away up there. Maybe Cam had said something to him, who she was and what she meant to me. What she meant to Chloe. Maybe Cord knew Chloe was getting yanked off the ranch and these were his last few hours with her until… Next summer?

Despite the accident sending the summer off-kilter, this was still, contractually, Cord's time with Chloe. *I* was the intruder. I had to tread lightly, if I was gonna renegotiate our agreement.

Exhaling, I leaned across the bed. Chloe already had half a muffin in her mouth. "I'll be back soon, Clo."

"No problem, Daddy." Somewhere my daughter grew to be a tough little cookie.

Like her mother.

Lord help me…

The sun coming up outside the window to Chloe's hospital room answered my curiosity. Growing up in Wild Heart had done that to her. I'd tried to keep things as real as I could for her in Nashville, but the music star lifestyle got in the way. Parties. Children's Charity Galas. Private school. Me, the glam king of country.

What an eye-opener.

I set my hat on my head and said, "Be back soon, Clo. Oh, Cord?"

He narrowed his eyes on me like he expected an invitation out in the hall so I could chew him out. "Yeah?"

"Thank you," I said, but didn't try to shake his hand.

I didn't think he and I were there…yet.

Harper

My phone stayed silent all night. Nothing even from Gigi, who'd gone off to a hotel with my father. I rolled my eyes again and again over that one and they were starting to hurt. I drifted off on the couch in the living room, a comfy blue corduroy sofa with an afghan draped over the back, that I eventually pulled down and used for a blanket.

With the morning sun peeking through the lace curtain panels, I pushed the blanket away and found a bathroom. From the bag I packed very quickly back in Nashville while Billy got his pilot on the phone, I grabbed a toothbrush. My hair needed more work than the horsehair brush I grabbed. The vanity's drawers were empty and I wouldn't have asked any questions if I found a woman's hairband. Remembering I probably had one buried in the bottom of my purse, I finished brushing my teeth and then wandered back in the living room.

The door opening startled me. Assuming it was Cam, I relaxed until the shadow had my body seizing with need.

Jamie.

I rushed to him and he let me fall in his arms.

A pickup truck left the driveway and headed back up the gravel lane toward the barn I saw deeper into the property. We held each other for a moment without a word, until I broke the silence. "Where's Clo? Why are you here?"

"Cord relieved me." His voice sounded hesitant.

"Cam filled me in when he picked me up last night on the missing pieces of your relationship with him."

"I don't want to talk about Cam or Cord right now. Chloe's feeling better and we're just waiting for a doctor to release her. I'm here to get cleaned up and…"

"Yeah?"

He kissed me. "This. Time to heal my heart."

"We still have to talk," I said against his mouth.

"I know." He buried his head on my shoulder. "I can use a hot shower, but there's a clawfoot tub in the bathroom. I'm sore as shit from sleeping in a chair."

"Let me draw up the water for you and we'll see how you fit in it."

*

After ten minutes in hot water and me rubbing his tense shoulders, Jamie's head tilted back against the rim of the tub. I kissed him, soft at first, my tongue gently brushing against the lush surface of his lips. His body rocked and his hips shifted. I peeked into the water and shivered at how hard he'd gotten, so fast.

"Touch me, please. I need it," he moaned in my mouth.

I dipped my hand under the surface of the water and tightened my fingers around his hard length. Jamie moaned in response, his hips arching higher, a thrill rushing through me of what a simple touch of mine could do to the man.

"Stand up," I whispered in his ear. "Let me take care of you."

He gripped the side of the tub and rose as a whoosh of water sluiced down his body. Poseidon never moved water so elegantly. All the hair on his chest, stomach, and groin area had darkened making me wonder why on earth *Sports Illustrated* didn't feature male swimsuit models.

Jamie stepped out, and I wrapped a towel around him just to keep my head on straight. There were still so many questions, but the man had a need right now. If he were willing to walk away from a multi-million-dollar contract for me, hell's bells, I was going to give him what he needed.

Not that I'd let him walk away from his contract.

Quick and furious, I lifted my wrinkled dress over my head and backed up until I found a bed in the adjoining room.

Jamie dropped the towel, ran a possessive hand across my body, and muttered, "Mine. You're mine, now."

"I want that." I drank in the possessive stare and melted with a need to be taken. Marked. And claimed.

"Let me take you. Let me love you." Strong hands gripped my thigh and even before I thought of removing my panties, Jamie roughly pulled the lace down and then off. Without needing to aim, he entered me, deep. He groaned, low and guttural.

Feeling him inside me, bare, connecting this way spurred my own possessive need. I wanted to wrap him up and hide him from the world. How dare they try to destroy him. He was just as much mine.

Jamie's body draped forward, and he pulled me in. His body shook and he cried out, his face buried in my hair.

"Damn it," he cursed because he came so quick.

Him being so on edge tipped my emotions and I shuddered along with him.

We lay connected for a few minutes, tangled together, getting our breathing back. My eyes drifted to the room we were in and the window across from the bed. Elegant roman shades were pulled part way down and with the daylight's help, I caught a glimpse of the ranch.

"Hey," I whispered.

"Hey," Jamie answered, but kept still.

"I want to meet this horse."

Jamie lifted his head and with one eye open said, "You're not gonna yell at her, are you?"

I scoffed a laugh. "No. I'm not a snobby city mouse. I know horses get caught up or confused. Wires crossed with the rider. Chloe loves that horse and I want to meet her."

"Let's go see the horse." Jamie checked his watch. "Then we're going to the hospital."

"I have to check on my parents."

"You said last night they got two rooms. Do you think they—"

I covered his mouth. "Don't say it. Don't even *think*

it."

Jamie hugged me. "I can't wait to watch the Gigi and Billy show 2.0."

Chapter Twenty-Five

Jamie

With Chloe's vitals looking good, I checked my daughter out of the hospital the next afternoon. Cam got all my appearances moved so I could stay in Wild Heart for a few days. Make sure she was all better. Then we'd get on a plane.

That morning, Chloe asked me to go with her to see her mom in the memorial park Cord created in the northeast corner of his land.

I trekked up the hill with Chloe quiet at my side. All the summers she'd spent on the ranch, her mother lying just feet from where she slept every night. Feet from where she died after being thrown from her horse.

Staring down at Layla's headstone reminded me of my responsibilities.

I swallowed seeing her name carved into the sparkling black headstone.

Layla Renner
Beloved Daughter and Sister
Mother to her angel daughter.

That last line always killed me.

I hated that gravestone with its shiny surface that reflected my sorry ass face every time I cried in front of the damn thing. Again, and again, I'd begged this inanimate object for forgiveness.

Chloe looked up and smiled. "Harper!"

In the thin space between my shades and my Stetson, I watched Harper and Cam crest over the hill. In her hands were wildflowers wrapped in a green ribbon. At the bottom of the hill, a dark-haired giant and glistening golden ringlet curls milled around a rented SUV. For a moment, I thought I was watching a bird's eye view of me and Layla.

With nothing decided between us, Harper handed me the flowers, but my breath hitched when Chloe gripped her hand. I looked down, Chloe had linked us together. It was always Chloe, wasn't it? Harper had stomped into that contract signing, spoiling for a fight then tried frosty indifference. Chloe had shattered that in Harper.

Harper must have detected I was ready to break down, so she asked Chloe to show her other family members. That left me with Cam who turned to his sister's resting place and removed his hat.

I couldn't imagine the hole Cam and Sierra felt without their sister. I was an only child. Harper, too. One thing was clear, if Harper and I figured this shit out, Chloe would have lots and lots of little baby sibs.

"For what it's worth, Layla loved you." Cam nudged me from behind. "You guys were young. We were young."

"I should have fought harder. We had a kid. It was the right thing to do. I should have stood up to your father." I sniffed.

"That's not what she wanted. Would you want some woman marrying you because she had no choice?"

I thought about that. "I guess not."

"I know you better than anyone, your behavior for a long time was because you hated yourself for what happened," Cam said, solemnly. "And I've kept my mouth shut. You've given me a great living, so I don't need my father. You have no idea how important that independence is for me. I was never going to make it as a musician like you. So, I thank you. But it's time to grow up." Cam kissed the top of the headstone. "If you think for one minute, wallowing after all this time was what *she* would have wanted, then that disappoints me more than *anything* you've ever done."

Chloe came back with the flowers and fell into me. I noticed the ribbon was the color of my eyes. Chloe's too. Was that an accident? Or Harper acknowledging what Chloe and I had? How our blood bond kept us together, like that ribbon.

Chloe put the flowers down and tapped the stone over Layla's name. "Bye, Mama."

I choked up, and prayed as Harper had said that Layla somehow knew I had stepped up to take care of our baby. Turning away with Chloe's hand in mine, Harper's dark hair caught my eye. She talked to her dad at the fence line. Her *daddy*. Billy Cross had a ton to make up for with that woman. I gripped Chloe's hand tighter, so happy I'd had much more of a head start. I hoped Billy made things right by that woman.

And I'd be there to make sure of it.

I was quitting music once my contractually obligated appearances were completed. Time to get off the ride. I would figure out a way to support Chloe. I could make a living as a songwriter like Harper had. It was doable.

Her job was keeping us apart, but I wouldn't make her quit. And I wouldn't recommend she run from Ronny Kravet. Harper worked at Blue Rock to make artists' dreams come true. Considering Kravet's new strategy was to whore out her artists, Harper needed to be there every day to fight against that madness.

My chest swelled with adrenaline when my life flashed before me. Not the life I'd lived, but the new life.

Me, Chloe, and Harper. As a family. I could think of no better role model for my daughter, if she couldn't have her own mother. If Harper and I couldn't be in a relationship because I was her artist, well dang, I'd stop being her artist.

Approaching Harper and Billy though, I realized I was entering a war zone.

"Help me out here, son," Billy said, catching my interest in their conversation.

"What's going on?" I came into the circle, feeling Chloe slip away from me and next my daughter was...leaning against Harper. The way she just relaxed against Harper, told me my decision was the right one.

But what was Billy trying to force my woman to do?

"I don't want my little girl here working for Ronny Kravet, let alone taking orders from him," Billy said.

I adjusted my Stetson. "I can't say I disagree with your daddy, darlin'. But Billy, Harper shouldn't be run off from a job she loves."

"She can if I can give her a better one," Billy said with a devilish grin.

"Better one?" I met Harper's eyes.

"Billy wants me to run his radio station." Harper folded her arms.

A spike in my heart set me back on my boot heels. "Run?"

"You saw my office, son," Billy said to me. "I don't want to deal with programming, and promotions. I want to play music. I need someone to run the business. Poppy, you decided not to record music and I know your mama gave you hell about it. I respected what you wanted. And what you wanted was to work behind the scenes. Come work for me. You can still support artists."

Harper rested her hands on Chloe's shoulders, her eyes off in the direction of Layla's memorial. Then it hit me. Billy's radio station was in Houston. A thirty-five-minute plane ride from Wild Heart. My hometown. Chloe's hometown. I cast my eyes in the same direction as Harper. Layla…

Chloe would no longer be torn between her families. I wouldn't spend my nights worrying about the next knock-down drag-out legal fight Cord was cooking up if I lived there in Wild Heart. Gave them access to Chloe. All year long.

"Harper, darlin', come take a walk with me. Chloe, can you stay here with Billy?"

My daughter looked up at Harper's dad. Some other little girl would be wary, but Chloe grew up on Renner Ranch sassing off to tall brutish cowboys like Logan and even Walker, Cord's horse vet. My cheek ticked up with happiness imagining the friendships I could rebuild.

"Show me this horse of yours, Chloe. Sweet Bell?" Billy reached out to take Chloe's hand and she gripped on to Billy, her face soft and easy.

I caught Harper by the waist to steady myself.

Our families were meant to be blended together, weren't we?

Steering Harper by the elbow, I walked her off to the edge of the field, and leaned on the fence post. No more going day by day. No more seeing how it went. I'd screwed up seven years ago, not realizing my second chance was right there. After not finding that connection anywhere else, I realized now, Harper had been my *last* chance.

"Marry me," I said, holding her chin. "I'm sorry I don't have a ring, or a sign, or a scoreboard to say it. I'll get you all of that."

"I don't want any of that," Harper said, her chest rising and falling.

"Do you want me? And Chloe? We want you. We need you, Harper. I love you. I'm sure I loved you that summer, but I was too stupid to put my heart, *your* heart first."

"Jamie," she breathed out my name. "I wasn't sure what I felt about you seven years ago. When I saw you again last month, it crashed into me. I was in love that summer, too. I should have told you that instead of just trying to fall into bed with you."

"My head was messed up. I may not have responded the right way. I had all this music madness ahead of me. It was all I could think of. This is better, isn't it?"

She gently nodded. "I believe everything happens for a reason."

"Harper?" I held her face. "I told you I love you. I want to marry you. You're not…answering me."

"Did you discuss this with Chloe?"

"Don't need to. I see how she is with you. If she's not in love with you, I know she will be. You're what's best for me, that makes you best for her. She'll see it. She..." I choked on my words.

"What?" She pushed the hair out of my eyes.

"She cried when she couldn't say goodbye to you."

"Oh, Jamie. Okay, here it is." She squeezed my hands. "I love you. Of course, I love you," she said it like it should have been obvious. "I'd love nothing more than to be part of your family with Chloe."

"No."

"No?"

"You're not *part* of my family, you *are* my family.

You're the center pillar, darlin'." He breathed. "We're not complete without you."

"Us getting married will cause a storm with—"

"I'm quitting music. The heck with Kravet and that contract."

She stepped back. "Jamie, that's not an option. Your talent will not be stifled. Especially because of me."

"Before I came down here, I made that decision. I don't want you to run away from Blue Rock. But I also agree with your daddy, I don't want you to work for a man who doesn't respect you."

"His radio station is in Houston."

"I know." I smirked. "We could…live here."

Harper's breath hitched. "Chloe could be near her grandparents."

"And her horse."

"And her horse."

"*And* Layla."

"And Layla." She threw her arms around me and I lifted her up.

I held her tight and kissed her a few more times, taking in the feel of her lips, every kiss feeding me with strength. "I love you."

"I love you, cowboy," she answered back. "This setting fits you so much more than Nashville. There you seemed out of place. Like you were trying too hard. And here, you didn't have to be."

Then she loosened herself from me and stepped back, her face serious. Like she was about to break my heart with rational b.s. No…

"Here're my conditions."

"You have conditions?" I folded my arms.

"I'll marry you. I'll take the job at the radio station.

I'll live here with you and Chloe in Wild Heart. I'll try to be…" She stifled a sob. "I'll try to give Chloe—"

"It's not something you'll have to work that hard at. You're a natural with her." When she nodded, I said, "So you'll do all this if I what?"

She narrowed her eyes at me. "You're not giving up music. That's non-negotiable."

Music had been my second beating heart. I'd needed it as much as my actual heart. But I was ready to cut it out and make it with just Harper's love. Now she handed it back to me. Picked it up off the floor, dusted it off, plugged it back in. Like a hole in a boat. To stop the sinking.

"So how would it work? How would I tour? I can't deal with leaving you behind. It destroys me to leave Chloe." The words made me breathless.

"Here's the good news for you."

"If you're agreeing to marry me, that's fantastic news."

Harper gripped my collar to bring me down for a kiss. "You're not alone anymore, Jamie. You don't have to figure it all out by yourself. You have me. And you no longer have them fighting you." Her eyes strayed to the Renner main house, a mansion that terrified me for years. "Your fight with the Renners is over. They can see Chloe whenever they want. And…"

"What, darlin'?"

"I have one more condition." She took a step back. "Formally renounce their money. Prove to anyone who takes all the pieces of your past and tries to create a picture of a man who claimed his daughter for money."

"That's the picture Kravet painted?" Anger hummed in my veins. "Did you believe it?"

"Everything I knew about you told me that wasn't true."

"I don't need to formally renounce anything, Harper—"

"Hear me out."

"I already did, darlin'." I scooped her back into my arms. "I got another piece of paper buried in my house that names a third-party trustee for Chloe when Cord dies. I don't want his money. I *never* wanted his money."

Harper looked weepy. "Of all the things Kravet dug up about you, why didn't he find that trustee paperwork?"

"It's under seal. Even Cam doesn't know about it." I grunted. "I don't want to be that rich. I've seen what it does to people."

"I have some *really* bad news for you, Jamie."

My heart pounded listening to the dread in her voice. "Hit me. I'm in the mood to fight if it'll lead to make-up sex."

"If you marry me, one day you *are* going to be wealthy beyond your wildest dreams."

"How's that?"

She scoffed a laugh and next tears filled her eyes.

"Now I'm scared," I said.

"You should be." She turned me around. "If you want me, you get those lunatics."

Down the hill, Chloe petted Sweet Bell in the training ring. On each side, holding her up, showing her horse love too, were Gigi and Billy.

Oh…them.

Marrying Harper meant I'd have legends for in-laws. I had a feeling wherever Harper went Gigi was coming, too. And considering how Billy looked at Gigi… Oh, lordy.

"*And* their money," Harper added.

"What do you mean?"

"Their royalties are worth billions. Their wealth makes the Renners' look like chump change."

I stepped back. "Wait, you're an heiress?"

"Looks that way."

"I guess I'm gonna get a killer pre-nup in the mail."

"Not a chance." Harper smiled. "But you need to keep making music because I knew from day one back in Austin, you didn't care about money. You could have gone the songwriting road with me. No, you wanted to sing. You wanted the stage. It's yours, Jamie. All of it. All of us. We're yours."

Then I finally saw the big picture. By agreeing to Harper's terms, by having it all, I was giving Harper it all, too. I was giving her a chance to repair the relationship with her father. She needed that in her life.

All I had to say was…yes.

Chapter Twenty-Six

Three months later…
Harper

My breath still hitched every time I saw Jamie in his worn jeans, plaid button-down shirt, cowboy boots, and that damn sexy charcoal gray Stetson.

In Nashville, he wouldn't blip the hottie radar. Here in Wild Heart, Texas, he turned heads. Not that he wouldn't otherwise.

"Keep the head up, honey." He held the handy stick and string as Chloe's horse trotted in the round training ring.

"I'm trying, Daddy. She's not behaving," Chloe answered with the kind of authority that gave us both confidence she had control over the horse.

Jamie's album was still selling strong. Michael, God love him, had called an emergency board meeting. Spilled all the dirt on Kravet, what his plans were for Blue Rock's artists.

The prim and proper prudes that made up the board were none-too-pleased at Kravet's dark past and secrets, but they were also money people. Appalled at how Blue Rock would look dropping damaging information on their own artist! Who the heck would sign with them after that?

Kravet was fired on the spot, and Michael was named CEO. Me, I loved running my daddy's radio station in Houston. My number one DJ and I didn't always get along, but I figured out that was normal.

Billy and Gigi? They were getting along a little too well, but I stayed out of it. And ignored all the giggling when he called her. To talk business, of course. And about me. *And* Chloe, who they already considered their grandbaby.

I made my way closer to the training ring and waved to the man I loved and his daughter, too, as they both smiled at me. They looked so damn alike it was scary.

"Hey, Harper!" Chloe waved. "Can I show her how we taught Sweet Bell to walk backward, Daddy?"

"Sure." He scooped up the lead rope nearby so the horse didn't trip with his daughter on her back and shuffled out of the ring.

Chloe flapped the reins to nudge the bridle, clucked her tongue, then Sweet Bell dropped her nose, and backed up.

Jamie strode toward me and it still made my heart go *pound pound pound*. I'd never seen him so happy and relaxed and sure of himself. Offstage, that is.

His arms were tight scooping me up, the earthy scent was as striking as his smile. "God, I missed you," he whispered, kissing my cheek.

"Back at ya." I kissed him softly, but turned to Chloe, letting Jamie hold me from behind. "I packed up tons of paperwork at the office so I don't have to go back to Houston until next week."

With our houses in Nashville sold, we'd been living in Jamie's guest house on Renner Ranch. And going a little stir crazy.

I reached into my pocketbook. "Here. What do you think?"

Jamie took the photos I printed of the house I'd found in a gated equestrian community not too far from Renner Ranch. "Oh, this will make Chloe lose her mind."

"Speaking of losing your mind." I handed him another photo.

A little square print out with a dark charcoal background and a creamy little body floating in the center.

Jamie's face fell and his grip on me tightened. "Is this?"

"Yes, Daddy." I took his hand and put it against my stomach. "You got another little one cooking up right here."

Squeezing me hard, he said in my ear, "We need to get married as soon as possible. No more waiting."

I knew the news of our baby would stir some old weariness. How when Layla was pregnant, she refused to marry Jamie. It scarred the man and I was slowly repairing him.

"Soon, I agree."

"Oh, Poppy Montgomery. You're really mine now." He kissed my cheek, but hovered and let his hot breath warm my face. As much as I wanted to bury myself against Jamie and kiss him until we couldn't stand up, living with Chloe, we learned a little vital thing called restraint.

"How was that?" Chloe yelled out with glee, atop her horse.

"That was amazing!" I slipped from Jamie and stepped to the post around the ring.

Chloe clucked her tongue and the horse trotted our way. She always smiled looking at me and Jamie.

"That was great, honey," Jamie said, stroking Sweet Bell's nose over the riser.

I swiped at his hat. "Hey Chloe, show me that backward move again."

"Definitely!" Her eyes lit up as she made the clucking noise and tightened the reins in the combination for the command. "Hi, Logan!"

Cord's lead trainer and ranch foreman strutted from the barn and into the sunshine.

"I got this. You two look cozy." Logan hopped the riser gate and took the lead rope, urging Sweet Bell and Chloe back to the center of the ring.

"You can be cozy, too, Logan," Jamie needled him.

"Don't get him riled up when he's in the ring with Chloe." I found out, Jamie, Cam and even Walker regularly bugged Logan about a nerdy plain girl from high school he used to bully which of course meant he was crazy about her. Only, Walker warned me not to say her name. Hearing the name Delsey Mackenzie, the now beautiful successful cosmetics CEO made Logan's jaw twitch.

Delsey lived in Houston, and I'd been figuring out a way to…bump into her.

With Jamie's eyes fixed on his daughter, he whispered in my ear, "Damn, I love you."

"I love you, more," I responded, knowing that meant more than any compliment about music he'd ever received.

"Impossible." All Jamie Miller needed was love.

Shuffling of boots against the dusty lane leading up to the ring turned me around. The ranch's veterinarian team, Walker and Emma approached us.

Emma waved to Chloe and then smiled at Jamie and me.

"Hey, Walker, how's the Thoroughbred doing?" Jamie asked. "He's a beast compared to the other horses Cord's got in there."

My neon cowboy had fallen into the horse ranch lifestyle. I loved watching the four of them, Walker,

Jamie, Cam, and Logan go off riding in the meadow. I preferred my boots on the ground, especially since I was carrying Jamie's baby.

"Savior's looking good," Walker said.

"Heart's strong," Emma added. "I wish I could say the same for that stubborn old goat up there." She pointed to the main house, meaning Cord.

I swallowed, thankful Chloe didn't hear us. Cord Renner's heart had been giving him serious trouble the past few months. It'd shaken up everyone on the ranch. We tried to keep much of the details from Chloe.

"Cam's arranging for him to see that specialist again," Jamie said, watching Chloe. She loved her granddaddy and it would devastate her if something happened to him.

"That's *another* stubborn goat.".

"Emma, let it go," Walker grumbled, tucking her against him.

"Are you still trying to set him up?" I mumbled to Emma.

"I don't want to make it *too* obvious." Emma made friends with a girl at another ranch who apparently was sweet on the handsome Cam Renner. "She's been here checking out Savior. And trying to get him to notice her. No-go so far."

Cam had his hands full managing Jamie, whose world had expanded and he'd been touring more now that I was in the picture and home with Chloe. Plus, with all of us living back in Texas, Cam had been thrown back into his father's world.

The pressure to take his place on the ranch was mounting.

"Emma's from Chicago," Walker said over her

shoulder. "Doesn't realize the apocalyptic fallout she'll unleash on this town hooking up a Renner with a Sutherland."

"Like Montague and Capulet hatred, between Cord and Old Man Sutherland," Jamie said.

"Old Man Sutherland?" I asked. "What's the guy's name."

Walker and Jamie snorted in laughter, "No one knows!"

"Whoa," Chloe popped off when Sweet Bell spun around abruptly.

"Excuse me." Jamie glided back into the ring. "I got it, Logan." He helped Chloe off her horse and the little girl skipped and dashed right to me.

Chloe sank into my tight embrace, testing the strength of my own heart, then turned to Walker's lady. "Hi, Emma."

"You're looking good up there, Chloe." Emma smoothed my girl's inky dark hair and sweet face.

Jamie strutted back over. "Hey, Clo-Clo. Why don't we let Sweet Bell have a rest and then you, me, and Harper take a stroll along the fence line? Chill out in the meadow for a while. We have something to tell you."

"Two things," I reminded him, discreetly patting my belly, although Emma squeaked and punched Walker, figuring it out.

"Okay," Chloe said with a confident nod, taking charge. "See ya, Emma."

"I'm here, too." Walker spun around, laughing.

"Sorry, Walker." Chloe gave the burly vet a hug.

"Now go take that walk with your daddy and Harper."

Winking, Jamie held his hand out to me, and

adorably so did his daughter.

With Chloe holding each of our hands, we walked toward the fence line, the setting fall sun behind us. Jamie scored the ending he never dreamed of.

He got the girl.

Both of us.

Thank you for reading The Cowboy's Last Song.

Strap in for a good time with the Wild Hearts of Texas.

Save a Horse. Ride a Cowboy! (preferably mine :)

The cowboys of Wild Heart, Texas are here!

The Cowboy's Forbidden Crush: An Age-Gap Professor-Student Forbidden Romance

The Cowboy's Last Song: A Country Music Star Single Dad Romance

The Cowboy's Accidental Wife: A Marriage Mistake Romance

The Cowboy's Rebel Heart: An Enemies to Lovers Romance

The Cowboy's Christmas Bride: A Secret Child Amnesia Holiday Small Town Romance

ABOUT THE AUTHOR

Deborah Garland is an Award-Winning author of emotional, funny, steamy romances!

She lives on the beautiful North Shore of Long Island with her very patient husband and their mischievous pug. She had to learn how to make her own Cosmopolitans and right now there's a bartender who will NEVER see her again. She eats cheap mac and cheese with expensive red wine, her heroes are ALWAYS over six feet tall, and they fall, hard, HARD for the girl.

STAY IN TOUCH WITH ME...

My newsletter followers get not only a good laugh each month, but also updates on new releases, sales and giveaways. Sign up at my website:

www.deborahgarlandauthor.com

Don't forget to follow me on any of these great platforms:

Amazon
Goodreads
BookBub
Twitter
Facebook & Instagram

Printed in Great Britain
by Amazon

80508938R00171